Mirror, Mirror

Mirror, Mirror

Paula Byrne

**WILLIAM
COLLINS**

William Collins
An imprint of HarperCollins*Publishers*
1 London Bridge Street
London SE1 9GF

WilliamCollinsBooks.com

First published in Great Britain in 2020 by William Collins

1

A catalogue record for this book is
available from the British Library

ISBN 978-0-00-830709-7

Printed and bound in Great Britain by
CPI Group (UK) Ltd, Croydon

MIX
Paper from
responsible sources
FSC™ C007454

This book is produced from independently certified FSC™ paper
to ensure responsible forest management.

For more information visit: www.harpercollins.co.uk/green

For Christine Marie

A sister is both your mirror – and your opposite
Elizabeth Fishel

Mirrors from Lohr were so elaborately worked that they were accorded the reputation of always speaking the truth *and became a favourite gift at European crown and aristocratic courts. Uniquely, the mirrors also* talked, *in aphorisms like one that reads in the upper corner of a frame:* Elle brille à la lumière *(She is such a beauty).*

Karlheinz Bartels, *Schneewittchen: zur Fabulologie des Spessarts* (Lohr am Main, 2012)

I don't remember who started the rumor that Mars was scheduled to collide with the Earth that summer of 1938 … the next summer, not Mars, but a little man in Berlin changed the course of human history.

Maria Riva, *Marlene Dietrich by her Daughter* (New York, 1993)

Prologue

Berlin, 1993

Die Deutsche Kinemathek

My mother was still alive when the wall came down, but she made no comment except this: 'I have cried all my tears for Germany. They have dried and I have washed my face.' She had the loveliest face since Helen of Troy, but her beauty was in flight, like Nike of Samothrace.

When she died alone, in her Paris apartment, she left no will. Her millions had been spent. But she had kept every possession in cardboard boxes: hats, scarves, gowns, shoes, clocks. I sorted 45,000 pages of correspondence, 16,500 photographs, and over 3,300 textile objects, and I sent everything I had to the Deutsche Kinemathek.

She was finally being honoured. Berlin's most famous and infamous child. I could never imagine her as a girl. She was a goddess; unknowable, unreachable. When I was a child I had a doll called

1

Heidi. She was the most beautiful doll, with golden hair, and nobody could have loved her more than I. But every day, I prayed that I would never have a daughter. Dolls could not feel pain. Could not be hurt. I feared girl children. I would not know how to be a mother to such complex creatures.

And now the last box has been sent. As I enter the museum, I find myself in a mirrored lobby, like a jewel box. A hundred images of myself are reflected back at me. I am old now. I see an elegant, white-haired lady in a smart suit. There are eyes everywhere, and with a sudden burst of grief and clarity, I know how she must have felt. Every aspect, every angle of her life scrutinised, photographed, filmed, analysed and judged. Nowhere to escape, and nowhere to hide. And now I understand what she meant when she told me 'Kater, I was photographed to death.'

The Devil is a Woman

It's funny how I can remember every single person who's ever been kind to me.

When I look back now, I see so much, but I guess that's the way it is for most people. I never knew my age in those days when we first went to Hollywood. That was because Mother constantly changed it, so I never had a chance to celebrate my birthday. To her friends and fans, I was a baby, to others, I was a young girl of nine, or maybe eight. All I knew was that I had the most beautiful mother in the world and that I was ugly.

My face was covered with pimples. Mother blamed the cream pastries I ate. It was one of the things I most loved about America: the food. For breakfast, the maid would bring me a stack of pancakes with maple syrup and whipped butter. There were strips of salty bacon 'on the side'. American waffles with cream and blueberries. Gloriosky!

Mother glared at me, sipping water mixed with Epsom Salts. This was how she stayed pencil thin.

'Sweetheart, hurry. The car is here. That Big Girl's Blouse will be weeping into his coffee if I'm even five minutes late.'

Her co-star was English. Peter somebody. On the whole, she disliked Englishmen, 'thick, white ankles, fingers like uncooked sausages'. She was obsessed by the beauty of her own slender ankles. 'Aristocrats have thin ankles, only peasants have thick ones.' She looked at my fat ankles, accusingly, as she said this.

I felt sorrow for my mother because she had given birth to such a plain child. I looked exactly like my father, but what was handsome in a man was plain in a female. In the mirrored dining table where we were eating a hurried breakfast I could see my reflection: high forehead, large flat nose, and deep-set eyes. My bushy eyebrows made me look perpetually cross. My hair was fine and a pale shade of ginger. I had blotchy brown freckles that I tried to scrub off with lemon juice. It never worked. But I had a lovely mouth, with a Cupid's bow. It was the only feature that I had inherited from my mother. I decided then that it might be best to avoid mirrors.

As usual, it was an early-morning call. Mother was expected to be in Make-up at 5 a.m. Her car and driver were already outside the house. A hot Santa Ana wind had been blowing that week, and the Hollywood hills were sharp-edged and the colour of elephant skin. The morning air was cold, however, and I wrapped a warm rug around Mother's legs. On the way to the studio, she talked non-stop: 'It's fine for stage actors, they're the fortunate ones, they don't have to be acting a love-scene at 9 a.m. after being in Make-up since 6 a.m.'

'Any country that can make a dog a film star is not to be taken seriously.'

'Harlow was at the dinner. That shows you the level of intelligence there last night!'

'Abominable country, America.'

Mother was always edgy during pre-production. I listened and nodded and smiled and tried not to get carsick. I longed for the studio, and the hum of the carpenter's saw. Only then would I know I was home.

She continued to complain that no drawings had been sent to her, and Nellie, her hairdresser, had not seen a single wig sketch. Von Goldberg, she knew, was still making adjustments to the script. What was everyone doing at Paramount? Hiding W. C. Fields' gin bottles?

We drew up at the Bronson Gate. In those days – before the big earthquake – there was an elaborate stone belfry framing the famous archway. I nodded to the frieze of Shakespeare, who seemed to be presiding over the studio lot.

'Good morning, Miss Madou. Good morning, Miss Kater.'

'Harry, take me straight to Wardrobe. I need to speak to Travis.'

'Yes, Miss Madou.'

That was the day I became my mother's dresser.

* * *

Like most little girls, I thought my mother was perfect. Except my mother really *was* perfect. Everyone told me so, and she had the face and body to prove it. I guess that's why I never told anybody the truth. Who would believe me? It's strange how people refuse to think badly of the beautiful.

I remember the first time that my mother went to an airport full of 'civilians' – that is, not 'Hollywood People'. She was horrified by the ugliness, the commonplace, the fleshy bodies. At the top of her voice, she exclaimed, to whoever cared to listen: 'No wonder they pay us so much!'

In later years, when she had left the film industry, she was bemused by modern actresses, who relied on their talent and not their good looks to succeed. Not that she truly cared about her beauty; it was a commodity: 'Glamour is what I sell. It's my stock in trade.' Mother liked her maxims: 'Darling, the legs aren't so beautiful; I just know what to do with them.' Another favourite: 'The Possible we do immediately. The Impossible may take a little longer.' And another: 'Nothing bad can ever happen to you when you're with your mother.' But the one she liked best was this: 'Kater, remember, the mirror never lies.'

Someday I'll Find You

Here they come, podgy daughter trotting alongside her, little piggy on the way to market. They've buffed and polished me so that I'm ready for her. And I go wherever she is. They all need me, the stars and the starlets, but nobody loves me more than Madou. The feeling is mutual. My passion for her remains unimpaired. Even when she is tired, she is staggeringly beautiful. I live for the moments when she gazes into me, and we become one.

Madou is to play a Russian empress. Perhaps the most famous woman of all time: Catherine the Great. Mr Goldberg (everyone knows that he added the *von* to make himself appear noble) could not resist. And who can blame him, darlings? The transformation from vulgar tart to sovereign ruler is just too delicious.

Naturally, his star cannot envisage the role until she has first created the wardrobe. Every seed pearl, every sequin, every feather, has to be perfect. Travis, head of Wardrobe, a man of indescribable and imperishable charm, will set her right. Travis dresses impeccably, like an English gentleman, exuding elegant masculinity. He always looks as if he has just stepped off a yacht, so unlike that vulgar imposter, Mr Moses *von* Goldberg, who looks like a Jewish schmatta tailor. Never trust a man with short legs, I always say, his brain is too near his bottom.

Travis's rooms are exquisite; book-lined and stuffed with antiques. I reside in the right-hand corner: a huge floor-length looking-glass, dotted with bulbous lights. The daughter never looks my way, studiously avoids my gaze. Well, who can blame her, when she looks like a baby porpoise?

Madou looks directly at me and speaks.

'She must look young, Travis. But who will believe that Madou is virginal? You must overdo the image. We need frills and flounces for the early gowns. Then later, when she gets to Russia we will need pelts; sables, mink, ermine, white fox, not chinchilla. So vulgar, so Garbo.'

Travis chuckles: 'Kater, dearest, have a sandwich. It's an American standard, egg-on-white. Delicious.'

Madou casts a critical look at him. She dislikes other people feeding her child: 'Now, where are the sketches? Kater, lay them on the floor, so we can see.'

Madou emits a sigh of appreciation as she scrutinises the gorgeous designs: 'Travis, sweetheart, that black velvet gown trimmed with ermine is magnificent, but it must be bottle-green. You understand? It will film better. And the fur should be mink, the white of the ermine will make the trim too distracting against the dark material.'

'Joan, my dear, are you absolutely sure about the dark green?'

Travis is one of the select few who is permitted to use her first name, just as she is one of the select few permitted to use Goldberg's, which she shortens to Mo.

'Of course I'm sure, sweetheart. You must remember how difficult black is to light well. The wedding dress is good. The antique silver lace is perfect, and the white seed pearls and diamonds. But the hoops should be wider. I need to check the width of the doors. Mo will need to make them bigger. The fur hat should not flop over the face, the face is important, Travis, not the hat. Kater, let's go and ask Mo about the doors.'

Before she leaves, she turns to look at me, and there, reflected in me, is her image. Venus could not look more lovely. Joan Madou: you are the fairest of them all.

The Scarlet Empress

Oh boy, there it was. The familiar smell of sawdust lingering in the early-morning Californian air. And then I was whizzed through the soundstage door into freezing St Petersburg. Gee, it was busy; horses neighing, cameras being pushed around on wheels, carpenters moving planks, grips high above, on ladders and scaffolds, rigging lights into position. I could smell glue, spirit gum, and the disgusting smell of sticky, fake snow.

In the centre of the winter set was a beautiful ebony carriage, the royal coach. Its silver lanterns sparkled in the bright lights, and a team of eight black stallions strained against a heavy, ornate harness. Extras, dressed as Russian soldiers with resplendent black moustaches, sat around waiting or stroking their Siberian horses. I later learned that they were polo ponies, rented from the Riviera Club's team, and given fake manes and tails, courtesy of Hairdressing. But, as Mother would say, why spoil the illusion with the bald truth?

When I first came to America, it was Mo who taught me my first important English words; *Hair and Make-up*, *Wardrobe*, *Dressing Room Row*, *Soundstage*, *Grips*. Mother insisted that we speak German at home, and even our maid was sent over from Berlin. One of the reasons Mother refused to let me go to school was because she didn't want me to speak English with an American accent. But Mo understood that I needed to try to fit in a little, in this curious world of make-believe that is 'Hollywood'.

Mother's stand-in was at the door of the coach, wearing an imitation cape, made of brown squirrel, not the silver-tipped Russian sable that Mother had insisted upon. She kept up her joke about the head of the studio, and his origins as a furrier.

'Sweetheart, he knows the cost of good fur. But I bet he never sewed on real sable.'

She chuckled, and there was a malicious glint in her eye. She loved it when she got one over on the studio bosses. They would be furious when they found out about the expensive sable. The thought was delicious to imagine: 'But Mr Zukor, I thought you *liked* fur.' Mother scanned the set for her director, until she found him astride a boom mic, like a witch on a broomstick.

'My mirror, Kater.'

I held it aloft as she donned her sable cape and pulled the hood over her golden hair. Dot from Make-up daubed glycerine onto those perfect lips, and with a 'We are ready for you, Miss Madou' from the assistant director, she was primed.

She stood perfectly still, in front of the door of the coach, gazing in wonder at St Petersburg in the depths of winter. The last time I had been in the studio, I had been to Shanghai. I remember Mo painting cloud formations on the top of a real-life express steam train. I didn't need to go to the real China or Russia. I had it all right here. That day in China, I had learned that when the director uttered the words 'Quiet on the set' I dared not move, even breathe.

Mother could stand still for hours without even taking a bathroom break. She was as still as a statue, just like Queen Hermione in my book about Shakespeare. That was a winter's tale, too. The queen was accused of a bad thing and, to avenge her husband, she locked herself away for sixteen years until she returned as a statue who magically becomes human again – right in front of the audience.

Thus she stood, Even with such life of majesty – warm life –

I stood in the shadows, fidgeting, clutching her hand mirror. Travis had made me a white coat, in honour of my new occupation as 'assistant to Miss Madou'. My stomach rumbled and groaned. I was so hungry. I hoped no one could hear. The commissary had a new sandwich. I wondered if I would be allowed a Coca-Cola. Or one of those wonderful vanilla milkshakes, with ice cream. My mind wandered.

'Make-up.'

With those words, I dashed onto the hot set. Mother took the hand mirror and scrutinised her face. A false eyelash had dropped onto her cheek. She removed it expertly, handed back the mirror, and smiled at me. I had done well. I escaped back into the shadows.

'Cut. Print.'

Back in Mother's dressing room, there was a buzz of activity. I knew that the first sign that Principal Photography was about to begin was the influx of slim white boxes containing flowers. Her director always sent her tuberoses or white lilacs, the studio sent snapdragons or lilies, her new co-star sent her red roses, a bad mistake, as she loathed red roses, especially 'American Beauty'. She loved yellow roses, but they were only to be given at the end of the affair. Never at the beginning.

I put the roses on one side to be given away to the maid, then I began my job of filing away the flower cards, not so that Mother could send thanks, but so she knew who had *forgotten* to send flowers.

That morning, she had swept into her dressing room armed with white vinegar and bleach. She took it upon herself to clean every room she occupied. Surgical alcohol was used to sterilise the bathrooms. She would never sit down on a toilet seat for fear she would contract a disease. Many years later, I discovered the reason for her paranoia. At the time, it was just another mystery to be kept 'from the Child'.

Then we unpacked the boxes. All of them were marked in German so that only we would understand their contents. The first box contained her African doll, her lucky mascot, her 'savage'. He was a present from Mo, and he sat on her dressing table, propped up by the mirror. He was always the first to be unpacked and the last to be packed. I never liked him.

Besides, I had my own doll, with silky flaxen-blonde hair, like Mother's, and enormous blue eyes. My Heidi. Mother said she was very expensive. She came from a famous shop on Regent's Street in London. When I lay her down, her eyelids closed, like magic. When I pressed her tummy, she cried 'Mama'. She had her own wardrobe: an outfit for every occasion. I loved to dress and undress Heidi. No one could be a better mother than I was to my doll. On special occasions, I would allow her into my bed.

Travis, one of the kindest of Mother's friends, made doll clothes that were miniature versions of the ones he made for Mother. He even made Heidi a real sable coat and matching muff to keep her warm. He would wrap the doll clothes in fine tissue, and tie them with pink grosgrain ribbon. Travis was a man interested in detail. He told me that he was born in Texas, where the men rode horses and wore cowboy hats, even to the office. He spoke to me as he would to a grown-up, and if I didn't understand a particular English word, he would take out his pencil and draw an image to explain it.

Travis had a secret. When he thought that no one was watching, he would take out his hip flask and pour amber liquid into his coffee, his hands trembling. He had such beautiful hands;

slender and elegant, with perfectly polished nails. On his pinky finger, he wore a gold and black ring. I think he knew that I was watching him, but he knew that I would never tell on him. I was so good at keeping secrets.

After I unpacked Mother's savage doll, I undressed Heidi and put on her white lace nightdress. I brushed out her long blonde hair with a doll brush that was made of real silver. I popped her into her doll bed. Then I got back to work.

Mother and I decanted vases, gramophone, records, ashtrays, cigarette boxes, pens, pencils, writing paper, special padded hangers, towels, bath mats, flasks. Thermoses, containing her beef tea and chicken soup, soon lined the shelves. Mother was the only star to have her own kitchen appended to her dressing room. Her famous goulash would bubble away on the stove, scenting the air with caraway and sweet paprika.

I went to the studio every day with Mother because of the Lindbergh baby who was taken away and killed in the woods. Mother, hysterical with fear, hired a bodyguard, who stationed himself outside her dressing room. To keep me busy, Mother gave me a list of duties.

Shine the shoes
Pass the hairpins
Pour the coffee (morning)
Pour the champagne (evening)

File the flower cards
Open the mail
Put cufflinks in boxes
Sharpen the black wax eye pencils
Pop out the top hat (this was probably my favourite)

The one duty I didn't like very much was tidying her vanity table. It was always cluttered with pots of cold cream, flacons of *No. 37 Veilchen*, make-up, brushes, sponges, photographs, and the savage who stared at me with its tiny red eyes.

I kept my eyes averted from the silver and black glass triptych … mustn't catch its eye. But I knew he was watching me, trying not to laugh at me, keeping his disdain at bay.

I Like America

Night falls quickly in Hollywood. The Child removes her mother's shoes and leaves them to cool. Later, they will be stuffed with tissue and stored away in their chamois bags. Slippers are placed on Madou's feet; she is wearing natty cream silk lounging pajamas, with a black velvet trim.

She looks at me, her reflection in threes. The Holy Trinity. A nimbus of light frames her face. She rubs on cold cream, flannels it off, stares again with deep concentration. Her fair hair is damp and swept back from her face. Her skin is pale, slightly pink, translucent like the finest porcelain. She resembles a beautiful boy. Beautiful boy triplets. How divine. I hum softly:

Mad about the boy
I know it's stupid to be mad about the boy
On the silver screen
He melts my foolish heart in every single scene …

Madou picks up the telephone. As usual, she's booked a call to the husband she never sees, back in Europe: 'Papi, sweetheart, Chevalier told me Lombard smells of cheap talcum powder, so I said, "What place did you smell it?" So, of course he was stuck and couldn't answer. Can you imagine his face? Mo was magnificent today. Do you know what he said to me? "No one lights you like I do, because no one loves you like I do." He knows now that he should never have abandoned me. That last picture was an abortion. We belong together. With this picture, we will make history. *She* has never looked more beautiful, but it's all down to Mo.'

The Child pours a glass of champagne from the ice bucket, and places it on the *poudreuse*. She is reading something; fairy tales by the Brothers Grimm, no doubt she'll skip over *Schneewittchen*. She's munching on potato chips, stuffing them into her cakehole, in greedy, fat handfuls.

Madou squints at her reflection, and then relaxes into a state of dreamy contemplation as she continues her telephone conversation: 'Peter has as much sex appeal as a dish of leftover potato salad. Of course, that pleases Mo. He's so jealous, unlike you, Papi, who have every right to be jealous, but is never. I have to go now. Kisses to you.'

Tonight, Madou is gay and jocular, but I, for one, have not forgotten her agony when her director ran away. Memory is viciously insistent on such occasions. Again and again, late at night, tired and alone, she's gazed into me, eyes half-closed in recollection, and told me, told herself, the story. How Mo had discovered her in the filthy backstreets of Berlin, brought her to Hollywood, made her a star, and then left her to the mercy of this nest of vipers.

She was just nineteen and the mother of a baby girl when she boarded the boat train at the Lehrter Bahnhof for New York followed by the long train ride to Pasadena. The little man was dismayed when he first saw her in her grey two-piece suit, looking like a lesbian; he instructed her to lose weight, and to buy better clothes.

Just like that – 'lose the weight' and, good soldier that she is, she did. She stopped eating. She took up smoking, sipped beef tea and hot water with Epsom Salts and drank endless cups of coffee. She loathed American coffee, but she drank the 'gnat's piss' all the same.

She adores Mo, refusing to believe the stories that he began his working life as an errand boy in a lace-making warehouse in New York. In her eyes, he was a genius of aristocratic Prussian stock. Her saviour.

In Hollywood, he set about the business of lighting. He despised most actors. 'Directing actors is practising *puppetry*,' he told her. 'It's about light and shadow.'

That first day on the hot set, she complained about her Slavic nose. He smiled, took out a phial and painted a silver line on the centre of the nose – then climbed onto the set to adjust a tiny spot to shine directly on the line from above her head, reducing the nose by a third.

Madou was a quick learner. From that moment on, she would sit before me or some other mirror, and draw a line of white paint down the centre of her nose (in a shade lighter than her base), lining the inside of her lower eyelid with white greasepaint – using the rounded edge of a thin hairpin.

Then she held a saucer over a candle, where a black carbon smudge would form on the underside, and mixed in a few drops of lanolin. Warmed and mixed with the soot, it created a perfect kohl for the eyelids, which she applied with a hairgrip – heavy at the base line, then fading up towards the eyebrow.

Together, they created the famous look, the mysterious face with the sculpted cheeks. The play of light and shadow created with diffused light. *Nobody lights you like I do, because nobody loves you like I do.* He is a painter of chiaroscuro who sees everything in terms of light and shadow. He places his light, and only then builds a scene around it.

Who else would think of using veils and nets to create shadows? To the amazement of the crew, he removes his cigarette, and burns holes in the net to make the individual spots shine through. Then, when he is satisfied, he sets her in the light he has created for her. He is a magician, a sculptor. She is Galatea, with skin as white as milk. He is Pygmalion. Herr Direktor, her master, Lord of Light. She is his willing slave.

Together they create magic. It is a perfect partnership. He is in love with the image on the silver screen, and so is Madou. But there is a third person in this relationship. *Moi*. I am the mirror, that never lies.

The Garden of Allah

Mother slipped off her travel pajamas and dressed herself in tailored tweed trousers and a silk shirt. She was cooking goulash for Mo. She tied a lace apron around her waist, and twisted a scarf around her hair.

Mo had found us a new house in Beverly Hills, just north of Sunset Boulevard, on the corner of Bedford and Benedict Canyon. It was a low, white Spanish-style villa, set in an acre of manicured lawns, with the requisite blue swimming pool, 'for the Child'. I loved the sun-drenched garden; a riot of colour, with huge red and gold trumpet-shaped flowers, orange and lemon trees, figs, camellia, gladioli, and lush green palms, which rustled like paper in the warm breeze. Beside the guest house was a miniature rose garden. Hummingbirds, tiny mechanical jewels, hovered and spun. My bodyguard showed me how to make a bird feeder with sugar and water, which I hung from a tree in the shade.

The Mirror House was perfect for a movie star. Inside, the walls were lined with exquisite hand-painted wallpaper, and lacquered

floors were strewn with animal skins. The sunroom was dominated by a large jungle mural, and the sofas and armchairs were
covered in butter-soft white leather.

I thought it was oh-so-elegant. Mother thought it vulgar and
'oh-so-Hollywood'. She lowered the blinds to black out the sun,
and rarely ventured out into the garden for fear of ruining her
milky-white skin. The only rooms she liked were her ivory and
gold bedroom, and the stunning mirrored dining room; its *verre
églomisé* panels depicted towering palms, and wild jungle
animals.

Mirrors. There were mirrors everywhere. It was a mini-
Versailles. They lined the walls of the interiors, and if that weren't
enough, there were mirrored fireplaces and mirrored furniture; a
French-style dressing table, a backgammon table, and mirrored
lamps. The doors were framed with mirrors. In Mother's bedroom,
there was even a mirrored ceiling.

Wherever I wandered, I would catch a glimpse of a pudgy little
girl, dressed in lurid puff-sleeved organdie dresses, which did little
to conceal the rolls of fat around her middle. How horrid she
looked. How she must be avoided. I resolved from the first to
spend as much time as I could outdoors. That was easy to do if
one lived in Hollywood.

Floating on my rubber ring in the blue pool made me feel
weightless. Under the watchful eye of my bodyguard, I spent
hours in the water as soon as I returned home from the studio.

But I was always careful to ensure that I was dressed and ready for dinner when Mother called.

Today, Mother was in the best of moods. The rushes of *The Red Queen* were a triumph. Mo was happy. As soon as he arrived, Mother removed his shoes, washed and massaged his feet, and encased them in soft Turkish slippers. I poured him a glass of ice-cold champagne. Mother stirred the goulash. I always wondered how she managed never, ever to get a single drop on her clothes.

'Oh Mo, those long dresses mean that for once they can't see the famous Madou legs. Serve those damn furriers right. What a joke.'

Mother chuckled. She had also taken a hearty dislike to her handsome co-star, which made her director very happy.

'Peter … that … useless abortion. Do you know he orders ice-cream for dessert? A grown man! Only Americans eat like children. You know he has Kotex stuffed down *there*. That *mennuble*.'

Mo puffed on his pipe and listened. Then he took a deep breath.

'Sweetheart, have you thought about Kater's schooling? She needs to be around friends her own age. She shouldn't be in a soundstage all her young life. It's not healthy. There will be no kidnapping. She is well protected.'

'But Mo, she speaks only German. It's impossible. I will engage a tutor. Maybe you're right. You are always right.'

I froze. I wanted to learn more English, and I wanted to go to American school, but I couldn't bear not to be with Mother in the studio.

'Mutti, who would fetch your hand mirror? And sort the flower cards, and thin your fake eyelashes?'

I need not have worried. Mother had not the slightest intention of sending me to school. She was terrified of me becoming 'American', and I was never allowed friends of my own. I worried that I would not be allowed on-set the next morning, as Mother was filming the 'Examination' scene. It was my favourite costume, and I longed to see her under Mo's lights.

When dinner was over, I excused myself from the table and prepared for bed. First, I took my bath. The water turned a rosy pink. My tummy hurt. I called aloud for Mutti who screamed when she saw me: 'No, this cannot be. She's only ten.'

(Oh, I thought, so I *am* ten, not eight or nine.)

'It must be the Californian weather. Look at the Italians, and the Mexicans are even worse. I should have kept her in Berlin, where it's cold.'

She was striding around the bathroom.

'Kater, you must not go near a man. Do you understand me? Stay away from men. Why have you done this to me?'

She towelled me down and gave me a pink silk sanitary belt and a napkin, told me this would happen every month, and sent me to bed. I had no idea why I should stay away from men. Did that mean all men, like Mo, and the pool man? And what about my bodyguard, who helped me to feed the hummingbirds? Life with Mother was so confusing.

I knew she was angry with me. Later, she phoned her mother in Berlin to share her disappointment. I heard snatches of conversation: *just a child, Californian heat, never stops eating this terrible food, enormous, diet, tennis lessons, so dreadful for me, how can anyone bear to be a mother of girls* … and then I drifted into sleep.

Sigh No More

Long after the Child is fast asleep in bed, Madou cleanses her face with witch hazel and puts on a dusky silk nightdress. She has sent Mo home. She wants to be alone. She sits at her dressing table, staring at me, without really seeing. I tell her, over and over again, that she is even more radiant, even more luminous than ever before. She searches her face for fine lines, but there are none on Nefertiti.

It's that wretched child that has caused her to feel so bad. So selfish. So she's growing up. No longer a child. Puff-sleeved dresses will return with a vengeance. But Madou has nothing to fear. In this new picture, she will be at her loveliest. Goldberg will make sure of that. It will be his parting present. He will leave her, again, but he will give her his light.

There are times when I have to administer a finger-wagging to those I love. Madou knows the growl of the Black Dog. Her friends see the relentless energy, the commitment, the long hours, the discipline. I see the days spent in bed, with the drawn blinds and the refusal to eat. I shall have to be firm. This business with the Child is a blow; a set-back. I need to impart some 'Mother-knows-best' wisdom.

'Well,' she says, wearily. 'And what do you have to say?'

'You know perfectly well what I'm going to say.'

'That everybody worships me. I'm tired of being worshipped. It's nauseating.'

'There's hell to pay if they don't.'

She smiles.

'So you think I'm an egomaniac? I work hard to keep everyone fed and clothed. My life is not my own – I belong to my work.'

'You know what I always say, dearest: *work is more fun than fun*.'

'What will my fate be, mirror? I suppose it is written in the stars?'

'I don't believe in astrology; the only stars that I can blame for my failures are those that walk about the stage.'

She laughs. I can always make her laugh. She looks across to the window, and the inky-black night. It's nights like these that make her feel far from home. A necklace of bright stars arcs around the sky.

She lights a cigarette and blows blue smoke into my face. She smokes slowly and methodically, no matter how much nervous strain she feels. I leave her to her thoughts. She stubs out her cigarette, sets the alarm to 4.30, turns out the lamp, and slips into bed.

Stage Fright

In the morning, Mother called for me, and I breathed not a single word for fear she would remember Mo's admonitions, and send me to school. It was freezing cold as we climbed into the studio car; a reminder of the desert that Hollywood was built upon. I had learned to dress with several layers, shedding each skin as the sun rose and became scorching hot. I looked like a roly-poly caterpillar; a look not enhanced by Mother plonking a beige knitted woolly hat on my head.

It was pitch dark on the lot, except for the street lamps, which lined Dressing Room Row. Back in her dressing room, the lovely aroma of greasepaint, coffee and Danish pastries filled the air. Nowadays, people ask me if I hated my life then, but, no, I loved it. Sure, I was sometimes lonely, but never, ever bored. Besides, back then, I knew no other life. Even now, the smell of greasepaint mixed with coffee takes me right back to those days, and the memories are warm and comforting. Bodies betray us.

We sprang into action; we knew our duties. That day, Mo was shooting an important scene; the Red Queen's inspection of her Russian army. Mother would look her most beautiful, but there was much work to be done.

I placed her ashtray on a side table and brought a fine-boned china cup and saucer for her coffee. Mother undressed and was wrapped in a white cotton robe. Hair first. Always hair first. Nellie brushed her hair away from her face, twisting and plaiting with expert hands. Then Dot began her work. Nobody spoke. All was quiet concentration. I thinned out the eyelashes and handed them to Dot with the special glue. Mother scrutinised her face in the mirror. She took a hairpin, dipped it in white greasepaint and smeared it along the waterline of her eyes. They grew larger, magically. Then, the lips. The perfect Cupid's bow.

Finally, it was time for the review dress. It was the green velvet one we'd seen in the sketch that first day. Edged with mink. Travis had excelled himself. Everyone would remember this dress. Garbo *would* be mad as hell when she saw it. Travis had created an oversized muff that matched the trim and the hat. Mother was right to insist that her hair should be pulled back, so the Cossack hat, set at a rakish angle, did not detract from the face. On anyone else the huge hat would be absurd. She had never looked more ravishing.

How to transport her to the soundstage, when the dress was so wide she could only exit the door sideways? A horse and cart were sent to her dressing room. I leapt forward to help her into the cart.

'No, Angel. You must not touch the velvet or it will leave finger marks.'

Travis obliged, wearing special gloves. There was a special bucket seat at the back of the cart for me. Mother stood erect, holding onto a rail. The horse set off at a snail's pace, transporting his most precious cargo.

When she entered the soundstage, the crew burst into spontaneous applause. Piercing whistles reverberated around the set. A film crew has seen and heard it all. They are tough, hard to please, impressed by nothing. Mother bestowed a tiny smile in grateful acknowledgement. Mo took her hands and kissed them reverently. Then he led her to the set. I followed behind, curious to see Mo's latest creation. It was the most terrifying thing I'd ever seen.

Hundreds of grotesque, malformed gargoyles and hobgoblins writhed and screamed, or smirked insanely. They lined the doorways, corridors and tables of the Imperial Palace. Oversized Byzantine saints and martyrs glared menacingly from great heights. Wooden crucifixes with emaciated male figures peeked out between huge stone pillars. Flickering candles in iron-branched candelabras created shadows of frightening intensity.

Worst of all were the El Greco skeletons: they twisted over mantels, peered through windows; macabre guests at the long banqueting table, bent over bowls of rotting, waxen food. The figures were draped in mouldering shrouds and grave clothes, their lean fingers reaching out to me. On the wall, near the door, I saw a dried, withered body of a child hung up by its hair. On a pedestal, I saw a screaming man being forcibly sodomised by a metal pike.

Cleverly, these corpses only served to highlight Madou's ethereal beauty, so she had no fear of them. Not that anything or anyone could inspire fear in my mother. As for worry about her small daughter witnessing this set of cruelty, she had no such concerns.

Nor did she need to fear the width of the iron doors: they were gargantuan. Looking back with adult eyes, I know that those doors were *gigantic*! It took at least five people to open and close them, so heavy they were. The imperial throne was shaped into a double-eagle, and there was a huge mirror curved into a winged gargoyle.

Finally, Mo pointed to his living sculpture: three topless maidens, looped by their wrists to a horizontal cartwheel, twirled their contorted bodies around and around in a slow dance like erotic trapeze artists. Mother did not flicker.

'Mo, it's superb. But I want to see my troops.'

First, she called for her special huge mirror, and it was rolled on, cables coiled around its base, snake-like. When the lights were plugged in, she looked at her reflection. A nimbus of light surrounded her face.

The Red Queen in lush green velvet. Mo kissed the back of her neck – looked at her in the long mirror, and smiled as he went back to work.

Madou was incomparable in that scene. Hundreds of handsome Cossacks created two straight lines. If she felt nervous, it did not show. She walked between them, to inspect her guard, staring intently at their crotches. She halted and looked down at one of the troops, talking to his trousers, and not his face, saying, 'Hmm, you're new here.'

When a sword was pushed into her abdomen, she purred, 'Is that your sword, or are you just pleased to see me?'

She was magnificent, electrifying. She was in command. The spoilt German bride, transformed into an empress, ready to defeat her faithless, gormless husband and his army. Every male gaze was turned upon her, longing to kiss her hand, ready to die for their queen.

Then she turned, picked a piece of stray hay from a bale, and placed it seductively between her lips. She sucked the straw, staring boldly at her director. Teasing him, taunting him. He had not instructed her to do this. He who controlled her every movement, every gesture. I could tell by his face that she had overstepped the mark. There was a stunned silence. He stared at his star. She held his gaze, cool and still.

'Cut. Print.'

This Time Tomorrow

Tonight, back home, they quarrel fiercely. He stalks over to her desk, where he finds a love letter. She sits, with her stillness, looking at her reflection, while he rages behind her, waving the letter, with a theatrical flourish worthy of a Drury Lane actor. I have heard this all before. It is a well-rehearsed narrative. I am the only witness, the sole audience member, forced to endure this man's appalling arrogance.

MO: It was *I* who found you on the filthy streets of Berlin and brought you to Hollywood. My mistake was to fall in love. I ought to have known that you were unfaithful to the core.

MADOU: You knew about my history before you met me.

MO: Yes, I saw you posing for photographs with violets and lavender at your groin. I know all about Gerda. And that other woman who sang that song, Margo. Margo Lion.

Yes, he knew all about them. That stupid song they would sing at the cabaret. What was the song?

MADOU: 'My Best Girlfriend.'

MO: Yes, that absurd song. Drawing attention to yourself in that revolting manner.

MADOU: Why don't you stop bouncing up and down like a rubber ball.

MO: So it was Berlin. I know you were curious, and wanted to try everything, but don't forget it was my idea to introduce you to Hollywood with that Sapphic kiss. Full on the mouth. Dressed in men's evening clothes, and top hat. *My* idea. Not Yours. I changed your name from Maria to Joan.

As he continues his ranting monologue, her face turns very still. Only her eyes move. I know she is thinking over the Berlin scenes she has talked of so often when we are alone. Her mind is drifting back to the bare-breasted whores who chatted with clients at the Café Nationale. The rent boys, on every corner, flicking their whips, dressed in leather and feathers. The White Mouse, on the Behrenstrasse, where Anita Berber danced her naked dances of Horror, Lust and Ecstasy, wearing her drugs in a silver locket around her neck. The little hotels in the Augsburger Strasse, where you could rent a room for an hour. God, how she missed that life. So much colour, so much excitement.

Mo was a fool. She alone had taken her inspiration for Lola Lola from the cross-dressed boys from the cabaret. One of the blonde transvestites she especially admired wore ruffled panties, a feather boa, and a white silk top hat. The boys treated her like a sister, and they went dancing; she in her men's tails and top hat. She liked to wear her dead father's monocle. It made her feel close to him.

Of course she preferred women, but they were impossible to live with. Mo knew about her past. Why did he insist on being so bourgeois? She lights a cigarette and turns around.

'You know, Mo, in America, sex is an obsession, in the rest of the world it's a fact.'

He suddenly bursts into laughter. She can always make him laugh, even when he's angry with her. He bends down to kiss the nape of her neck. He is sorry. He should not have read the letter, which she left open for him to see.

Mo was obsessed by her from the first time he saw her in that beastly revue, *Two Neckties*. He had almost given up hope of finding his Lola Lola, when, by accident, he saw her in the play. The first time he laid eyes on her, she was standing offstage, leaning by a pillar, and she looked aloof and bored. She spoke only one line. She was wearing a conventional dress, but when she twirled around, she showed her underwear.

But it was her face – that face, so exquisite, but with the promise of devilry. What he loved was her nonchalance, and her cold disdain in the face of the knowledge that a famous Hollywood director was in the audience. She was equally indifferent when he invited her to his office for a screen test. She looked bored, and made no effort to be charming, and that was what interested him, poor little fool.

He asked her to sit on top of a piano and sing a ditty. She complied, but was sullen and dragged on a cigarette, blowing smoke out of the side of her mouth. She was asked to sing a song in English. The pianist, though able, was unfamiliar with the tune, although tried his best to accompany her rather mediocre singing, it must be admitted. Madou knew her limits.

Every time he made a mistake, she berated him, 'It's music, remember. Call that piano playing? How can I sing to that rubbish? You're not playing a washboard, jerk!' And again: 'What do you have for brains?'

Pale with anger, she climbed down from the piano, and she slapped him, hard, across the head: 'And I have to sing this crap – just don't screw up again, or I'll kick you.'

She knew that the studio executives, brought over from Hollywood, were horrified by her open contempt for a fellow artist, but Goldberg was delighted. This crass, uncouth, trampy woman was exactly what he had been searching for. He had found his Lola Lola; seducer of men, corrupter of morals, careless, contemptuous and carnal.

Mo knew that she could love no one, only herself. But that skin; white as milk, Parian marble, semi-translucent; pure white and entirely flawless.

He saw that she was so utterly beautiful, even *before* she was beautiful. He knew what he had to do; he would dominate her with his light to create perfection. That way she would never leave him.

The Lady is Willing

The review scene was the last time that my mother and Mo were really happy. All of a sudden, she had important issues to discuss with her leading man – the man she used to loathe, with fingers like sausages. For days, I was barred from her dressing room. Goulash no longer bubbled on the stove. Nellie kept guard and gave me dollars to spend in the commissary. There was a new chocolate malted that she wanted me to try. On the way, I saw Mr Goldberg. He looked sad.

Was I starving! I ordered hot dogs with onions, mustard, and ketchup; potato chips; corn on the cob, oozing warm butter. I crammed it into my mouth, relishing each morsel, away from Mother's prying eyes.

'You want apple pie, honey? Whipped cream and ice cream?'

I nodded. The lady was so nice.

'It's good that you enjoy your food, honey. I like to see a young girl who appreciates her food. You want more?'

My empty plate was my answer. I pushed it over the counter before she changed her mind.

People liked to feed me, I guess it's because they felt sorry for me. The more I ate, the thinner my mother became. I remember when I first began to eat alone. It was that day at the commissary, when the nice lady had pity in her brown, knowing eyes. I felt ashamed. That afternoon, I ate and ate. I took cookies and a huge tub of ice cream, and found a secret corner to eat. I ate quickly, not savouring the taste but stuffing my mouth as though my life depended on it. It felt so good to eat alone. All I could think about afterwards, was when I could eat again. And how I could get the food, without my mother knowing.

And here's the thing, I got to be good at it. Really good at it. The secrecy was thrilling. I had my favourites: Kraft macaroni and cheese, Wonder Classic white bread, Charleston Chews, Bumble Bee tuna, Lay's sour cream and onion chips, Wheat Thins, Yodels, Ring Dings, Cheese Nips.

When I had obtained my stash (often via my kindly body-guard) I would ask permission to go to my bedroom, and then I would turn on the electric fan to disguise the rustle of paper. One night, I ate half a chocolate cake. I especially loved candy, and when I'd finished, I folded the wrappers into tiny squares so that they could be hidden away. No one would know my little secret.

And how could it be bad when it made me feel so good, so warm inside? Here's the thing: food was my friend. It didn't insult me, or ignore me, or judge me. It was the gift that kept on giving. The discomfort was a small price to pay, the tightness of the waistband of my dress, which chafed my skin, the back ache, the stretch marks.

Compulsive eating: it creeps up on you, and before you know it, it feels like a thousand lead weights bearing down on you. But by then it's too late to stop. I ate when I was sad, when I was bored, when I was feeling bad about myself (most of the time), and when I was lonely. Can you imagine how it feels to be a child who is heavier than her mother? Here's another funny thing about compulsive eating. I truly believed that the more I ate, the more invisible I would become.

One day, I stole a cookie from my mother's dressing table. I tried not to look in the mirror, but I swear I heard it say, 'Go ahead and eat it, porker.'

Mo no longer appeared at the breakfast table for Mother's scrambled eggs. Never mind, more for me. She glared at me when I had extra helpings, and smoked her cigarette, puffing furiously.

'A bigger dress size. How can that be?'

Mother is ashamed, but nothing that anyone else says can hurt as much as the things that I say to myself. When I pulled on my bathing suit, over my hips and belly, I tried not to notice the soft rolls of fat. In the blue rectangular pool, I felt light as air. I spent hours floating until the skin on my fingers wrinkled.

I was sure that Mo would be replaced before too long, and I was right. The next morning a dozen long-stemmed red roses appeared in their long, white coffins. American Beauty. Whoops. I waited for the storm.

'Why can't the shop girls cut the thorns from the roses? But if they were not stupid, they wouldn't be working in a florist's shop.'

The sender of the red roses appeared in her dressing room. She cooked him a perfect omelette in her crinoline and wig, and somehow managed to never get a drop of oil on her dress. The next evening, he appeared at the house of mirrors for her famous *pot au feu*. Mother looked divine in a *Hausfrau* apron with a bandana tied around her hair. She removed his shoes, and massaged his feet. I poured the champagne into crystal-cut glasses that sparkled and gleamed. I loved to hear the hiss of the bubbles as they danced around the rim of the coupe. The breasts of Marie Antoinette, Mother said, with a smile.

At dinner, she smiled and tapped her finger on the side of his head: 'You see, there's nothing there. Quite empty. Nothing inside that pretty head. Not a single idea, and that's what I like.'

Nevertheless, there was talk over dinner about the New Deal. I liked the nice new president who seemed to be trying to help people who couldn't afford food. The thought of being hungry made me feel ill. Mother had her own views on why the bad times didn't seem to affect the motion-picture industry: 'Nobody wants to pay for reality during a depression – that's there for nothing.'

She glanced at the *LA Times* on the sideboard.

'All those millionaires jumping out of skyscrapers just because they lost some of their precious money. All they had to stop doing was being so dramatic and get a job.'

I had eaten so much at supper that my new pink organza dress split its stitches. I heard it tear as I stretched for the salt cellar. My cheeks burned hot, and I could feel the sweat under my waist and my arms. Mother was too absorbed in her new friend to notice. I asked permission to leave the table, and scarpered. On the way to my bedroom, I played my daily game of dodging all the mirrors.

Back on the hot set, Mo was displeased with his star. He barked out his criticisms, called her 'a fat cow' in German.

'Drop your voice an octave and don't lisp.'

'Look at that lamp as if you could no longer live without it.'

'You are the Empress of Russia, not a German milkmaid.'

He made her descend a staircase forty-five times, over and over again, until she got it right. She did it without demur. Her velvet crinoline, so magnificent, was heavy, and the intense heat of the lamps burned onto her face, but she didn't perspire, and never once complained of fatigue. She was so courageous. Didn't flinch, despite the insults, and the pain etched on her lovely face. Over and over and over again. Up and down. Down and up. Such a soldier, such a queen. She *had* 10,000 men. He marched her up to the top of the hill, and he marched her down again.

But I was furious. Why was Mo being so cruel to my mother? What had she done that was so bad?

Bonne Nuit, Merci

That gorgeous tart-face and her garter belt launched a legend. But, more than this, Madou knew how to *sustain* a legend.

The reflection is of a movie star, but as I know all too well, she is also a woman who reads. Knut Hamsun, Selma Lagerlöf, Hugo von Hofmannsthal, and Friedrich Hölderlin. She worships Rilke; she knows, by heart, the writings of Erich Kästner. Very fancy, very modern.

According to her myopic critics, her acting talent isn't supreme, her singing voice at best mediocre; she can't dance for toffee. None of that matters a jot. She isn't a celebrity; she is a Movie Star.

Here's what I think about Moses von Goldberg. He saw her as someone who could take his direction, someone pliant, and ready to be moulded. Poppycock! I once heard him say, 'I can turn you off and on like a spigot.' Their first film together set the tone for their professional relationship: the clever, gentle, sophisticated, older gentleman dominated and humiliated by a crass showgirl. He would return to this theme over and over again.

Lola Lola had to be able to inspire obsession in an *intelligent* man, and that was exactly the quality he was looking for. Madou had it naturally. It couldn't be faked. Eventually, inevitably, the girl destroys him. He should have known. But how could he have known that Professor Unrat's descent into a grinning cuckolded stage clown would mirror his own doomed relationship?

As I say, he wasn't counting on her intelligence. She was no statue, or puppet. When he deserted her, to save himself, she found her own way. He left Hollywood to make another picture, telling her that she'd be better off without him, that she would develop as an actress. But she was terrified of losing his light. Then she had an idea. She would steal his light.

For days, she watched Herr Direktor's films in the projection room, over and over again. The others thought she was vain, but she was mastering his art. Light and shadow. Shadow and light. Another director was found, and on the first day of shooting she asked for her mirror.

She looks at him scornfully when he brings her a hand mirror. She points her finger, and I am wheeled in front of her: an eight-foot mirror on castors, dotted with light bulbs. She looks around the set at the crew, who are half mesmerised, half shocked. She is terrified, but, always the warrior, she sets about her job. She instructs the electricians to plug in the lights, and the grips to position me, so that she can see herself exactly as the camera will see her.

Then she makes her next move.

'With your permission, gentlemen,' she issues instructions to the electricians high up.

'You on the right, come down, but slowly, there stop, set it.'

Then it is the turn of the small wattage lights, and then the all-important key lights. The spotlight near her face, but high, high above it, and a little to the right. She raises her finger, until she feels the exact amount of heat.

All the time, she stares at me, the mirror, and, like a miracle, shadows begin to appear. She is moulding, shading, highlighting. Then the face appears, in all its luminous beauty. A small butterfly shape flutters under the nose. She is ready for the camera to roll.

The crew, hardened and tough, begin a slow, appreciative, clap. She smiles: 'Thank you, gentlemen.'

She has taken control of Joan Madou, the Movie Star.

Mo was vanquished, and he knew it. Vanquished by a mirror.

The Little Napoleon

A bad day at the studio.

The crew was pale. Nobody said a word.

'Do it again.'

'Why are you so incapable of doing anything correctly?'

'Clear the set.'

This was the third time Mo had cleared the set. I waited outside in the blazing Californian heat while he screamed and shouted at her. Mother stayed silent.

This was the final scene. Madou was to ring the great cathedral bell, proclaiming herself the Empress of Russia. A huge steel crucifix had been attached to the end of the rope, which was weighted with sandbags, rigged onto a pulley. Every time she pulled the rope, using the full force of her body, the crucifix whacked against her inner thigh. She was required to ring the bell eight times.

'Cut! Miss Madou, what on earth are you doing. You are not ringing for the butler at an elegant dinner in Paris, you are ringing the bells of the Kremlin. Do it again!'

On the fourteenth take, he cried: 'Miss Madou. Try for a little expression on that beautiful face of yours. You are seizing a throne, not calling in the cows like an Austrian milkmaid.'

On the twenty-fifth take, her hands trembled and she began to perspire. The crew looked on in shocked silence. The tension in the air was unbearable. At that moment everyone on-set despised Mr von Goldberg.

On the fiftieth take, she could take no more. Her pale, lovely face was contorted, like the agonised screams of those gargoyles. She was not the Empress of Russia, triumphant, victorious, ringing the bells of her success. She was a hollow shell. And that's the one he chose.

'Cut! Print! Ladies and gentlemen, thank you.'

And with those words he left the set.

Nellie and I rushed to my mother. The metal edges of the crucifix had lacerated her inner thighs, blood seeped through her white long tights. Nellie begged her to see the studio doctor. Mother finally spoke: 'No. Do not let anyone know about this. Not a soul. Bring me a bowl, towels and alcohol. Take me to my dressing room and lock the door.'

I could hardly bear to look as she poured the stinging liquid onto her cuts, but she didn't flinch. Nellie and I bandaged her legs, and then we drove home in silence.

Back in the House of Mirrors, Mother prepared her goulash,

opened the wine, and waited for Mo. He didn't appear. At nine, she cracked and telephoned him.

When he arrived, she served him his food in the mirrored dining room. She was limping.

'Is it good? Would you like more flat noodles?'

He looked at her in sorrow and shame. But he said nothing.

'It's fine, Mo. You were right. You are always right. I was terrible in that scene. I am sorry for being so much trouble to you.'

I felt so hungry that my belly ached, but I excused myself and left the table. She would be angry with me for my appalling manners, and I knew I would pay for it, but at that moment I hated the little man. The Red Queen had made her final move. I didn't know why or how my mother had won. I just knew that she had.

The Party's Going with a Swing

As a rule, Madou dislikes Hollywood parties, mainly because of the low level of intelligence among her fellow actors. We have one of our infrequent 'discussions' about her profession. It is my belief that intelligent actors are seldom as good as unintelligent ones. That's part of her problem. She's too damn smart for this tawdry business.

'My dear Joan, acting is an instinct. A gift that is often given to people who are very silly.'

'Actors don't ever grow up. I have no real desire to be an actress. To always play someone else, to be always beautiful, with someone constantly straightening out every eyelash. It's a bother to me. I do it for the money.'

'They're made of papier mâché, creatures of tinsel and sawdust. You're not an actress, my dear, you're a personality. A star.'

'How do I look?'

'Charming. You're a permanent pleasure to the eye.'

She puts down her hairbrush and clips on her diamond earrings. It's time for the wrap party. One thing that can be said for Hollywood is that it really knows how to do a wrap party.

Madou adores her crew, and they adore her back. She admires their discipline, and their professionalism. She is generous to a fault. One time, a grip fell from a lighting rig, and damaged his back. Madou paid for all of his hospital bills, and sent packages of food to his family. If someone so much as sniffs around her, she fetches her thermos flasks of broth and advises on the best medications. Her wrap parties are legendary.

She is still angry with Mo, so she wants this party to be one to be remembered, insisting that it is hosted on the set of the Russian Imperial Palace. She is dressed to kill, in a Molyneux silk sheath and a white fur stole. Diamonds glitter at her earlobes and throat. She adds a ruby and diamond ring; a present from her latest conquest, knowing that Mo will notice and be furious.

One final glance, and she is off to the sound set. Once there, she asks one of the crew to wheel over her mirror. She wants me to see it all. What an enchanting spectacle! Mo's huge banqueting table, which formerly held rotting fruit and platters of painted food, is now home to piles and piles of presents exquisitely wrapped in gold and silver, gleaming in the spotlights.

Trays of champagne flutes hiss and sparkle with amber bubbles. Party food lines the table; egg sandwiches, platters of sliced ham, and bowls of Russian potato salad. The showpiece is a magnificent cake depicting scenes from *The Red Queen*. There's a snow scene of the entry into St Petersburg, complete with a gingerbread carriage frosted with ebony icing. Sugar-frosted pine trees glisten, and shimmery white chocolate snowflakes rest softly on the gingerbread window panes of the Winter Palace.

For the indoor scenes, marzipan gargoyles grin and leer, and sugar-crafted pillars are entwined with delicate garlands of pale edible flowers. In the middle of the creation is a sugar paste figure of the empress in the Imperial Palace wearing her white and gold wedding dress, and sitting on a white and silver-leaf throne. Naturally, this confectionary delight of a cake is too beautiful to eat. It exists merely to be worshipped, just like Madou herself.

The Child, I'm happy to say, doesn't see me, but stares greedily at the platters of food on the never-ending table. It is time for the present-giving ceremony. Twenty-dollar gold pieces are sliced open to reveal paper-thin gold Patek Philippe wristwatches, with personal messages signed inside. These are given to the men, along with cufflinks, leather wallets, gold cigarette cases.

For the women, diamond clips from Cartier, some with rubies, sapphires, then patterned gold. Others are given handbags, scarves, and perfume. Lower down the line, waitresses are given signed photographs. Madou bestows every present with a handshake and a beatific smile.

Finally, she calls for Mr von Goldberg. He doesn't want to be there. He is shifty, uncomfortable, so *déclassé*. He is despised by the crew. Madou kneels at his feet, and she kisses his hand reverently: 'Without my master, my Lord of Light, I am nothing.'

He presents her with a sapphire and diamond cuff. But it's me that she turns towards, twirling and twisting her slender wrist so the bracelet dances and gleams in the light. The Child, I see, looks on enviously. She is singularly unattractive. How did Madou give birth to such an unappealing child? No one will ever present *her* with fine jewels, fit for a queen.

I dare her to come closer, but she backs away and returns to the table. I regret to say that when she *thinks* no one is looking, she crams forkfuls of cake into her fat little mouth. Then she takes the sugar figure of the empress and bites off its head. She carefully places the decapitated figure back in its place on the marzipan throne.

The Woman One Longs For

Later that night, when the party was over, Mother and I went to the editing room with flasks full of beef tea for Mo. The studio was always a strange place at night. We drove through a silent New York street, a shabby Little Italy tenement, then BOOM, we turned a corner into a night shoot set in Victorian London. The commissary truck supplying sandwiches and hot drinks, lights blazing. On and on we went until we reached a three-storey building with blacked-out windows. The edit suite; Mo's domain.

He showed Mother his best results. She was respectful, gracious. She knew that he would work long into the night, cutting and splicing, wearing his special white gloves. He seemed happy. He talked away as he worked. This is poetry, Joan. You are more than an actress, you are a dramatic encounter with light.

There are many encounters between my mother and Mo that I have edited from my memory, but this one remains a cherished moment. He was so proud of his work. I can remember his exact words.

'You see, Joan, she has to become ruthless to compete with the men around her. She has been groomed for stardom by her mother, given a new image, presented to the public, and then become dehumanised, imprisoned by her own image. You see what she has become?'

If only my mother had taken the hint. Listened to Mo and his warning. Things could have turned out differently. For all of us. I wish I could turn back the clock to this moment, and tell her to stop, now before it's too late.

Mo told her to stick around for retakes, and then she could depart for Europe, as she wished. Then there were sittings for publicity photos. Mother presided over the contact prints, retouching them with her wax pencil, shaping the nose, the hands (which she hated), the corners of the mouth, and when the product was perfect, she ordered dozens of copies for herself.

Mo left a message to join him in the projection room to view the rough cut. Mother was luminous. As Mo intended, the corpses and gargoyles served to enhance her beauty, the purity of her white skin. *No one films you like I do, because no loves you as I do.* Mother knelt at Mo's knees, her golden hair fan-like against his trousers. He put his hand gently on her hair, his eyes sad.

* * *

In the morning, we stripped Mother's dressing room, and then we packed for Europe. Mother's clothes were carefully wrapped in tissue paper and stored in enormous steamer trunks, which looked like coffins. We packed the dolls. On the train we pulled down the blinds, locked the doors, took off her departure outfit, and packed it away in tissue. She removed her garter belt, then the expensive silk stockings, rinsed them and hung them carefully over towels to dry. A more comfortable bra was put on. She washed her face and brushed out the curls in her hair. Put on a navy PJ set and silk dressing gown.

'Soon, I will drink real coffee in Paris, not the piss that Americans drink.'

I ate my last cheeseburger and a slice of lemon meringue pie, and waved goodbye to the Big Green Lady with the torch, and I promised her that I would be back soon.

Mother was in a good mood when we boarded the *Europa* and entered our staterooms, which were already filled with huge baskets of flowers and bottles of champagne in ice buckets. The pungent scent of tuberoses and white lilac filled the air. The maid had already begun unpacking the coffins for Frau Madou; her tuxedos and evening gowns were hanging on padded hangers, and evening shoes and bags had been labelled and stored away.

Mother was chatting and laughing with the waiter and her steward. She was so relaxed, and I didn't understand why until I realised that everyone was speaking in German. So that's why she was happy! My heart swelled with love and pity. All those times when she was so edgy, it hadn't occurred to me that she could be homesick.

We ordered room service: liver dumplings, cabbage rolls, frankfurters, red cabbage, sauerkraut, liverwurst on black bread. When she finally finished eating, she worked her way through the large pile of cables, while I sorted the flower cards. She picked out one to read.

'Sweetheart, just listen to this: *Darling I yearn for you (stop) it is one week today since your beautiful naughty hand opened a white rose (stop) how will I live without my love and my life.*'

Mother was unimpressed: 'Nebbish, that woman is getting too vain.'

Mo's telegram pleased her more: I AM MADOU STOP MADOU IS ME STOP DO NOT FORGET TO COME BACK STOP

Then there was a cable from my father, telling Mother that she must not come to Berlin, and that they would reunite in Paris. But nothing could prevent her from bubbling over with happiness.

The captain had invited her to be his guest. We dined in the vast splendid dining room with its carved mahogany pillars, festooned with carved garlands and eagles. Everyone turned to stare when she made *La Grande Descente* and we walked to the table. Mother was resplendent in a low-cut gown of gold lamé that clung to her body as if she had been dipped in silky butterscotch.

I started to worry when the waiters began to bolt down the tables. As the ship began to roll, the dining room emptied. Mother held her glass of champagne firmly, and calmly carried on eating her pickled herring in sour cream.

Her mood only changed when she discovered a copy of *Mein Kampf* in the ship's bookstore. Luckily, it was the day that we docked, though she wasted no time in telling Papi, who was there to meet us at Southampton.

I kissed Papi and made my curtsy, and then they talked about stuff I didn't understand. The book burnings at the Opernplatz, how Mutti (he always called her Mutti) must not go to Berlin, how it wasn't safe.

'Papi, don't be so dramatic. Why doesn't someone just kill that dreadful little man?'

Papi chuckled: 'Mutti, the hotel outside Paris. It's beautiful. It's in Versailles. A hotel of mirrors. We shall go shopping.'

'Papi. May we go fur shopping? I stole my Russian sable from those damn furriers at the studio, and now I have a taste for it.'

'Darling, we shall go fur shopping in Austria, lingerie shopping in Paris, suit shopping on Savile Row.'

'And Berlin?'

'No, Mutti, not Berlin.'

*   *   *

We had a phrase for when Mother was not working: 'in real life'. In real life, she wore trouser suits and shirts with cufflinks. In real life, she ate as much as she wanted and let her hair dry naturally.

As Papi promised, we stayed at the Trianon Palace Hotel, close to Versailles. Our suite of rooms was fit for Madame de Pompadour: all mirrors, gilt, and rococo furniture. I imagined Cinderella dancing in the Salon Clémenceau, and losing her glass slipper on the wrought-iron and bronze-gilded staircase.

After we had finished scrubbing and bleaching the bathrooms, Mother bathed, while I set up her desk. I unpacked and laid out ashtrays, water glass, tray with pencils and Waterman pens, desk blotter and blue ink, two boxes of blue monogrammed paper and envelopes. Stack of Western Union forms.

The first day we ate beluga caviar and filet mignon, with white asparagus, washed down with pink champagne for the grown-ups, and freshly squeezed lemonade for me.

In Europe, Mother never seemed to tire: 'Papi, I want to go lingerie shopping. But I want silk only, not lace. Lace rolls into a wet sausage between one's legs. So vulgar, so low-class shop girl. Very Garbo.'

Papi chuckled indulgently and telephoned for a saleswoman to bring her wares to the hotel. She arrived in a navy serge suit with a huge suitcase while I was having my rest. Later, Mother called me into her room. Strewn over her bed were dozens of gossamer silk mousseline confections in champagne, coffee and ivory.

Satin, crêpe de Chine, so soft to the touch they slipped between my fingers.

Mother picked up a pair of pink silk panties edged with golden-brown lace, and, turning to Papi, announced: 'You never know, said the widow.' It was one of her favourite sayings whenever she handled beautiful lingerie. It was one of those adult jokes that escaped me, but I laughed along with her, because I loved to see her happy.

Fresh from *The Red Queen*, Mother had developed a taste for fur. We went fur shopping. She acquired a floor-length mink cape, and a silver lamé dress with a five-foot train edged in black fox. Two silver foxes, joined at the snout, were bought to be draped over her pinstriped suits. For me, she bought a white rabbit coat and matching beret.

Mother was getting fat on the delicious hotel food. We ate chicken poached with truffles, lamb, céléri à la grecque, artichoke vinaigrette, spring-pea soup, soufflé potato, leaf spinach, endive salad, caramelised pear, raspberries with cream, lemon soufflé tart, and soft cheeses. I still longed for melted cheese and bacon on white, and Paramount's coconut cream pie.

In the evening, we went to the opera. Mother wore a dress of pale chiffon, which clung to her curves like a second skin. She looked just like a Greek statue. I had taped her breasts with adhesive to make them appear naked and perky, just like we did at the studio. She often told me that I had ruined her breasts when she had fed me as a baby, so it was important that I make them perfect again, as they had once been.

Papi had given me opera glasses, and when I peered through them I admired the beauty of the dress extras, which caused great mirth to my parents, who explained that these were real people in real clothes. In Hollywood, central casting often hired old failed actors from a special list who came perfectly groomed and dressed in their own evening clothes. It was sometimes so hard to tell reality from studio life.

We visited Versailles and lingered in the Hall of Mirrors. Even for someone who feared mirrors as I did, it was a glorious sight. The seventeen mirror-clad arches echoed the seventeen windows looking out on the garden. I counted each of the twenty-one arch mirrors, 357 in all. The guide explained how Jean Baptiste-Colbert had enticed glass-makers from Venice to teach the art to French manufacturers. Mirrors were a symbol of power and status. The guide told us how the Venetian Republic sent agents to France to poison the workers who had betrayed the secrets of mirror-making.

The light reflected from the glass and the chandeliers and the windows bathed us in a golden glow. I heard Mother muttering darkly to herself as she caught sight of her iridescent beauty in the mirrors.

Later that evening, she confined herself to fish soup and coffee, smoking furiously in short, stabbing motions. Over dinner, there was talk of Berlin. Words I had never heard: *Nazi, Gestapo, SS*. Germany was not safe, so we packed for Vienna.

Mother had longed for coffee with *Schlag*, which, as she had promised, was delicious. The Viennese adore this rich, sweetened whipped cream, which they put on pies, fruit, cake and coffee. 'Papi, do you think the Viennese *do it* with *Schlag*?'

We shopped at the House of Knize for tails and tuxedos, bought tickets for the Mozart concerts in the Golden Hall of the Wiener Musikverein, and took strolls in Belvedere Palace park.

In Salzburg, Mother wore blue-flowered chiffon, and played 'The Blue Danube' over and over again on her gramophone. In Lanz of Salzburg, she dressed me in a Tyrolean peasant dress with a red bodice and full blue skirt.

'Sweetheart, another size larger? How is that possible? Here put this striped apron around your waist. Stand straight. Slouching does not help matters. Hmm, the blouse is too tight around the upper arms.'

A circle of customers gathered to watch the show. They pitied my beautiful mother, who was only trying to do her best with me. Salzburg was a disaster.

But then, gloriosky! A telegram arrived from the studio trusting that she'd had a pleasant rest and bidding her imminent return to California. Von Goldberg was to direct her in a film that he had written for her, and she was to wire her acceptance so he could proceed.

The phone rang: 'Mo, sweetheart, what is this madness? Those little Russian Jewish furriers think they are God. They should kiss your feet, not de Mille's behind. You tell them that *Mr* von Goldberg will tell me what to do, and I will do it.'

She hung up. I tried hard not to show my joy that I was going home. That evening we stayed in and had room service. Papi finished his accounts, and Mother read her book. It felt just like being in a real family that I had once seen in a movie.

Farewell Song

Madou stares into me as she scrubs her hands over and over again with Roger & Gallet sandalwood soap. It is time to teach that bastard a lesson. Ever since she returned from Europe, at his behest, he has been beastly.

Jealousy … such an ugly emotion, so demeaning, so low-class. He has become boring, joyless, with his cow-like eyes full of recrimination and self-pity. But there will be no undignified scenes. Better to behave admirably in the face of his ungovernable rage.

She knows this is their swan song. She's said it before, and gone crawling back to him, but this time, he's gone too far. She is contracted for one more picture, and then she is free. This movie will be her favourite because she has never looked more ravishing. It will be the only picture of which she will ever own a print, but sitting here, in the thick of it, all she feels is the pain, the humiliation.

Regrettably, she is, once again, playing a whore. Why? Because that's what he *truly* thinks of her. It's time for more finger-wagging.

'So you've come back for more, my dear? Glutton for punishment or Jacobean revenge tragedy? That type of man never changes.'

She takes a cigarette out of the case on her dressing table and lights it.

'Most women set out to try to change a man, and when they have changed him, they do not like him. I've never tried to change Mo. He is what he is. I accept him the way he is.'

'You're in for a bitter time.'

'Then I shall summon up my courage and face it properly.'

'You need to develop as an actress. Every picture you appear in is exactly the same; frivolous, superficial, and without the slightest intellectual significance. Don't you want to go down in posterity as a great actress?'

'I don't give a damn about posterity. Why should I care what people think about me when I'm as dead as a doornail?'

'You might feel differently when you're older, and wiser. Well, you have been warned. Better stop shilly-shallying and get to it. You're needed in the Canvas room.'

The setting of the new picture is Seville. There is lace everywhere; scalloped lace, Chantilly lace, antique lace in every colour imaginable. Mo loves lace because he can put his light behind it, creating patterns and shadows that enhance his star's beauty. In the

Canvas room, they unfurl flags of silks and muslin. The Child hovers, as ever, her eyes watchful.

'Kater, sweetheart, we must have Spanish combs. Tortoiseshell and ivory. And those silk carnations we found in Paris with Papi. I knew we would need them one day. Fetch Travis. And Nellie.'

Nellie crafts a braided wig that looks similar to Madou's blonde, wispy hair, and then sews the wig onto the large comb. Madou's hair is dragged so tightly back from her forehead it makes her scalp bleed. She loves the effect it has on her skin; a natural facelift. She never complains about the pain.

And nor does she demur when Mo explains his insane idea about his close-up opening shot. His plan is to fire an air gun into a mass of party balloons. When all of the balloons have exploded, the camera will reveal her perfect face. He tells her it is important not to flinch, not to blink. Not to show fear.

'Excuse me, Mo. I'm not sure I understand you. You are intending to explode balloons in my face? Who is shooting the gun?'

'I am, my darling, I would not trust anyone else. But you must not show any reaction. Not a flicker of an eyelash.'

'Then we will need to change the top of the dress, so it's lower. And we must have a very high comb, with a veil. And if you shoot me in the eye, we will need an eye patch.'

The Child looks on anxiously. She fiddles with her doll. She's far too quiet for a child. Easy to forget that she's around, except that I see everything. I also observe that Nellie has made a tiny doll comb and veil. Travis has created a ruffled Spanish doll dress, red with black silk spots. The Child forces the comb up into the hair of the doll, pushing the hair back from the face. The doll is exquisite; arms and neck made of the finest wax, dimples where dimples should be, eyelashes that look real. Ears like delicate pink shells. There she is; a perfect mini Madou.

Mo turns to his star.

'Joan. They have decided not to renew my contract. It's better this way. I can do no more for you.'

She pretends to be angry. She tells him that it's his own fault. He replays the same theme, over and over again, the man who suffers for his passion, who throws himself away on a vulgar guttersnipe who tortures him for her pleasure. She's sick of it. Why does she always have to play a cold-blooded whore?

He glares at her. 'Why do you think?'

In this picture he reveals his torture about their relationship: 'That woman has ice, where others have a heart.' He has her speaking a contemptible line to her lover: 'If you really loved me, you'd kill yourself.'

He tries to take it out on her with his art, but he is a fool. She doesn't care. Anyone could see that. He could never pull *her* strings. She is the girl tossing him into the air. One evening after a day's filming, she loses her cool and screams at him: 'You made me in your image. Now deal with me.'

But she suffers, too. One evening, she returns to her dressing room, exhausted. Her head aches. Nellie has made little braids of Madou's hair and wires a large comb to her head. A heavy mantilla is attached to the comb. Madou sits at her dressing table and Nellie takes out her wire cutters, snips the bands and releases the comb. Madou falls forward, exhausted from pain, and rests her arms and head on the table. When she comes up, tears are coursing down her face.

The film is a box-office disaster, but I have a feeling that one day, probably after Mo's death, the critics will reassess their verdict and pronounce it a masterpiece. While the rest of Hollywood is producing screwball comedies, he is the one exploring the agony of love.

I can imagine the scene. She will be an old diva. They will ask her if the film was a metaphor for his hopeless love and disillusion. She will laugh: 'We were just making a picture. It was our last collaboration. They say it was all about Mr von Goldberg and me. Such affectation. Nebbish. But I was most beautiful in that film. It was all down to *Mo*, of course.'

That appalling little lace-maker is finally out of her professional life, but there is one final, ugly scene that I am forced to witness. Although he will no longer work with her, he hasn't yet learned how *not* to be in her bed. But he won't stand for it, when she flaunts her love affairs in his face. Now, he will leave.

Mo kisses her softly on the back of the neck, and takes a last glance at her reflection in me. He is wearing a degraded brown hat, and absurd Turkish boots.

She isn't going to let him leave without a fight.

'So, you are again throwing me to the wolves? You bring me to this dreadful country and you throw me away, like a piece of rotting fruit. I gave you everything.'

'Yes. I have never denied that you have been a sublime inspiration.'

'Then why are you deserting me?'

'If you don't know the answer to that question, there's no use my trying to explain.'

'Mo, that's a woman's line.'

'Perhaps our roles have reversed?'

'Don't be clever. If you want to leave, then leave.'

'It is better this way. For us both. We have gone as far as we can together. Now I have to save myself.'

'So you are going?'

'Yes, my love.'

And he leaves. Just. Like. That.

She gazes into me for a long, long time. There have been endings before, fights, and reconciliations. But this one is different. I do my best to give comfort. She expects it of me. She has no one else to turn to.

'Darling Joan, in moments of private chaos, it is better to be alone. Loving advice merely increases the misery. But I will never let you down, and I will always speak the truth: *Thousands of people have talent. I might as well congratulate you for having eyes in your head. The one and only thing that counts is: Do you have staying power?*

She finally speaks: 'Yes, I do.'

She snaps on Mo's resplendent bracelet of diamonds and sapphires and she sweeps out of the dressing room.

Manpower

Mo vanished out of our lives almost overnight, and a new man appeared in the House of Mirrors. He was a tall, blond, blue-eyed Englishman, who loved Shakespeare, the theatre, and my mother. And I think he loved me. I know that I adored him. He listened intently when I asked him a question, and he spoke to me as if I were a grown-up. He was a classically trained actor, with the most beautiful cut-glass English accent. Of all my mother's lovers, he was the man I most wanted to be my father. His name was Lacy.

He gave me my first Shakespeare play, told me to read it slowly, and not to be frightened by the difficult words, but to keep a dictionary beside me. It was the start of a life-long love affair. The play was *A Midsummer Night's Dream*, and I was enthralled. There was a funny man called Bottom, and he was transformed into a donkey, and the Queen of the Fairies fell in love with him. She reminded me of my mother. The queen loved the changeling child, just as my mother loved only me, and said I belonged to no one else, not even Papi.

There was another Shakespeare queen, too, who was a bad queen. I told Mother all about her. She snorted: 'Lady Macbeth. Peculiar idea of hospitality!'

I had displeased Mother. I didn't know then that an adult could feel jealous of a child. She didn't like Lacy giving me so much attention. It was she who had insisted that the studio find her a new leading man, and they brought him over from England, especially for Mother. Mother wanted my undivided attention. When she was angry, she never raised her voice, she simply pretended that I didn't exist, or gave me 'the freeze' – that look of hers that was as cold as Siberia. Her mouth full of lemons.

In the morning, she left for the studio without me. For once, I could lie in bed. I remember waking to an odd sound, a low shuddering sound. I looked at the mirrored closet doors … they were rattling. The next thing I knew, the new maid ran in and grabbed me. She was gibbering in Spanish and I just about made out, 'the door frame … is the safest place'. The earth was moving, and I was excited and terrified in equal measure. As we headed down the staircase, it began moving up towards us, and the huge chandelier in the hall was shaking and jingling ominously. We just about made it to the huge oak front door, as the chandelier crashed behind us. Then all was silent.

Mother had no way of knowing we were safe. All the phone lines were down. Luckily, she had not even left her dressing room at the moment that the first tremors began. Lacy rushed to find her, shouting that at least they could die together. Mother was horrified. She pushed him out of the way and ran to find a phone.

On the way, she met another famous actress; she never would tell me her name.

'Joan, why are you running?'

'My child. I've left her at home. I need to reach her.'

'It will be fine. Don't worry, my children are at home, and I'm not worried.'

'Yes,' my mother cried, 'but *your* children are adopted!'

My memory is hazy about our reunion. How did Mother get to me? The phone lines were down, and people were terrified of the aftershock and hid under tables and door frames. All was quiet. I guess I've seen so many film sets that the sight of Hollywood diminished to rubble didn't seem so peculiar. I always had a problem distinguishing between appearance and reality, and who could blame me?

Find me she did. Our maid took me to her church, which was still standing, though its windows had been blown out. Long Beach was levelled, the House of Mirrors was a mountain of smashed glass, and so we moved into the Beverly Wilshire Hotel for the night. Mother and I lay together in the king-size bed, waiting for the aftershocks, Mother muttering, 'There are no earthquakes in Germany.' After running to stand under the door frame three times, we decided to get some sleep. Mother told me about Lacy's impertinence, reassuring me that she would only ever want to die together with *me*. I was expected to show my gratitude for the honour of dying with her, but all I could really think about were the delicious black and white ice cream sodas at the hotel's drugstore fountain.

Our suite at the Beverly Wilshire was so elegant. In the main room, greeting our arrival, was an enormous bunch of white roses and lilies, and a huge bowl of fruit. Mother hated all fruit except for apples. She took a red apple from the bowl and bit into its crisp flesh, and a dribble of apple juice trickled down her scarlet lips.

Dream Girl

They escape the House of Mirrors, but will not escape me. The most dangerous place to be in an earthquake is next to a mirror. Broken glass lines the streets of Long Beach; scenes of destruction and debris that look like a war zone in a movie, except for once, in Hollywood, it's real life. All those broken mirrors create a tsunami of bad luck. In the end, 117 people die in the earthquake, and many more are injured.

It's a good thing I wasn't shattered because that would have been the end for Madou. A broken mirror is seven years' bad luck. Seven because life renews every seven years. Every cell in the body renews so that the person is a different person. Shedding skin, like a snake. Every seven years, skin flakes off, hair falls out; nails break off and regrow. Regenerated cells in the hair, the skin, the liver, the stomach and intestines, the bones. Every seven years, they all become new people with new consciousness. How can anyone know themselves when every seven years the person is changing, the human body in constant flux? Seven years are enough to change every pore and every emotion.

Some people believe the seven years' bad luck could be washed away by immersing the pieces of broken shards of mirror in south-flowing water for seven hours. What an absurd superstition. No, you must apologise for your clumsiness and then bury the fragments of the glass in the cold earth, carefully and respectfully.

If the person happens to be looking into the mirror when they break it, then they fracture their soul. Breaking a magic mirror is even more dangerous. Magic mirrors reflect the shadow soul, and show the true nature of the person being reflected. Certain death will come to those who shatter a magic mirror. The Child wants to protect her shadow soul, so she covers me, especially at night, before she retires to bed. For extra good luck, she recites her favourite poem:

And moving through a mirror clear
That hangs before her all the year,
Shadows of the world appear.

. . . .

But in her web she still delights
To weave the mirror's magic sights,
For often through the silent nights
A funeral, with plumes and lights

And music, went to Camelot:
Or when the moon was overhead,
Came two young lovers lately wed;
'I am half sick of shadows,' said
The Lady of Shalott.

Are the gods of Hollywood speaking through the earthquake? I have a feeling that for the next seven years things may not go quite so well for Madou.

Song of Songs

'Papi, you will not believe this … now listen carefully and tell me what to do.

'"Applause for Joan Madou, who has finally dismissed the Jewish director who has always cast her as a prostitute or a fallen woman, but never in the role which would bring dignity to the great citizen and representative of the Third Reich. Now, Madou should come home to the Fatherland, assume her historic role as a leader of the German film industry and end allowing herself to be the tool of Hollywood's Jews!"

'Do they really believe that *I* will be returning to Germany, when eight million Jews are trying to escape? Papi, you must leave at once, and you must bring Mother with you. I'll send you more money. Now, speak to your daughter.'

'Hello, Papi. How is Sofi?'

I knew from the silence that I had displeased my father by my reference to his long-term mistress. But I loved her deeply, and it was so long ago that I had seen her, and felt her arms around me. I should have remembered to be more careful.

'I'm sorry, Papi. I've been rude. I miss you so much. I worry about Mutti. She's seemed so worried, and Mo has gone.'

'Do not worry, Kater. I need to speak to your mother, again.'

'Papi, may I have a dog?'

'Goodbye, Kater.'

On my father's advice, Mother contacted the studio's head of publicity, and later that day announced that she would sever all ties with Germany and apply for American citizenship. She also released a statement, praising Mo as her God: 'It is not my wish for our association to be broken. I would prefer to go on as in the past. He feels that this is the time for me to go on alone. So that is what I shall do.'

Many years later, Papi told me of the danger he was under. On the evening of Mother's statement, Papi was paid a visit requiring him to take on a senior position in the German film industry. He thanked the official for the great honour, and asked for twenty-four hours to think about it. As soon as he was alone, he packed a suitcase, threw it into his car and drove slowly and calmly all through the night until he reached Paris. Don't bring attention to yourself. Don't stop. Don't panic. He told me that he had never been so afraid in all of his life. He then telephoned my mother. She cried with relief. I wondered why she had forgotten to ask about Sofi.

My father was pleased when Mother told him that the studio had renewed her contract, making her the highest paid star in Hollywood. She celebrated by renting a new house in Bel Air, and going jewellery shopping. She went to Trabert & Hoeffer-Mauboussin and bought magnificent cabochon emeralds. People said they were a present from one of her lovers, but that wasn't true. They were a present to herself. They were to be one of her best investments.

I called them my sisters. The emerald and diamond cuff was 128 carats, and its huge cabochon stone, the size of a bantam egg, could be snapped into a ring. There were two clips, one pin, a necklace, and a pair of earrings. My green charges lived in grey, velvet caskets and they barely left my sight. I felt less lonely now that I had my emerald sisters. I hoped that Heidi didn't feel jealous, though she would always be my priority. But I had other responsibilities now. My mother had entrusted me with her most special possessions, and I vowed never to let her down. Nothing bad could ever happen to my sisters as long as they were with me. Sometimes, they appeared in her films, sparkling in the lights, for ever in posterity. Now they are long-gone, disappearing somewhere to pay bills and taxes. But will they ever grace a wrist, a finger, a neck as beauteous as my mother's?

Mother made her first picture without Mo. It was called *The Song of Songs*. Lacy was her leading man. Ah, so that's why he came for scrambled eggs in the mornings! In the absence of Mo, Mother was taking on 'Madou' as her personal duty. She tells me that she needs to protect and perfect what Mo has created. It will become a lifetime dedication. It will show how the pupil has learned from the master. She will create a legend. Yes, the looks, the costumes will stand the test of time. She and Travis concentrated on creating a series of breathtaking images. She remembered the lessons from her master, very well.

Travis and Mother created a fabulous black velvet, off-the-shoulder evening dress, with egret feathers. She was as ravishing as ever, but there was a terrible, unforgettable moment when she first arrived on-set, and spoke for everyone to hear: 'Mo, where are you?'

The scene everyone remembers was Mother posing naked. Lacy, who played a sculptor, sketches her naked, so that he can preserve her beauty in cold marble. Draped in black silk, Mother slowly removed her robe, revealing her milk-white body from shoulder and neck, the camera then dropping to reveal her naked legs. It was one of the most daring scenes in movie history.

Now that I'm old, I love to look back at that film, and witness Lacy's love for my mother. I wonder why she is so often compared with a statue. Perhaps because statues never grow old. I won't say because she was as cold as marble. That would be unfair. Lacy was so handsome, so English. The first man I really loved. Who made me feel safe.

Lacy encouraged me to read the *Song of Songs*, telling me that it contained some of the most beautiful language ever written about the love between man and woman. He told me that first love was precious and pure. He explained that this was the way he thought about my mother. One day, he trusted, my first love would feel this way about me. Ever-dutiful, I took out my bible.

I am my beloved, and my beloved is mine.
He feeds among the lilies.
Let him kiss me with the kisses of his mouth — for his love is
    more beautiful than wine.
Her breasts are twin fawns.
I opened for my beloved, but my beloved had left.

Lacy was right. It was the most moving description of love that I had ever heard. My mother was so darned lucky that a man like Lacy loved her so passionately. I wondered what first love might be for me. To this day, I am relieved that Lacy never discovered the truth.

I'm Old Fashioned

Her first film without Mo is a perfect disaster.

'Darling, the part is rather thin.'

'Next time, I'll ask for a fat one,' she snaps, glaring accusingly at the Child.

She is angry that I tell the truth. *She* has created the face. Yes, but Mo would have retouched the side of her neck to bring out the beauty of her jawline. Ha, I have her there. She cannot deny that I'm right.

'Nuts! You don't know what you are talking about. The face is perfect. Look at the cathedral arch of the lips, the hooded eyes, the height of the cheekbones.'

'But the talent, dear. Let's not forget the talent. Do not think that I criticise'.

'I love criticism just so long as it's unqualified praise.'

'Now, dear, remember what I always say: wit ought to be a glorious treat, like caviar. Never spread it about like marmalade.'

She smiles again, a wistful, sad smile.

'The human race is a let-down, mirror, a bad, bad let-down. It thinks it's progressed, but it hasn't. It thinks it's risen above the primeval slime, but it's wallowing in it, clinging to our hair and to our eyes and to our souls.'

'You know what I tell you, Joan. Refuse to be unhappy. And if life becomes insufferable … Sail away, sail away, sail away …'

'I know the film stinks. You're right. It's good that you tell the truth. True friends tell the truth.'

'My dear, it's discouraging to think how many people are shocked by honesty and how few by deceit. Success is far more perilous than failure. You've got to be doubly strong and watchful and weary.'

The Child, who has been listening, while buffing the emeralds, suddenly stands. She comes to her mother, strolling with her usual bovine listlessness. She puts her arms around her mother, sensing her unhappiness. Tells her that she's so beautiful in *Song of Songs*. How handsome Lacy is in the film. How Lacy loves her so. How she will always love her mother. How she will always be a good girl, and never cause her grief.

Madou is becalmed. She turns from the dressing table to address her child.

'I do it all for you. To give you this life in the sunshine. Now, kiss me and go to bed.'

*   *   *

And so it went on. The films were all flops. Entertainment, not art. Madou insisted that I was positioned beside the camera, so she could see what the camera saw, but it was to no avail. I regret to say that her new director could not create the mystery. It was vexing, but there it is.

When one sees her perform as Lola Lola, one sees what might have been if she had only allowed that raw talent to develop. Not that she cared. She didn't care one jot. She took her pleasures elsewhere. The men came and went. The women, too. Only her love for her daughter remained a constant.

I begin to despise her. The daughter, I mean. Her embonpoint distinguishes her from other children her age. So heavy, such a jiggly-puff. A girl of ample proportions. Bovine. Broad in the beam. A hefty, tubby butterball.

She might take a few lessons from her mother, for whom self-sacrifice is all. It can't be easy for the Child, being such a dismal mediocrity. But she is thoroughly greedy. Devouring sensational amounts of food in great gobbling gulps like a pig at a trough. Podge and Stodge. Pig-Wig. Little Miss Chunk-a-lot.

Madou seems to shrink, as her daughter bulges. I see Nellie letting out the daughter's dress (flowered crêpe de Chine), which is straining at the armholes. In contrast, Madou's dresses cling like scales to a fish. She smokes constantly, and sips beef tea. She is a woman of extraordinary discipline when it comes to food.

I see the daughter cleaning the Turkish carpets with sauerkraut. It is the perfect way to remove stains and refresh the colours. Whenever she thinks no one is looking, she grabs handfuls of sauerkraut and stuffs it into her fat mouth. That is the reason she volunteers for that particular job. On her hands and knees, scrub, scrub, scrubbing. Gobble, gobble, gobble.

And that face, so pimple-ridden, and her hair, a peculiar hue of lurid orange. One wonders how on earth a goddess could give birth to such a horror. But Madou adores her second self. When her child is ill, with flu, she nurses her with all the fervour of Florence Nightingale.

Madou works tirelessly at the studio, night and day. She constantly tells me that it is for the Child. Never complaining, never taking a bathroom break when she is in front of the camera for hours on end. Living for the moment that she can pack her trunks and leave the tinsel enchantment of Hollywood for Europe and civilization.

Madou is to appear in her first Technicolor picture 'on location'. It is to be shot in the Arizona desert masquerading as the Sahara. We pack as though we are never to return, Madou arranging things with military precision. Our hotel is in Yuma, and Madou sets about sterilising the toilets and unpacking the stockpiles of toilet paper that she has ordered from the drugstore.

Sand dunes stretch out as far as the eye can see. The Child has brought her cowboy boots and her snake stick, and she is on the look-out for scorpions. The hot wind flaps the canvas of our dressing-room tents. Despite the intense heat, Madou does not perspire. Her co-star does not fare so well. He peers into me and sees that his toupee has slipped in the heat. Madou glues it to his head with half a bottle of spirit gum.

Madou loathes her director, and takes every opportunity to express her contempt.

'Remember when Mo created the desert in the studio with nothing. It was wonderful, not like this abortion. All of these people with sunstroke. That old lady' – gesturing towards her male co-star – 'puts ice-packs on his wrists, while I sit under a hairdryer. Even the camels are dying of the heat. I was raised properly. To endure. Never to complain. A soldier's daughter never cries.'

The picture is another flop. Madou's magic is in chiaroscuro. She was made for the mystique of black and white. Technicolor always lets her down. Her director is frustrated almost to tears with her perfectionism. She insists on her hair being perfectly coiffed, even when the 'Sahara' wind is blowing. In despair, he sends her a memo: 'Surely a little reality can't do a great beauty any harm?'

Madou is furious. 'What does he mean by "reality"? Nebbish. We work in make-believe. We *are* make-believe.'

Follow the Boys

Lacy returned to England to make a movie, and Mother gained a new friend; a woman writer whom she called the White Knight. To this day, I never can remember her name, except that is sounded like an expensive automobile. All I know is that the White Knight claimed that she could get any woman away from any man. Among her many lovers were Isadora Duncan, Alice B Toklas, and Garbo. During one of her many rifts from Garbo, the Knight met my mother. Mother, who loathed the Swede, loved the idea of stealing her rival's girlfriend.

Mother's latest circle of friends included two freakishly hand-some, impeccably dressed young men whom Mother called 'the boys'. Ben was a party planner for the rich and famous, and Andrew sold real estate. They knew everyone in town. If you weren't invited to their parties, then you were nobody. You might as well leave Hollywood if you weren't on their guest list. They made Mother laugh until she peed her pants. After giving birth to me, she suffered from a weak bladder. The boys would regale her with the latest Hollywood gossip, and she would laugh until she cried and then dash for the bathroom.

The boys teased Mother about having the Swede's sloppy seconds. For once, when her rival's name was mentioned, she seemed amused: 'You know, the White Knight really has ideas above herself. She's terrified that Garbo will discover our affair, and so she's taken to wearing an oversized fedora to disguise herself. The other day, she climbed into the studio car with a controlled furtiveness that Sir Henry Irving would have envied.'

The boys howled and looked at Mother adoringly. They giggled appreciatively when she told them that the Swede was a peasant who wore dirty underwear and who didn't know how to please a woman.

One of their jobs was to watch over me as I swam in the new blue pool, and I hated to see them snigger when I appeared in my lurid red polka-dot swimsuit and red rubber cap, looking like a boiled lobster. I loathed the boys as much as they loathed me, but a small compensation was their King Charles Spaniel called Gus. He was adorable, and would splash around with me in the pool.

The boys encouraged Mother to join the Hollywood circuit. Mo Goldberg had never permitted her to go to social events; he wanted her to maintain her mystique. The studio was equally delighted that she was more visible and willing to be photographed at the latest party. Mother found it difficult to make friends with other women, so she relied on the boys to give fashion advice. They would never lie to her. OK, so Andrew was 'matchy-matchy' in the accessories department, but she knew they would never lead her the wrong way. Ben was a fan of sequins. Preferably gold. He was all about the dazzle.

Costume parties were suddenly all the rage in Hollywood. Mother was invited to a 'come as the person you most admire' party. She discussed the possibilities with me.

'Angel child, I should come as myself, but I think it would be more compelling if I came as Leda and the Swan. Get Travis on the phone. We will need real swan feathers, and lots of them.'

They put me straight through and I handed the phone to Mother.

'Travis. You don't know the myth of Leda and the Swan? I thought you were intelligent. Let me remind you: "*He holds her helpless breast upon his breast.*" Now, the swan must look enfolded within her. Order long feathers from the wings, and short ones for the neck. How about real emeralds for the eyes?'

Travis was jealous of the boys, but he could not resist the challenge. He had always loved feathers. Could my mother look more beautiful? Swathes of billowing white chiffon festooned with feathers sculpted her body, and the swan curled around her legs, her neck, and rested its head on her right breast. Goddess and swan entwined.

I asked Mutti about Leda and the Swan: 'You and your obsession with stories. Why don't you ask Lacy when he's next in California?'

She took a young starlet as her special guest, dressed as Madou in top hat, monocle and tails. They were the sensation of the evening.

I was to go to a party of my own. I had never been to a children's party. Travis made me a new dress, and Mother tied a huge satin bow on top of my head. I looked like a huge Easter egg. Bridges, the new driver, delivered me to a big house in Hollywood.

All of the American children knew each other. I was worried about my German accent, so I hid in the shadows and watched them.

'Do you like parties?' a voice whispered.

'I don't know. I've never been to one before. My mother arranged for me to come to this one.'

'Who is your mother?'

'Miss Joan Madou.'

'Oh she's so famous. Do you like being her daughter?'

Nobody had ever asked me that before. Before I could think about it my reply slipped out …

'No, I don't.'

The voice trilled a laugh, the loveliest laugh I had ever heard.

'Do you hate being fat?'

'Yes. I do. And I hate this stupid dress and bow. But where are you?'

I heard the creak of a porch swing.

'Come and sit with me.'

'Whose party is it?'

'It's mine.'

'Really, but why are you sitting here all alone?'

'I worked at the studio today. I'm so tired.'

'Oh, which studio?'

'MGM. But I don't really like it. No one lets me eat. They weigh me and measure me, and tell me to do this and do that. I like it when I sing, because then they all stop talking and listen.'

A scent of hotdogs wafted over.

'I wish I could have a hot dog.'

'Wait there.'

I went over to the barbeque and took two hot dogs, corn on the cob, and Coca-Cola. I made sure there were onions and ketchup and mustard. I put it all in a cardboard box and returned to the porch swing. We feasted, and the juices ran down our chins, which made us giggle. Then we told our secrets. We became friends. Whenever we met throughout the years to come, we returned to being two fat girls on the porch eating hot dogs. We were shadow children.

When I got home, Mother asked, 'Did you like Judy Garland's party?'

I chose my answer carefully because I wanted to see her again.

'I prefer our parties, Mutti. They're more interesting.'

Mother was pleased with my answer. I had done well.

Poor Lady in the Throes of Love

Each night as she takes off her face, she tells me everything; the good, the bad and the ugly.

Madou is Paramount's darling. The pictures are second-rate, but it doesn't seem to matter very much. She is never late for the studio, takes direction, and learns her scripts on time. Always the consummate professional. Always so disciplined, so diligent. She never seems to tire. The harder she works, the more money she sends back home to her family in Berlin. The *Hollywood Reporter* announces that she is the highest paid actress in Hollywood. Mo's desertion is proving to be a triumph.

But without his protection, and without Lacy to pay court, she is lonely and bored. The boys arrive, on cue, and report that the White Knight is reconciled with Garbo. Madou is livid. She sits at her dressing table and removes her hat. She takes out a cigarette, and picks up her favourite gold lighter; a gift from the studio when she renewed her contract. It is encrusted with rubies in the shape of her initials.

'The Swede plays around. She's in hospital with gonorrhoea. And she's mean. You know she counts the sugar cubes so the maid doesn't steal anything.'

The boys shriek.

Madou swivels around to face the boys, takes a slow drag from her cigarette.

'Calling herself the White Knight. What pretension. But she is a welcome relief from this Hollywood mentality. You know, they should build their churches out here in the shape of a box office.'

When they have left, she telephones an order to her florist to send weekly bouquets to the White Knight; lilac and lavender, naturally. Flowers are supplanted by expensive presents; an engraved cigarette case, a diamond pin, silk lingerie, a silver-framed photograph of herself, dressed in male clothes.

Madou bans everyone from her dressing room, sending the Child to sit with Travis or Nellie. Madou feeds her White Knight with her famous coq au vin, believing that she is consumptive. It is her job to comfort and console. And, even better, to steal her away from her rival, Garbo.

The relationship reaches a new level of intensity when Madou presents the Knight with a doll; the symbol of Sapphic love. She telephones her husband to tell him of her latest conquest.

'Papilein. I met someone interesting at Thalberg's party. A woman with jet-black short hair, like a toreador. She wears a tricorn hat and a cape. An heiress. Garbo is crazy about her. She calls me her Golden One. I will send you her love letters for you to file. I kiss you, Papilein.'

Madou is in between films, and needs to be distracted, but I know her better than most. She will tire of adoration. She hates to feel suffocated. The White Knight will go the way of all the others. Personally, I find her rather humourless. She shan't be missed.

The Child falls ill with influenza, and Madou, a believer in the healing benefits of sea air, demands a beach house in Santa Monica, *not* Malibu, 'where all the nouveaux riches like the Schullbergs live'. The studio obliges, and off we pop to the seaside.

Suddenly, tennis parties are all the rage. A famous tennis star, name of Fred, comes to dine, wearing pale flannel trousers and a creamy silk shirt. Madou is entranced, and insists that everyone wears flannels. She adds a white beret to her look, and ties her hair with a cream silk ribbon. Even the Child wears flannels and a beret; she looks like a swollen field mushroom. Fred teaches Madou to play tennis, in between flirting and kissing, but she is ever skilful at keeping him away from the White Knight.

Mo returns for one night. He despises himself for his addiction to a woman he no longer respects. He leaves, knowing he's not welcome, that he's outlived his purpose. Poor scoundrel. He catches himself in the mirror as he leaves, and I notice that he's wearing white flannel trousers.

A Modern Dubarry

Mother's friendship with the White Knight was brought to an abrupt end. A love missive had been sent, which Mother deemed excessive. She read it aloud to the boys, her ever-appreciative audience.

'Watching you in the darkness made me think of a black tulip, and gave me exotic and uneasy dreams.'

I never thought it unusual that my mother took women to her bed. She inspired complete devotion in everyone. Later, when I was a mother myself, I asked her why she went to bed with so many lovers. She simply replied, 'But they asked so nicely. Wouldn't you?'

I deeply resented Mother's friendship with the boys. I expect I was jealous. I was convinced that they were hangers-on, fair-weather friends, and not to be trusted. Fame begets scavengers. But I misunderstood her need for a different kind of adoration. Later, she confessed that she felt safe with pansies. They were the only men who didn't pounce. They were kind and so much nicer than 'normal' men. In the case of the boys, she appreciated their wit, their style, and their love of Hollywood gossip. They bestowed uncomplicated veneration, wanting nothing more than to be in the orbit of her dazzling presence.

I guess I felt left out, ignored. But I was relieved by the departure of the White Knight, who had made a false move on the Red Queen. No more bunches of lavender and lilac were exchanged. The Chinese doll that the Knight gave Mother was banished to a linen chest. The boys were temporarily exiled from Bel Air. And, best of all, Lacy was home for Christmas.

Santa Claus did not come to our household. Mother refused to be upstaged by an old man with a white beard bearing presents. She was the giver of gifts. Our German custom was to celebrate on Christmas Eve. In Berlin, Mother would play '*Stille Nacht*' on the gramophone, and then I would open the door of the drawing room to gasp in wonder at the candlelit tree. I can still remember the aroma of pine and chocolate.

Now that we were in California, we went to Bullock's for our Christmas shopping. I loved the store with its bitter chocolate and beige carpet, and pillars of gold and glass. As we came into the foyer I gave a gasp and even Mother stopped in her tracks. There it was: a huge white Christmas tree, draped in glass baubles and real electric lights. The lights were blue. The tree looked like it was frosted in snow.

I talked and talked about the blue tree for days on end. On Christmas Eve, I dressed in my new organdie dress and Mary Jane white leather shoes. Mother and Lacy each took a hand, and led me into the drawing room. There behind the heavy double doors was the blue tree. Now it was my blue tree.

Mother had persuaded the manager of Bullock's to sell it. They delivered it to the Bel Air house. Later that day, carpenters from the studio came to saw the tree branch by branch and build it back together in the garden, so that the studio could take press photographs. In the blazing California sunshine, the glue melted, and thick oil paint began to drip. I posed under the branches in my new silk dress, looking up towards the great glass star that perched on the uppermost branch.

Later, Mother invited the press photographers to take some more pictures. In the sitting room there was a fireplace with a large gilt mantel mirror. There was only one light source, a single pinpoint spot above the mirror. She leaned against the mantel and tilted her head, her face and cheekbones perfectly illuminated. There it was: the 'look' that she and Mo had created.

Lacy watched adoringly. Later he presented her with a ruby and diamond ring. He gave me a book about a little girl and a white rabbit who fell down a rabbit hole. He said if I liked it, he would buy the sequel, which was about the same girl falling through a looking glass. Lacy didn't know about my fear of mirrors, but I promised I should love the book, and made my best curtsy.

When they disappeared to Mother's bedroom I made my way to the fireplace mirror, with the spotlight. If it worked for her, perhaps it could work for me. Maybe my nose would be smaller, my skin smoother, and my cheekbones sharper. I knew what magic Mo's light could create. Perhaps if I faced myself I could stop dodging mirrors, and I could be brave enough to read Lacy's book about the girl and the looking glass. I switched on the spot. I just needed to lean against the mantel, and look upwards.

But I just couldn't do it. I couldn't do it. I was frightened of what the mirror might reveal to me. I walked to the window, opened the blind, and took a last look at my blue tree, melting in the sun.

There are Bad Times Just Around the Corner

An old pal pays us a visit. His name is Billy. He wants to set up a fund to help Jews escape from the Nazis. Billy and Madou meet in her dressing room on the lot, so that they can talk in private. Madou wheels me into the corner, and switches off my lights. No matter. I can see everything from here.

Billy tells her that it is the Jews who have turned the movie business into a success, into a Golden Age. That at first they came to Hollywood because of their talent; Lubitsch, Lang and Goldberg, and now there are those who come to escape the Nazis. Madou sits and listens, nodding her head at intervals, allowing him to talk.

They speak about the old days in Berlin. Old stories of how he used to sit for hours in the Romanisches Café with his portable typewriter. He liked the noise and activity, the smell of good coffee, the sight of rich layer cakes (his mother ran a cake shop in Austria, he reminds her), the sound of conversation, the dancing of dishes.

'You know, Joan, I arrived with one suitcase, and a letter of introduction, and before I knew it, I landed a reporting job at *Die Nachtausgabe* and a furnished flat on the Pariser Strasse. Then I got a job …'

'I know, Billy, I know. At UFA, now where the hell is this going?'

'Hella and me, we left at the Reichstag fire, and fled to Paris. We got out, we were the lucky ones. My mother is still in Vienna.'

He does not need to explain. Madou will help. She never refuses to help those in need. It's her duty. She tells Billy that another approach has been made for her to return to Germany. They want her to be the face of the Third Reich. She refuses to return to the homeland, even though she fears for the safety of her mother and her sister, Birgitte.

She tells him how she has heard how her films are banned in Germany, and that Hitler has destroyed every copy of *The Blue Angel* but one, and that one he keeps to himself, filthy beast. She has heard that there's a rumour of a list, a black book, and her name is in it. She has become an undesirable. Imagine that? The most desirable woman on the planet! It's a badge of honour for her to be on Hitler's list.

She writes a cheque and Billy kisses her hand and makes his farewell.

Madou sits in front of me and lights a cigarette. She thinks of her mother and sister in Berlin. She knows that her refusal to return to Germany has put them in danger. She has put herself in danger. And what about the Child? At least Papi has escaped to France and will be safe. She has just heard that the studio has loaned her out for a film in London. She will see Papi there, and he will give her news of her mother.

People say there will be no war, but she doesn't believe them. Those pansies who used to hang out with her at The Lady Windermere and Eldorado are now parading around Berlin in Nazi uniforms. Let's face it, they always loved dressing up. She has to admit to herself, the uniforms were beautifully cut, especially the SS uniforms. Hugo Boss is a superb tailor, maybe he should make some suits for Madou?

She wonders who else might be on Hitler's list, or if it does indeed exist.

She is glad that she has helped Billy with his fund.

Many of her closest friends are undesirables, but perhaps she is the one Hitler would have most liked to get his hands on. Noël Coward, also on the list, sends her a telegram: 'My dear, the people we would have been seen dead with.'

Desire

'Good morning, sweetheart. What would you like for breakfast? Shall I pour you some orange juice?'

I was speechless. Mother hadn't eaten breakfast for twenty years, she hated all salutations, and she rarely spoke to me in English, only German. She forked crisp Beechnut bacon onto my plate and turned back to the oven where she tossed buttermilk pancakes.

She was playing Gershwin (gloriosky!), and was looking ravishing in tennis whites. Her hair was tied back with a white ribbon. Something very strange was happening.

'Sweetheart, you are about to meet someone special. Maple syrup? I met him last night at a party. Wait until you see his smile. For a Hollywood actor, he is quite fascinating.'

Mother despised most Hollywood actors ('they have peanuts instead of brains, and they are all impotent'), and only tolerated Lacy because he had been trained in the English theatre. I was intrigued to meet this latest actor, though I worried for Lacy, who seemed to have disappeared. I prayed that he would return, and see off this imposter.

Junior arrived clutching a bunch of American Beauty roses (ouch! she wouldn't like that).

'Good morning, Pie Face. You are looking mighty beautiful this fine morning.'

I held my breath, waiting for the storm, but Mother smiled serenely and beckoned him to a seat. Really, wonders would never cease. Pie Face! He called this goddess Pie Face!

This man was *so* American. I loved him on the spot. He was the most handsome man I had ever seen (with the exception of Lacy), with startling blue eyes, and the whitest teeth behind a perfectly manicured moustache.

Mother, who hated the sun, and rarely went out in the sunshine, ordered bathing suits from Bullock's and we headed off to Palm Springs, then a tiny town with a few Indian shops, one swanky tennis club, and a riding stable. Mother bought me real cowboy boots and a snake stick. For once, Heidi was left behind. She was far too delicate a doll for the desert, and I didn't have time to ask Travis to make her some Indian clothes.

We stayed at the town's only luxury hotel, El Mirador (now burned to the ground), flanked by the magnificent San Jacinto Mountains, which looked to me like a Paramount film set. In the warm evening air, the katydids sang, and I swam in the huge pool surrounded by date palms.

Junior loved to be seen at Hollywood premieres. Mother disliked being in the company of other stars. She didn't like her allure to be dimmed by competition. But knowing that her last film was a flop, she conceded that Junior was right, and she should be more visible than just attending a few crummy parties. The Paramount publicity department was ecstatic that Mother was suddenly so accessible, so un-European. They put it down to Mo's departure, but it was more to do with Junior's influence.

Mother was invited to a premiere of a new film. She disappeared for a few days, and I was longing to hear all about it as everyone was talking about Walt Disney and the new feature film.

'Sweetheart, you should have seen it. There was a red carpet, klieg lights, everyone in furs and jewels. The crowds went wild when I got out of the car. I couldn't fit into the white chiffon because you weren't there to tape the breasts. But I wore the emeralds. And guess what? All this glamour for *hopping rabbits*. Now who is going to see that film? Those ugly little men, and the prince who looks like a pansy. There was a scene where she is cleaning the house, I almost peed my pants, and the birds and squirrels are helping the village idiot. Now who is going to pay good money to see that abortion; he should stick to Mickey Mouse. The only good things were the magnificent stepmother and the talking mirror.'

I longed to see *Snow White*, and when I did, I adored it, singing birds and all, though it was different to my story book.

Lacy arranged for me to see it, and took me in his car. In the movie, there was only one attempted murder of the daughter – death by apple. In my book, the evil queen had first tried to suffocate her daughter by tightening the laces of her bodice, and, when that failed, had brushed her hair with a poisoned comb.

I shuddered when I saw the queen in her ermine-lined velvet cloak speaking to the magic mirror: 'Through wind and darkness, I summon thee, Speak. Magic Mirror on the wall. Who is the fairest of them all?'

On the way home, Lacy, who was upset with Mother, teased me about the movie. 'Now, Kater, does she remind you of someone? The beautiful queen talking to her mirror?'

So Lacy had noticed, too. Gloriosky! It was our little secret. But I was no Snow White, with hair black as ebony and skin white as snow. And my mother loved me, unlike poor Snow White. How could the queen ask the woodsman to cut out the heart of her daughter? The queen was the heartless one; ugly inside like the old crone with the apple.

Lacy saw me to the door of the Mirror House, but he refused to come in. He kissed me on the cheek and waved me goodbye. He smiled with his mouth, but not with his eyes; they looked sad. His last words were, 'Say hello to your mother.'

You're the Top

She stands in front of me, swaying, finding the most flattering angle. She is trying on Travis's latest number. A gown with a nipped-in bodice and padded shoulders, which emphasise the tininess of Madou's waist. It is trimmed with 4,000 black paradise feathers.

This is just like the good old days in Wardrobe, except that now the fittings are at our place. Travis has a new occupation. He has left the studio and designs evening gowns for Hollywood's movie queens. As ever, Madou is his muse and his model. He will design *gratis*, provided that she wears his gowns to the best parties, and tips off the photographers in advance.

This first creation is a nod to her enduring love of feathers. No French *plumassier* could compete with Travis when it comes to feather design. He has studied Madou's body a thousand times, and knows every inch of her flesh. When she wears plumes, she wears them as the birds and animals wear them, as if they belong to her body.

Everyone wants to duplicate the look, but they can't source the feathers. She glides into the party, enjoying the gasps from the other women; admiration from her peers is far more delicious than from her adoring public.

Travis wonders how he can outdo the feather dress. He enjoys the challenge, and creates a fish-scale dress, made of iridescent celluloid scales, hand sewn onto silk chiffon. Their sea-green shimmer makes her look like a mermaid.

At parties she likes to make a late entrance and arrive unaccompanied. She looks predatory; fierce in her plumage and scales. At any moment she may pounce on an unsuspecting mortal. A bird of paradise. Solitary and territorial.

She tells Travis: 'Most people who make movies are a disappointment in real life. I, on the other hand, am so much better in real life.'

The key to her allure is her mystique. She rarely gives interviews, exudes an air of unavailability, and she refuses to mix with the other stars; that way her light won't be dimmed. She has the same trusted circle of friends, Travis, Nellie and Dot; they all know how to make her look exquisite, how to create and sustain the legend.

Above all, she trusts the Child. She has an unerring ability to suggest the extra touch. When Madou wears a simple white trouser suit to a party, the Child suggests that she adds ivory rhinestones to the lapels to reflect light onto her mother's face.

The Child knows exactly which piece of jewellery will work with a particular look. She has a gift for choosing the right accessories: scarf, gloves, hat. She tries the looks out on her doll and then makes suggestions to her mother, who always takes them seriously. Madou never speaks down to any child. She talks with them as though they are intelligent adults; that's why all children are enslaved and worship at the shrine.

Some people think that Madou was the synthetic creation of von Goldberg, but she was her own invention. Like Shakespeare's Cleopatra, she makes hungry where she most satisfies – she is all things to all men, and to women, too. She is sex without gender. When she wears a tuxedo, she wears it better than any man.

'In my heart,' she says, 'I am a gentleman.'

She understands, better than anyone, that Hollywood makes dreams. Its business is illusion and invention. Nothing is real. She tells the Child, 'It's all smoke and mirrors, sweetheart, smoke and mirrors.' Then off she sweeps, to another party, yet another secret assignation.

I see the Child watching her carefully like a little sharp-eyed ginger kitten, mincing up little bits of experience for future use.

I Loved a Soldier

Severing her ties with Germany seemed to make Mother more nostalgic than usual. That Christmas, she told me wonderful stories about her childhood in Berlin. She remembered her mother's beautiful Dresden cookie plate and a hand-painted Austrian milk pitcher with tiny painted snow scenes encircling it. The birthday when her mother gave her a hand-painted music box from the family shop.

Her mother's family, the Felsings, were famous clockmakers and jewellers. Apparently my great-grandfather donated a golden clock to the famous Kaiser Wilhelm Memorial Church. Mother inherited her obsession with punctuality and precision from her own mother.

Felsings had elegant premises on Unter den Linden. Mother could remember childhood visits to the store, where she was taken by her grandmother. Her grandmother – she called her Oma – encouraged her to try on pieces at the store. She explained to her which jewels should be worn with each outfit. She also taught her to dress correctly, and to select accessories, especially purses and scarves. Perfume was an accessory to be well chosen.

Oma told her that she had a good eye, which confused the little girl. She wondered why she said that, because she had two eyes. Was only one of them good? Oma wore wonderful jewels, especially brooches. She taught her a trick to sew the brooches onto her dress, lightly but securely.

Oma took her for tea at the Adlon Hotel. There were sparkling chandeliers, beautiful marble and oriental hangings. The food was wonderful – pheasant, smoked salmon, caviar, and best of all the pastry cart loaded with sweet delicacies.

The very high cream layer cakes: they were a favourite childhood memory of Berlin. Cream cake was always at the end of an afternoon excursion with Oma. German eclairs are totally different to French eclairs … larger and fatter and delicious.

Mother's memories recalled descriptions of food that made my mouth water. On Sundays, when Grandfather was still alive, they would purchase chocolates and vanilla creams, then onto the Café Bauer on the Friedrichstrasse to drink coffee and hot chocolate.

Huster was the renowned gourmet store – their horse-drawn carriages clattered through the streets of Berlin, carrying lobster, salmon, caviar and salads to restaurants and private patrons in the Bellevuestrasse and the Voss Strasse. On special occasions, they would visit the Scala Theatre to see the famous variety show, with Rastelli the juggler, and Grock the Clown.

She told me that Grandfather was tall and imposing, with a smell of leather and cigars. She remembered standing at the window of her home in Schöneberg and listening to the sound of the soldiers marching in step, the *clip-clopping* of the horses.

The house came to life when there were guests, and she remembered the sparkling chandeliers, the fine goblets, the candles, the porcelain dinner service. Her mother would play a Chopin waltz.

'I could smell her perfume, she would be wearing a beautiful gown, her fingernails touching on the keys with a delicate little click.'

But then the war came. One of her early schoolgirl memories was passing a POW camp for French soldiers. She impulsively picked up some wildflowers and handed them to a soldier, who put his hand through the barbed wire and clutched them like a gift from God.

That winter, they ate nothing but potatoes and turnips; turnips, turnips and turnips, turnip marmalade, turnip cakes, turnip soup.

She remembered Germans pushing wheelbarrows full of deutschmarks for a loaf of bread, and people burning them for fuel and using the banknotes for toilet paper. It was so, so cold. No heating, little food … the freezing cold winter of 1917. Her cousin Hans who gave her her first kiss. Everywhere, there are red flags. Rain and more rain. The soldiers singing 'Hail to Thee in the Victor's Wreath' and 'Hold Firm in the Roaring Storm'.

Mother loved ice skating. It came naturally to her. She would just put on a pair of skates and off she went. The skating rink in Berlin twinkled with fairy lights. Her sister did not like to skate. When Mother twirled around on the lake, all the boys gathered around to watch, with hungry looks in their eyes.

People said to Grandmother: 'What a beautiful daughter you have.' They said it in front of Mother's sister. She never seemed to mind. Grandmother was proud of her daughter's beauty, and her long, golden hair that reached down her back, but she forbade vanity.

Once, when my mother was very young, her mother scolded her when she saw her standing in front of their full-length mirror. She was standing so close, she was almost going into it. She seemed to her to be too pleased by her reflection, and to like what she saw excessively. She was not hiding her pleasure.

'Very bad,' her mother scolded, 'revealing your feelings, even to yourself.'

Grandmother was a cold parent. She never kissed her daughter or hugged her, as did my mother, who was constantly kissing and holding me to her side; especially when there was a camera around to record the moment. Grandmother's constant refrain was '*Tu Vas*' – 'Do Something'. What my mother thought she was really saying was 'Be Something'.

Mother remembered that her father was affectionate. He would stroke her golden hair, and when she sat on his lap she could smell the leather and tobacco-smoke up close. He would allow her to twirl his moustache. He was so handsome with his blond hair and high cheekbones. And then suddenly he was gone.

She was just nine. She remembered her mother polishing his high boots after his death, which she kept in her bedroom. Grandmother called her daughter her 'little soldier'. When she was feeling sentimental, she called her by the name Paul; the name she would have been given if she had been born a boy-child. She liked being Paul. He was strong and sometimes naughty, but very loving. When she was called Paul it meant that her mother was in a good mood.

The only time she remembered her mother being happy was when her father bought her a yellow dress with a matching bouquet of yellow flowers. She watched through a crack in the door as her mother stared at herself in the full-length mirror. When Grandmother saw her daughter looking, she closed the door.

My mother's account of Grandfather's untimely death varied, according to her mood. Sometimes, he died in the war, with full military honours; at other times he fell from his horse and cracked open his head like Humpty Dumpty, and they couldn't put him together again. I only learned, much later, that the truth was much less noble. When Mother was dying, she talked about Grandfather's death. She remembered Grandmother taking her and her sister for a walk outside a hospital building in Schöneberg, so that Grandfather could look out of his barred window and see the young girls.

He died of syphilis – a disgrace to Grandmother and the Felsings, so she told no one. It was bad enough that she had married beneath her, but this ignoble death must be concealed from everyone. Grandmother was terrified that the disease might have been passed on to her daughters.

I sometimes wonder whether my mother's obsession with germs stemmed from her father's death, and I was convinced that, deep down, she knew the real ugly truth of his death. But it was another thing that, in her mind, it did not happen that way, simply because she didn't want it to. The truth was always her truth. It was the same with what happened to me. She would never have believed me, even if I'd tried to tell her the truth. Why bother with facts when a pretty lie would do?

'*Quid est veritas* ... What is truth?' she would say, in that husky, lispy drawl. 'Well, sweetheart, it's all *quatsch*. Now go to bed.'

World Weary

On Madou's free days away from the studio, she shops with manic energy. Piles and piles of shopping are stacked in a corner of her dressing room. She buys scarves and gloves for her mother and sister, silk ties and dressing gowns for Papi, books for the Child, and gramophone records for herself. She loves Richard Tauber, and listens to him over and over again.

Today a new gold clock from Cartier is placed on her mantelpiece. She is proud to be a clockmaker's child. *Tick tock, tick tock.* She runs her hands over its surface and goes off to clean the bathroom, scrubbing away on her hands and knees.

She has other uses for the bathroom, too. She discovers a new way to stay slim, while eating whatever she wants. She binges, and then runs to the bathroom and puts her fingers down her throat. Then she feels purged and new.

For once, she can eat in an unrestrained manner, like her daughter. She guzzles down all of the delicious pastries and cakes that she usually denies herself in order to stay pencil-thin, in the

American fashion. As with the Child, she enjoys eating in private, although I am always there. A silent witness to her greed and gluttony.

In terms of sex, she has always been a woman of lusty and unashamed appetite. In her manic phases, she devours men, choosing who she wants. 'Daddy, I want a piece of that,' she whispers when she sees a young handsome actor go by. She's rapacious and seldom satisfied, seeking the next thrill, the next conquest. She's careful not to get caught. She doesn't want another brat. Her trusty douche is her best friend, and she buys Heinz vinegar by the gallon.

One of her swains said that every time a waiter waltzed past with a vinegar salad dressing he would think fondly of Madou.

She gets everything she wants, because she wants it, and because nobody ever says no. This, I believe, is very bad for the soul. As her truth-teller, I shall intervene. She won't like it, but she will listen to her conscience.

Tonight, she is immaculate, dressed in an ivory silk and lace nightdress that has the delicacy of a cobweb. She sits down at her dresser, to brush out her hair.

'You give too much of yourself, Joan. Free love is hateful and sordid and cheap.'

'Don't be pompous, darling.'

'Your hormones are working overtime, rushing madly in and out of your blood like busy messenger boys.'

'It's not a crime to be loved. It's my temperament. I require passionate love.'

'You never love anyone, you only love them loving you.'

'You're cruel to torment me.'

She twists her mouth into a half-smile.

'Most of the world is greedy and predatory, and if you give them the chance, they will steal unscrupulously the heart and soul out of you, without really meaning to.'

'It's my opinion that love affairs are the only real education in life.'

'Poppycock. Personally, I'd rather have a nice cup of cocoa.'

She laughs softly.

'I mean it Joan, one gets carried away by glamour and personality and magnetism – they're beastly, treacherous things. You need real friends. The kind that you can call at 4 a.m.'

'That's why I have you. I have my child. I don't require anyone else.'

The telephone rings to interrupt our rendezvous. Her telephone is her constant companion; her link to her family and the Europe that she loves, and sees crumbling to dust. One day it will be her only friend.

A Foreign Affair

Memory is a treacherous thing. When my mother took to her bed in her dotage, she would reminisce about old times. She would say over and over again, 'Kater, didn't we laugh?' I know that we did, but I just can't remember the moments. Mother had always had a weak bladder, and there were times she would rush to the bathroom, howling with mirth. That I *can* remember, though I don't remember myself losing control in that way. But then I see a photograph of us both, one when we are wearing matching white bathing suits, standing by the pool in Hollywood, and we are laughing together, so I guess it must have happened at least once.

Some memories are hazy; houses we lived in blend into one another, another dazzling green lawn here, another sparkling blue pool there. Smells take me right back to the past. Orange blossom at a wedding transports me to the train arriving in Pasadena. In those days, there was no air conditioning. The windows would be flung open and a rush of heady orange blossom filled the air.

Those were the years when travel was an experience, not an expedient. Nowadays, I spend too much time in noisy, crowded airports, in cramped airplane seats, on freezing train platforms. It wasn't always this way; long distance travel was civilised. The studio chartered a private train to bring us back and forth from Hollywood to Europe. The Pullman sleeping cars were luxurious, built by craftsmen. They were the private jets of the era.

I remember the dining room, with Cuban mahogany tables and chairs, and the bedrooms richly upholstered in pale green. Mother had a dressing room, with a fireplace and a chaise, and a dresser with a large mirror and brass lamps. Pullman joked that he ran the largest hotel in America, except that it was a moving hotel.

Mother, proficient at forgetting about the past when it suited her, had no romantic yearnings for our long, slow journeys. In her later years, she loved to travel by air; the speed, the convenience, the ease. She flew around the globe with nauseating energy, never once succumbing to jet lag. I, still in love with the past, recall the slow boats that brought us home.

I can remember every detail of the *Normandie*. She was the greatest ocean liner of them all. Oh boy, was she a beauty. A fabulous, floating art deco palace. Where do her bones lie now? During the war, she was set on fire and utterly destroyed. But I remember her glory days.

Mother was always given the Deauville Suite, which boasted an oval salon, with a honey-coloured baby grand piano, four bedrooms, five marble bathrooms, and a circular dining room, which opened out onto our own private balcony. It was all the colour of dusky rose-gold, with Aubusson carpets and ebony furniture. Even now, I can see the swirls in the carpets. I can see Mother changing from her travel clothes, ready to scrub and bleach the already gleaming bathrooms.

The first time we sailed on the *Normandie* was a magical time. I remember pouring Mother a glass of champagne from the several ice-cold bottles nestling in their silver tripods. Before sorting the flowers, I begged Mother if I could say goodbye to the Lady.

'Really Kater, you are as American as a coloured girl. You know the French designed the Statue of Liberty. Americans are too stupid.'

I took that as a yes and scrammed before she could change her mind. I got up to the sun deck just in time to say goodbye to the Green Lady with the torch. I could just about see the broken chains around her feet. I closed my eyes and made my wish: 'Please let me get back home to America.'

Mother was not expected to dine the first night, so I tucked her into bed and set off to explore the greatest ocean liner in the world. First, I took the elevator to the grand lobby, which was more fabulous than the Waldorf. The band played Cole Porter and Irving Berlin, not fusty old Mozart. Gloriosky!!

I made my way to the first-class dining room, another mini Versailles. It was longer than the Hall of Mirrors and boasted twelve tall pillars of Lalique glass, flanked by thirty-eight matching mirrored panels. I counted them one by one. Sparkling chandeliers, like upside-down wedding-cakes, hung at each end of the room. The tables gleamed with Christofle silver, Lalique glassware, and Baccarat crystal. Little wonder that the liner's nickname was the 'Ship of Light.'

I discovered smoking rooms, reading rooms, tea rooms with Limoges porcelain, a playroom for the children (Babar the elephant adorned the walls), a huge swimming pool, a chapel with stained-glass windows, a library, a full-size movie theatre, which led from the Grand Salon. My favourite place was the Winter Garden. Large, comfortable wicker chairs nestled among orchids and ferns. Snuggled among the lush foliage, I looked up at the huge domed glass lantern to see the moonlight and the twinkling stars beyond.

We were expected to dress the part on the *Normandie*. Three different outfits a day, and never the same outfit twice. The next evening, we dressed for the captain's table. Mother wore a dress of oyster silk, and Mo's sapphires. I wore a blue dress of uncrushable velvet. Mother took my hand and off we went.

The Grill Room, all etched-glass panels, black calf and gleaming steel, was even more exclusive than the first-class dining room. That was for the rich, this was for the rich and famous!

The waiters, dressed in scarlet and black, ladled out bowls of caviar.

The highlight of the evening was the Grand Descent, when all of the rich and famous passengers walked down the main staircase, showing off their eveningwear like glittering peacocks. The people looked like dress extras in their white tie and tails and Patou gowns. 'Straight from the costume department', as Mother would say.

They gaped at Mother as she descended the stairs with all the grace and poise of Nike of Samothrace. She made her way to the captain's table, who was waiting to greet her and kiss her hand. He led her to her chair, as a waiter approached the table with a flute of champagne. Mother took a sip, smoothed her gloves, and remarked loudly: 'All the women here look like Kay Francis.'

One year (was it that year?), she met the Writer. The captain's table was laid for thirteen, and mother, who was always superstitious, beckoned to the handsome man who looked uncomfortable in his tuxedo. The Writer was transfixed, and they spent the evening speaking only to one another.

She called him Papa, he called her 'my little Kraut'. Mother told me that they had never been free to pursue a sexual relationship at the same time, but, boy, could they flirt. That first time they met, he became her devoted slave. His first words to her still resonate over the long years of their friendship. 'What do you really want to do for a life work? Break everybody's heart for a dime? You could always break mine for a nickel, and I'd bring the nickel.'

There were times, over the years, that I thought of confiding in Papa Hem. He was a big bear of a man, and a man of unimpeachable courage. But then I knew that his first loyalty would always be to my mother. So I wrote him down on my 'not to be disturbed' list, and worshipped him from afar.

The Stately Homes of England

The Child thinks she can escape me, but I am omnipresent, just waiting for her to catch a glimpse of me when she least expects it. And, of all places, the family come to Claridge's of London. They are in England to see Lacy. An attractive man of considerable charm, though his acting leaves a lot to be desired. He thinks too much, that's his problem. Actors should never think.

Claridge's is a paean to the age of glass; a glittering, sparkling, silvery wonderland. From the moment one steps through the revolving doors, therein lies enchantment. The lobby floor is marbled chequerboard, Gershwin tinkers on the piano. The flower arrangements are as tall as houses, flames flicker in the Victorian fireplaces. The chandeliers dance and reflect the light that bounces from the mirrored walls of the lobby.

The tables in the dining room are laid for afternoon tea; the tiniest silver spoons on gleaming china, thin-cut sandwiches, silver teapots of Earl Grey, and delicate cakes of pink and white.

Those in the know make their way to a secret doorway at the foot of the sweeping staircase. This is the Fumoir, where bad girls go for cocktails. It is constructed to resemble a mirrored jewel box, with deep red and aubergine velvet seats lit dimly through Lalique cut glass.

Everyone in England is talking about the King of England and Mrs Simpson. Madou has a plan. Lacy has arrived, and they sit in the Fumoir, smoking and sipping cocktails.

'Dear heart, I need to save the monarchy. I need to prevent history from taking a tragic course. I am going to see the king. I spoke to the Duke of Kent last night and told him that I can do *it* better than Wallis Simpson, and I won't try to be the Queen of England.'

Lacy tries to conceal his smile.

'She must be very clever to get a king so mad about her. You know what everyone says about him, and men like that always love their mothers. But men like that cannot be kings. She is clearly very good at doing what he likes.'

'What exactly do you propose, Joan?'

'I shall show him that there are plenty more fish in the sea.'

'Darling, what about us? I can't stand aside and let you seduce the King of England.'

She glared at him.

'Don't be so old-fashioned. We are doing it for England, which we both love. Some sacrifices must be made.'

That evening, she prepares herself, spending hours at her dresser to look her very best. An hour later, she returns. She summons Lacy to her bedchamber. She is livid.

'I drove to Buckingham Palace, and I was refused entry. I demanded to see the king. I suspect that woman knew of my plans. Well, so be it. It will be his funeral. He'll be as miserable as sin. You mark my words.'

Lacy looks mightily relieved that his lover won't be bedding the King of England. He tells her that a telegram has arrived from the studio instructing her to return to Hollywood. He wonders if he could take the Child to the Natural History Museum. She is annoyed and snaps, 'Why on earth do you want to see all those old bones? Do as you wish. I'm going to bed.'

The Ship of Lost Souls

The past is never where you left it. The main memory I have of England, as a child, was afternoon tea at the Savoy with Lacy. We ate paper-thin finger sandwiches (cucumber and Gentleman's Relish), and the waitress brought a cake tier with several different cakes; Victoria sponge, coffee and walnut cake, and scones with jam and cream. We sipped Earl Grey tea. Lacy never looked at me when I ate, or made a comment when I piled my plate high.

Lacy returned to Hollywood with us, and we moved house again. This time we rented a beach house in Santa Monica, 'so the Child could play on the beach'. That lasted only a short while as it was deemed too far away from the studio, and we moved back to the Mirror House, which had again become available. Lacy fell out of favour, and a new, older man appeared. He was Mother's new leading man, and, as usual, she insisted on a love affair to create the right chemistry. That he had once belonged to Joan Crawford amused her. 'That low-class woman who beats her children.'

He moved into a house just down the street from us. 'Wasn't it a funny coincidence?'

Travis welcomed us back with open arms. Mother had zipped over to Paris before we left Europe and bought clothes to wear in the new film. Travis was desperate to see them and to chat about England.

'You know, darling, it's true about tea. They stop working at four o'clock to drink tea and eat cakes. I didn't believe it until I saw it for myself. No wonder Kater is so fat. I saw Noël in London, and Cole Porter in Paris, they say he can't live without his cocaine, and I must say his nose looked most peculiar. I saw Lombard in that black monkey fur dress you made for her. Really, Travis, it made me want to feed her a banana …'

Travis giggled and sipped his coffee. I got the feeling that he had really missed my mother.

'Did you see what Adrian put on Crawford? Nothing but bugle beads, like a second skin. Beautiful, but with those hips, it just looked vulgar. But then everything looks cheap on Crawford. Now what about this new film? What have they told you? I know she's supposed to be the wife of an English lord, so I thought white chiffon blouses, a simple black velvet suit, white kid gloves.'

The House of Mirrors, our mini Versailles, was unchanged. The exotic birds perched on their silver branches, and the panthers prowled. Once again, I played my game of dodge the mirrors. Mother's new friend bronzed himself by the pool wearing tiny white shorts. The hummingbirds hovered over the rose bushes. We were home.

The studio had redecorated Mother's dressing room as a welcome home present. The art deco chairs and chaise longue were covered in the softest white fur that looked like polar bears, and the carpet was geranium red. I thought it looked incredible. Mae West, whose dressing room was next door, thought Mother's white bears were hideous, and told her so.

Mother waited to exact her revenge. It came when Travis told her that he had made Mae a beautiful silk-chiffon robe trimmed with ostrich feathers. It was to be sent to her dressing room, but Mother intercepted the package and sent the wardrobe girl on her way with a present of a signed photograph.

Mother stripped naked and put on the sheer robe, and waited for Mae's return. She let out a scream when she saw Mother: 'That is *my* robe, wait until I get my hands on that low-life Travis.'

'Oh Mae, I'm sure you're mistaken. A girl of your taste would not be seen dead in this abortion. You don't think it's too vulgar?'

Mother twirled around, leaving nothing to the imagination. Mae's horrified expression turned into a grin: 'Why, honey, don't you look just divine? I suggest you come into my dressing room to discuss lil' ol' Travis's treachery.'

Mae gave my mother a gentle but firm pat on the bottom, and they disappeared together, locking the door.

I Wonder What Happened to Him?

This is how she tells me about it, a crystal tumbler of bourbon in her shaking hand: *He lies upon me, gasping with desire, and then, all of a sudden, the gasps turn to groans, and then gurgling in the throat.*

'John, darling, what is it?'

'My chest, my chest.'

'My darling, you need help.'

She summons up all her strength and pushes him out of her and onto his back. She knows he is dying (he has suffered two heart attacks in the last few months), and she knows that she can't be found in his bedroom. She must move quickly. She calls her driver, stuffs her belongings in her overnight bag, including her silver-framed photograph of her daughter, and then she calls for the doctor.

*   *   *

Back in the House of Mirrors, she goes over the scene in her mind, again and again. Finally she spits it all out, looking frightened and ashamed. With her hands still trembling, she lights a cigarette and tells me about her love for him. His desperately unhappy childhood in Utah, the parents who abandoned him, and then his success as a silent movie star, until the talkies destroyed his career. He was known as the Great Lover. But he was an artist. A man of keen intelligence and integrity. She remembers how he told her that the movie game was like shoot-the-chutes; one minute you're in breathtaking ecstasy, and down in the doldrums the next. You can't live for your art in this game. You've got to keep a weather eye on the box office, and that means you're going to do a lot of things and play many a part you don't want to. He tells her that he hates poverty like a snake. That he wants respect for his work.

She knew he was an incorrigible drunk, and she thought she could help him. She wanted to protect him, and look after him. She wanted to save him. But he couldn't be saved. He calls her 'Love Face'. She keeps every note he ever sent. 'Angel. Keep loving me. Rush home to me. I love you so.'

When the news comes of his death, she can only think of the headlines that say that he died alone. No one will ever know that he died in her arms. Later, she attends his funeral. She wears no make-up, and her face is deadly pale. When his possessions are sold, she buys his bed linen. That's all that she has left of him.

Then she takes to her bedroom, and there she stays. She lights a votive candle under his framed photograph, and doesn't come out for days.

When she finally surfaces, she looks ghastly. I must be gentle, and kind.

'I wish I were dead,' she says.

'Life is for the living, Joan. It doesn't matter about death, but it matters terribly about life.'

'I'm not afraid of death. I'm afraid of life.'

'One must be aware of moral standards. The dignities of life. It's Fate. It can't be helped.'

'Don't be pert.'

'I like it when you're being all beautiful and sad.'

'I *am* beautiful and sad. I was weaning him off the drink. Feeding him properly, moonlit drives.'

'My dear, the damage was done. There were demons eating away at his soul. There's only one rule in Hollywood, and that's to survive.'

'I'm a soldier's daughter. I am a wife and a mother. Papi is on his way to me. But for now, allow me to be sad.'

The Spoilers

There are many ways to destroy a person.

It is time for me to talk about Sofi. Now that I am a grand-mother, I find myself mourning my father's lover. She was Russian by origin, and a very beautiful woman. More important than her fragile beauty was her kindness. I remember when I met her the first time with Papi she was wearing Mother's cast-off clothes. She was gentle and sweet. I wanted Sofi to be my mother, but I knew my mother would never allow this to happen. I had to hide my love for my father's mistress, because that way I would keep her.

Twice a year, Sofi and Papi would come to Hollywood. She would help me to dress Heidi, brush out her hair and choose her shoes. She would cradle my doll in her arms, singing softly. In those moments, Sofi was happy. She was like a child herself. Then my father would call her to come to him, and the smile would disappear and she would scurry to obey, fearful of rebuke. I remember how her head would be bowed, eyes lowered, hands trembling.

There are many ways to destroy a person. Whenever my mother and father were photographed together, Sofi was always asked to walk a long way behind them. No one seemed to see the girl in the shadows, dressed in my mother's old clothes.

My father chose her food, her wine, her place of living. Mother gave her only the things she had out-used, and berated her for her weakness of character; '*schwache limonade*' she would mutter under her breath.

She plied her with sleeping pills and champagne and then scolded her for sleeping late and missing breakfast. Sofi would finally appear pale and withdrawn, hands shaking. Papi would shout at her for her laziness, for not helping Mother, who had done so much to look after everyone. I desperately wanted to say something in Sofi's defence, to show how much I loved her, but I was cowardly and contemptible.

One bright sunny day, Sofi took out her scissors and neatly cut off the heads of the roses in the garden. When she realised what she had done, she was horrified.

'Katerlein. What have I done? What will Papi say, and Mutti?' She was sobbing, terrified.

'It's OK. We will put them in vases and tell them it was the gardener's fault.'

That evening we had guests. Now that Mo had gone, Mother was enlarging her inner circle. Nobody seemed to be surprised by Sofi's presence. That morning, she had broken a china teacup, its fragments shattering onto the hard, unforgiving floor.

My father spoke.

'Mutti, we have to fire the gardener. He cut off the roses from the bushes. Sofi, do you have something to say to Mutti?'

She looked horrified.

'Remember, about the cup that you broke this morning?'

'Mutti, I'm so clumsy. I am sorry I broke a cup. I will repay you.'

'I will take it from your allowance.'

Sofi cleared the plates, and I rose to help.

'SIT. We have guests.'

The guests looked highly amused by the whole set-up. My mother had a malicious glint in her eye that worried me. Later, when the guests had left, I heard her lecturing Sofi in the pantry. Sofi apologising, softly.

The next day, Mother and Papi went away together for the weekend. There had been rumours about their marriage, and Mother had arranged for a photographer to turn up at their Palm Springs hotel. Sofi and I had four precious days together. It was utter bliss, and I never wanted it to end.

We ate whatever we liked, and watched movies, and at night, she let me sleep in her bed. When the lights were turned out, I told her about the pink water, and the sanitary belt that I had to wear every month. She told me that I should be very proud to have become a woman. That I had inside me a lovely room that would one day house a beautiful baby. Every month, the room had to be cleared out, to be made nice and clean, so that when the baby came, the room would be perfect. I drifted into sleep, feeling the warmth of her body, and the softness of her skin.

Mother and Papi returned, looking tanned and happy. The press had taken many pictures of Madou and her handsome husband. Then Sofi and Papi left together for Europe. Mother promised that she would send plenty of money.

I wondered if, now that I was a woman, it was still all right to play with Heidi. I decided that, perhaps, I wasn't yet ready to be a woman. That evening, when I was undressing and putting her to bed, I overheard my mother on the telephone.

'Can you believe that Sofi's done it again? Now I have to find the money. And who will look after Papi when she's gone away?'

She emitted a tremulous sigh.

'Such a selfish woman. Hasn't she heard of a douche?'

Down with the Whole Damn Lot

Madou doesn't know that this is going to be the end, but she has a hunch that the film will be a disaster, despite everything she's doing to save it. Nothing seems to work. She stretches across the bed on her belly, looking hard into me, her special floor-length mirror. I have taken up position next to the camera. As ever, she directs the lighting: 'Move the main spot higher, I need two more lights below.' She waits for the butterfly to appear above her mouth so that she knows that she looks perfect.

She whispers to me, 'How can I save this abortion?'

She knows I always speak the truth.

'Two things should be cut. The first part, and the Child's throat.'

She chuckles at my joke. But there's nothing worse than working on a film that everyone knows is a flop. The death of her leading man has not helped matters; his replacement is wooden as a rocking horse. Her contract states that she has final say over the script, and she fights with her director, who refuses to work with her on the grounds that he is not going to allow a star to have so much authority over a story that he is supervising.

Another director is found. He has no rapport with Madou, and things take another wrong turn when the supporting actress stumbles and trips on my lighting cables, and breaks an arm in two places. Madou is furious that her supporting actress is also a blonde; she will allow no other woman to steal her light. When the actress accuses Madou of complicity in the accident, there is a quarrel, and she storms off the set.

The script is lame, her part is a cliché, and the ending is pure kitsch. She can hardly bear to attend the premiere, but she puts on a brave show with a new gown designed by Travis, and a new, shorter, more blonde, hairstyle designed by Nellie. The haircut makes her look younger than ever.

As Madou applies the final touches to her make-up, the Child reads out the stack of good-luck telegrams. There is a loving one from Papi, who sends his apologies for his absence, and one from Mo, wishing her success. There is also one from the White Knight, who is in India, trying to find enlightenment. Hers is the telegram that elicits Madou's approval: 'My Golden One. I miss you. Hope you get a warm hand on your opening.'

Nobody is surprised when the picture bombs, but the final blow comes when the president of the Independent Theatre Owners of America declares Madou 'Box Office poison'. She is on a list of major movie stars who are deemed the 'Poisanalities'. She telephones Mo and reads out the article.

'Mo, listen to this: *Wake up! Practically all of the major studios are burdened with stars – whose public appeal is negligible – and receiving tremendous salaries necessitated by contractual obligations.*

'Now, admittedly, I'm not at the very top of the list; that honour belongs to Garbo … but *they are poison at the box office*, blah blah blah. Now, Mo, I must tell you Mae's response to this, it's a hoot. She says that the only picture that has made real money in the past year is *Snow White and the Seven Dwarfs*, and they'd have made twice as much if they had me play Snow White. Now, isn't that hilarious?'

The studio cancels her contract, and for the first time in years, Madou is unemployed. I am wheeled away, but she seems unconcerned: 'Box office poison? Thank heavens. We shall leave for Paris immediately.'

I Kiss your Hand, Madam

Mother called Papi on the telephone: 'Papi, we are leaving America. Even Hepburn is on the list, and the pop-eyed one, who can act but is ugly. Bette someone. Who would want to pay money to look at her? Crawford, too.'

We packed up her dressing room and left without a word. That was how she wanted it. No drama, no teary farewells. We had always been gypsies, but I still felt empty inside. No more humming-birds or blue swimming pools or orange trees. Just grey, drizzly Europe. There was no talk of returning. Mother was overjoyed.

Even being back on my beloved *Normandie* did not help. I waved goodbye to the Green Lady, wondered if I would ever return. I guess it was a good thing that I didn't know then that it would be years before I saw her again.

Mother was worried about me. As soon as we saw Papi and Sofi at Le Havre, she launched into another of her monologues about me: 'Of course, she's never been a dainty girl. It's the German in her. She's big-boned. I could put her on a diet, but she's a child.

She's so happy when she eats. It's the sign of a good mother, feeding your child. It's the American food. I need to call the doctor. Nothing fits. Something is wrong. Her bones are growing too fast. Look at her feet. They are huge.'

I reminded myself to slouch more. But it was true. I was almost thirteen, and I was colossal. My bosoms were capacious. Fleshy pumpkins, not like mother's creamy globes.

Papi kissed me and assured her that my height was normal. I was tall like he was. He would arrange more tennis lessons. They would buy new clothes in Paris. I hoped they would stop buying those organdie dresses with puffed sleeves and wide cummerbunds. Sofi smiled at me with a smile that reached right up to her beautiful, gentle eyes. Hollywood smiles were not like this. As ever, she was dressed in Mother's hand-me-down clothes, and though she was slim and attractive, I had to admit that they never looked as good as they did on Mother.

'Kater, sit up, stop slouching. Papi, maybe we should send her away to school. Like the English do. The food will be terrible and she will lose weight.'

It was confusing, as back in California she insisted on cooking my breakfast potatoes in a whole packet of butter, alongside four-egg omelettes. She encouraged me to eat all the puddings that she forbade herself, staring greedily at me as I gorged.

At our hotel on the Champs-Élysées, The Lancaster, I decided to eat modestly.

'Eat. It is good for you. Are you sick? Good, then finish what is on your plate.'

Over breakfast, they gossiped. Mrs Simpson was finally married to the former king. Mother was still upset that she had been refused entrance.

'Mutti, you know she cannot be called Your Royal Highness. Nor any of their children.'

'Well, we all know that they are never going to have any children. Duchess is already too good a title for her. She's an American and a divorcée.'

There was talk of war. Mother was anxious to hear news of her mother and her sister. She told Papi how no one in Hollywood talked about the situation in Europe. There was talk of Herr Hitler.

Paris was the most beautiful city in the world. I could understand why my mother loved it so. We became tourists. Mother disguised herself in a black wig and oversized sunglasses, and we set off to explore the sights; Notre Dame, with its heartbreakingly glorious rose windows, the Louvre, and the Tuileries Palace. My favourite outdoor space was the Jardin du Luxembourg, where I sailed a wooden boat on the lake. Mother pointed out the Medici fountain, and I saw the naked lovers, Acis and Galatea, watched over by the terrifying giant, Polyphemus. Galatea had marble-white skin, just like my mother.

Hem was in Paris. Papi, who was never jealous, also became a friend and admirer of Papa Hem. This was the year of writers:

Colette, Scott Fitzgerald, John Dos Passos, George Bernard Shaw, Noël Coward, Gertrude Stein, and a truly wonderful man, perhaps the best of them all, who became one of my closest friends. His name was Boni.

Love a Little

She snaps open her compact mirror and examines her perfect lipstick for smudges.

Of all of her many lovers, Boni is the superior. No one can hold a candle. He is utterly exceptional. They meet in Venice. She is with Papi. A tall, handsome man, extremely well-dressed, approaches and asks to introduce himself. Madou is dismissive of such bad manners, but as soon as she hears his name, she is all charm. She motions him to sit, and her husband makes his excuses and leaves.

'You look too young to have written one of the greatest novels of our time.'

'Madame, you have made me so happy. Perhaps I only wrote it to hear your magical voice says these words.'

He lights her cigarette with his gold lighter. They talk until dawn. She tells him that she loves poetry, but he doesn't believe her; after all, she's an actress. Not a great brain. But she surprises him. Her favourite poem is Rilke's 'Leda'. She recites in her husky voice.

And she, all openness, already guessed
who it was coming in the swan, knew that

the thing he asked of her, her dazed resistance,
could no longer hide from him. A swoop,
and his neck butting through her hands' weak hindrance,

the god unloosed himself into love's grip.
Then feeling in his feathers for the first time gladness,
the god became a real swan in her lap.

That voice. If she had nothing more than her voice, she could break your heart with it. He is falling hopelessly, helplessly in love with a voice. He doesn't know it now, but she is the great love of his life.

He is a German exile, who has escaped to Switzerland. He is despised by Hitler and the Nazi Party, who deem him a liar, claim he never fought in the war, and burn his books. Later, she will see his shrapnel scars, in his legs and neck.

He follows us to Paris. He collects art and fine wine. He has smuggled his Impressionist paintings out of Germany and to his house in Switzerland, where he always keeps a suitcase, ready-packed, just in case he has to leave quickly. That, he says, is the life of the refugee. He tells her that one day he will write a book for her. It will be another masterpiece, like his first novel, but it will not be about war and death, it will be about love.

Angel

Mother was madly in love. She knelt at Boni's feet, and worshipped. She lavished him with presents. She cooked him mushroom soup, and veal and rice. He was a gentle, softly-spoken man, with a passion for great wine. Everything I knew about wine I learned from him. He told me that he threw a bottle of his finest vintage wine into Lago Maggiore in a ceremonial gesture of 'Thanks to the Gods', for allowing my mother into his life. She was in his words, 'the apotheosis of Beauty'. He called her 'Golden Puma' – his blonde, melancholy panther.

There was something childlike and vulnerable in this most charming of men. His eyes were particularly beautiful, and he always listened to me carefully, just like Lacy. He was always saying marvellous things that made me think. For example, that pious people are the most disloyal, cynics have the best character, and idealists are the least bearable.

I badly wanted Boni to be my father. I prayed that my mother would not play her little games this time. He was intelligent enough to see that she could not truly give herself to anyone. When she withdrew, he sent her love letters in the persona of an eight-year-old boy called Alfred. She said that Alfred's were her favourite love letters. I wanted to meet Alfred, as I thought he might like to be my brother.

Boni loved my mother with an intensity that she found hard to bear. He told her that she was like a mirror that gives a wonderful reflection, but which holds nothing. She was Diana of the woods, with a silver bow. Invulnerable and deadly.

She told me that it was he who introduced her to calvados, instructing her to drink it in one gulp, to warm her veins: 'Sunshine that has lain all through a hot summer and a blue fall on apples in an ancient windswept orchard of Normandy. Only the old Greeks had gods of drinking and the joys of life. Bacchus and Dionysus.' She was enthralled by his words.

She took her time telling Papi about Boni. He was not just one of her actor conquests, whom she trifled with and then cast aside. She respected the writer and the artist in him. She admired him for his stance against Hitler and the Nazis. When she finally told Papi about her love for Boni, she had a tenderness about her that I had never seen before. 'And Papi, best of all. He told me he is impotent. So we can just be cosy together.'

Papi threw back his head and roared with laughter.

'Mutti, they can't *all* be impotent.'

In fact, Papi adored Boni. There were many occasions when we all went out for dinner in Paris; Papi, Sofi, Mutti, and Boni. As usual, my memories of my childhood were food related. This was the time of *filet mignon*; delicate white asparagus; tiny, crumbly strawberry tarts. For once, Papi allowed someone else to choose the wine; such was his respect for Boni's taste and judgement.

Papi ordered my citron pressé, and I prayed silently that the lemons would be fresh, so he wouldn't make a scene. Papi always tasted my juice and would think nothing of leaving the restaurant if it were not fresh. It was mortifying when he made a scene. I think now that he was trying to show the world that he was someone other than Mr Madou. He was not to be treated like a fool by a bunch of cooks.

Suddenly, I had an idea. When the sommelier asked what I would like to drink, I blurted out 'Mineral water, please.' Papi shot me a glacial look. Later he reprimanded me, furious that I dared to show such entitled independence.

Mother and Boni were gazing at one another, excluding everyone from their bliss. Sofi was too afraid to show her concern, merely bowed her head, hoping for the storm to pass. I apologised to Papi for my thoughtlessness, promised I wouldn't do it again, and privately thought that maybe Papi minded about Boni more than he was letting on.

Don't Let's Be Beastly to the Germans

Two blond men in handsome black uniforms, with silver eagles on their caps, guard Madou's anteroom in The Ritz. The door opens, and a man walks out with a cheery *Heil Hitler!*

Madou looks into the glass, smooths her hair, and lights a cigarette, and then another, and then another. Her husband hurries into her chamber.

'Mutti, what happened? I was very anxious for you. They refused to let me come in.'

'Papi, how can an intelligent man like Ribbentrop believe in Hitler? I had to hide Boni in the bathroom. Did you see that uniform? The fit of the shoulders. They have the best tailors. Probably Jewish.'

Boni enters, with a cold white fury.

'Joan, if you ever do that to me again …'

'But darling, they burned your books. They will kill you if they find you. They keep telling me that I should return to be the Great Star of the Third Reich. Nebbish. Hitler saw me in my first film in that garter belt and wants to get into my lace panties.'

Boni roars. He so rarely laughs, but she can always get him to loosen up. He is prone to melancholy, fits of despair.

Madou makes a joke of her encounter with Ribbentrop ('that used-up ex-champagne seller'), but she is more worried than she allows. She knows that she must renew her German passport. Her husband insists on accompanying her to the embassy. They have one of their rare disagreements, in her bedroom.

'Mutti, I am coming with you.'

'If you step one foot across the door of the German embassy, you will be on German territory. They would not dare to detain me, but you are another matter.'

'Mutti, do you think I'm afraid?'

'You ought to be. Now, don't worry. You stay here with the Child and let me go alone. I will be as formal and proper as the occasion demands. They won't try anything.'

She makes a final adjustment to her hat. It's important for her to look her very best. I know that she is more afraid than she looks. Her clothes are her armour. She wears a severe, but beautifully cut skirt suit, with extended shoulder pads and a nipped-in waist. The skirt sits just below the knee, enough to show her glorious legs encased in the finest silk stockings.

When she returns, several hours later, she is calm and quiet. She removes her hat. Her face is pale as parchment. The room darkens, and Papi switches on the lamps. Outside, soft rain falls. He pours a strong drink.

'Where is the Child?'

'With Sofi. Mutti, tell me everything. Every detail. From the beginning.'

'When I arrived at the embassy, I was taken down a long corridor, and into a large room, which was decorated with a huge Nazi flag. The ambassador, Ernst vom Rath, a handsome man, he looks like a child, was sitting behind an oversized walnut desk. He was flanked by two guards, who stood rigidly as he spoke. He told me that he was authorised to make an offer to me, by the highest authority in Germany, which would assist my movie career. Papi, he was studying my face, and I knew that if I said the wrong thing, the situation could change in a flash.'

'Please, Mutti, tell me more.'

'He said that the German film industry is expanding its productions of films and if I return, they could guarantee lead parts of my own choosing, and the budget would be no problem.'

'And how did you respond to this pack of lies?'

'I asked Herr Rath if I could have choice of director? There was a pregnant silence, and he asked who I had in mind. Papi, I told him Moses von Goldberg. You can imagine his face. He said to me, "Miss Madou, he is a Jew. You will be working in Germany, with your own kind."'

She takes a sip of brandy, and continues.

'I rose to leave, and said to him, "I'm sure it can all be arranged. I shall await to hear from you." His last words were, "Miss Madou. Your passport has been renewed. Please collect it from reception when you leave. I will pass on your request to Berlin."'

'Papi, I almost fainted. You must never go back to Germany while that madman is in control. These people will stop at nothing. I know it. I felt it in there.'

'Darling, you have been so brave.'

'He was just a boy in a Nazi uniform. And there's something else. He's homosexual. I am sure of that. He never once looked at the legs. Not once, even when I crossed them and hitched up the skirt.'

The husband embraces his wife, and leaves to attend his mistress. Once again, she is alone. She undresses, slowly, unpeeling the silk stockings, which she rinses in the bathroom basin, and then hangs over the towel rail. She has her German passport for now, but as she glances at it, the black eagle, with the swastika at its centre, she knows what she must do. And what she must do will put her family in the greatest danger, her beloved mother and her sister, Birgitte.

I Am a Camera

Who was it who said that the past is a different country? The museum in Berlin, who have asked to buy my mother's chattels, has no idea of what an inveterate hoarder she was; she saved everything. It is my task to sort through her possessions; clothes, shoes, papers, jewels (most of it paste; the real stuff lost long ago), books, records, and thousands of photographs. In one drawer, I find her American passport. In the same drawer, I find yellowed newspaper cuttings, denouncing her as a Jew-lover and a traitor to Germany.

My mother renounced the country that she loved at the very time that Hollywood had turned its back on her. She could have returned to Germany in a blaze of glory, but she despised Hitler, and she knew, long before others were willing to believe it, that he was evil. She never underestimated him, or the damage he could cause. The Nazi Party were used to getting their own way by intimidation, and did not know what to do when someone stood up to them, like my mother did. It was a lesson that Europe was very slow to learn.

Nobody knew, except maybe Boni, what it meant to her to give up the country of her birth. Despite the fact that Hollywood and the fickle public had let her down, she felt that America would be a safe haven, and would embrace her as an American citizen. She would always be grateful to the country she had once despised.

Now that the studio had cancelled her contract, the money ran out quickly, but Mother knew the importance of keeping up appearances. She began a lifelong habit of hocking her jewellery in times of need. When the money returned, she bought more jewels. She refused to buy property, or paintings. The jewels could be worn, and sold quickly when needed. I prayed that she wouldn't sell my emerald sisters. She agreed to my supplications. Goldberg's sapphires were the first to go.

That summer, in Europe, was the last time I saw my grandmother. I had spoken with her on the telephone many times, but my memories are hazy. Her voice was harsh, and she told me that I must always be obedient to my mother.

Papi arranged for us to meet Grandmother and Birgitte in Austria. For once, Sofi was left behind. Mutti did not intend for her mother to discover anything about her unconventional lifestyle. We took the train to Salzburg, via Switzerland. Just as when we had last visited Salzburg, Mother insisted that we all dressed for the part. I wore a patterned blue dirndl with a huge apron that disguised my girth, hiding everything that Mother thought needed hiding. She plopped a straw hat on my head, which had a large feather that bobbed about when I walked. Papi wore leather shorts and Tyrolean knee socks. Mother looked like a divine milk-maid in a pink dress, with a rose-coloured apron, and a loden cape.

She had insisted that Papi should find her an Austrian farm-house, with green shutters and red geraniums in window boxes. She squealed with delight and clapped her hands when she saw what he had done. It was exactly as she had imagined, down to the cut-out hearts in the wooden chairs, and working cuckoo clocks.

In the mornings, we sat around the old farmhouse table, devouring warm, soft bread rolls, and drinking fresh milk from the cow in the barn. Mother was in cooking mode, and ordered vast amounts of butter and sugar from Salzburg. She insisted that I ate breakfast potatoes fried in liberal amounts of butter, and ordered in fresh cream slices, with delicate, layered pastry as light as air.

My weight ballooned, and I split the bodice of my costume. Mother was alarmed, as Grandmother was on her way for her much-anticipated stay, and she could not tolerate criticism from her mother.

'Papi, the Child is so fat that she looks ugly.'

'Papi, I know they say that a well-fed child is a loved child, but really this is too much to bear.'

I was relieved when Grandmother and Aunt Birgitte arrived, and my mother had something else to do other than fuss about my eating habits. I loved my gentle, shy Aunt Birgitte. She was an ugly duckling like me. We picked field flowers together and made them into little bouquets. My grandmother scarcely noticed me. She shook my hand and wished me good-day.

Grandmother's first words to her daughter were severe. She admonished her for extravagance in sending a driver to meet them at the station, complained about the smell of the old barn, the size of her bedroom (too large), and the lack of good lamps for her to read her book. Her biggest complaint was the abundance of mirrors in the house. I was on Grandmother's side. Mother had insisted on ordering mirrors from Vienna and having them delivered to the farmhouse. Her favourite was a large Biedermeier wall mirror with a thick walnut veneer.

Grandmother scolded her daughter for her vanity. Mother apologised, over and over again. For the first time in my life, I realised that Mutti was afraid of another person: not Ribbentrop, not Rath, not even Hitler, but her own mother.

Cowardy Custard

So the old trout doesn't approve of mirrors? It's hardly surprising when she looks like a cross between a washerwoman and a toad. How on earth she could have given birth to the world's most beautiful woman is anyone's guess. The mirror in her bedroom has been turned against the wall. No matter, I make my presence felt elsewhere.

She constantly complains to her daughter, criticises Birgitte, ignores the Child (well, I can't complain about that one), and only shows respect to Papi, probably because he is a man. No thanks are ever expressed to Madou for everything she does for the family, the money she sends, the time she gives. You ought to remember, my dear, sugar catches more flies than vinegar.

On her final evening, there's a beastly quarrel. My poor Joan is distraught, beside herself. It is almost unendurable to witness this row, but I am always here for her, will never let her down. They argue about Germany.

'Mother, you must leave Berlin and come to America, where it is safe. If the Nazis are willing to bomb Spain, there will have to be a war. The French will never allow such behaviour, the English can never make up their mind, and Americans simply don't realise that any country exists outside of their own.'

'No, Maria, Franco is a great friend to Germany. All this talk of a small Basque village being bombed is propaganda. It never happened.'

'It did happen, Mother, terrible, terrible things happened. It's not anti-German propaganda. Nobody is stopping them ...'

Birgitte, wringing her hands, looks shocked at her own audacity. Her mother interrupts, her face white with fury.

'Birgitte, you are speaking out of turn. You are not intelligent enough to give an informed opinion. You are an embarrassment to this house and I will not have you making a fool of yourself. Now go and pick flowers with Kater.'

Birgitte slinks away, cowed and afraid, probably thinking that even the flowers in the fields are Gestapo informers.

When they leave, it is a blessed relief. But Madou is shedding silent tears as she watches the Packard wend its way down the valley of St Galgen. She is afraid for her mother, for her sister. What they might have to endure on her behalf. Now that she has been unable to convince her mother to leave Berlin, she has nothing left to do here. We shall depart for Paris and before too long, Hitler will add Austria to his list of shotless triumphs. Madou doesn't know it, poor darling, but she will never see her sister again.

In Paris, she invites Boni to her suite in The Ritz. She asks, why can't some Jew kill the little man and get it over with? She tells him that she will take matters into her own hands. Perhaps, she alone can stop this German madness.

'Boni, I have heard that Hitler admires me. Despite everything, they still want me to return to Germany. You know, to be Queen of UFA.'

'What is UFA?'

'Universum Film Aktiengesellschaft. Their studio. They want me. I shall agree on the condition I'm left alone with Hitler.'

'But, darling, there will be guards to search you.'

'Then I will go naked.'

'But what will the murder weapon be?'

'That's where you come in, with your connections. I was thinking of maybe a poisonous hairpin.'

'But darling, they will kill you.'

'Everyone has to die some time. Life is wonderful, but to kill Hitler would also be wonderful.'

Boni prevents himself from smiling at the thought of Hitler's death by hairpin. She is looking particularly lovely this evening. She paces up and down in front of the mirror, and he watches her walk towards him with long, lithe strides. His golden puma. Her face is bright and open. Her shoulders shine out of her black evening dress.

'Has anyone you loved ever left you?'

'Yes,' she replied. 'One always leaves the other.'

'You do love me, Joan?'

'My head is full of silver when I think of us.'

'Your happiness is too easy. You didn't know me a month ago.'

'Why do you always talk of leaving and being left?'

He looks at her with tenderness. Those eyes ... as if behind them lightning were flashing.

'Joan, I'll tell you a story. Once upon a time there was a wave who loved a rock in the sea. The wave foamed and swirled around the rock, she kissed him day and night, she embraced him in her white arms, she sighed and wept and besought him to come to her. She loved him and stormed about, and in that way slowly undermined him, and one day he yielded, and sank into her arms.'

'And?'

'And suddenly he was no longer a rock to be played with, to be loved, to be dreamed of. He was only a block of stone at the bottom of the sea, drowned in her. The wave felt disappointed and deceived and looked for another rock.'

'What has this all to do with us? Should he have remained a rock?'

'Things that move are stronger than immovable things. Water is stronger than rocks.'

'Boni, are you making fun of me? You will be the one to leave. I'm sure of that.'

'That will be your last statement when you go. You'll explain to me that I've left you.'

He looks at the bright face, with blue eyes and high brows, the bold sweep of the hair. The cool bright face that doesn't ask for anything, which simply exists, waiting – it is an empty face, he thinks; a face that could change with any wind of expression. One could dream it into anything. It is like a beautiful empty house waiting for carpets and pictures. It has all the possibilities – it could become a palace or a brothel.

'When the time comes, Joan, you must remember not to say goodbye. Farewell is better than goodbye.'

Around the World in 80 Days

Mother is in her room in the Paris Ritz for days on end, with only Boni for company. Sofi, whom everyone thinks is my governess, takes care of me. I take care of Heidi, and the emerald sisters, and all is well with me and my little family. Sometimes I think that maybe I am too old for dolls, but I can see from Sofi how it is possible for adults to take pleasure from toys, especially those as beautiful as mine.

When I'm finally permitted to see Mother, she crushes me to her body and kisses my eyelids. She wants to know what I have been doing, and I tell her all about the Paris Exposition; the German skyscraper with the twenty-foot eagle crushing a swastika to its claws, the Siam golden temple with jade buddhas, the Spanish displays of bright toreador suits under glass, the Eiffel Tower, which had been illuminated for the occasion, and, best of all, a huge, terrifying mural called Guernica, by an artist called Pablo Picasso.

Mother sniffed.

'I don't like that Picasso. Why does he paint such ugly faces? He's a madman. I don't know why Papa Hem likes him so much. Though everything associated with that civil war is sacred to him. Now, sweetheart, stop all this gabbling and let's plan our evening. I want to eat the fish in dill sauce in the Danish pavilion, and Papi wants to sample the Turkish baklava and those little wild blueberries in sour cream. You and Sofi can go and eat those disgusting red cakes that you like so much.'

Mother was in good spirits. She had heard that the studio was thinking of renewing her contract in light of all the good publicity about her defection from Germany. My mother was so beautiful that winter.

When she left for America, leaving me behind with Sofi and Papi, she cried, kissed me, and promised that she would write to us, and telephone with all her news. She had to prove to Hollywood that she was still a star, and not a 'has-been'. She didn't want to take me, just in case the new contract didn't come through and it would all be a wasted journey. On the way to California, she shopped in New York for hats, and fell in love with a woman called Beth. I wondered if Boni knew about her new love affair.

Mother wrote to say that she had arrived safely, that Tauber sang German songs outside her door on the train to Pasadena, and that she had written to Beth to tell her that the affair was over. She wrote that she was 'Lost without the Child', but was in negotiation for another film that would restore her to her movie star status. She told Papi that she was spending money like crazy to appear glamorous and not have 'out-of-work' written all over her face.

I felt stabs of remorse for not missing my mother. What kind of a daughter would feel only relief at the absence of a devoted parent? The last thing my grandmother said to me in Austria was to remember that the only things that mattered in life were loyalty and duty. So how was it that I felt more loyalty to my father's mistress than my own mother?

My happiness, however guilt-ridden, was short-lived. My parents sent Sofi away to another sanatorium, to 'pull herself together'. Maybe my mother could really see into my mind and heart and find only her absence.

This is a Changing World

Hallows' Evening comes; the day before All Saints' Day. The time to remember the saints, martyrs, and all the faithfully departed. Time to light a candle on the graves of the dead, so that, for one day, when the magic is most potent, the spirits and fairies can make contact with the physical world.

Feed the children with soul cakes to commemorate the dead. Bake them with allspice, ginger, nutmeg, and raisins. But let the children observe the rituals of Calan Gaeaf, the first day of winter. The day when children rush home to their parents, before the black sow and the headless woman devours your soul. The last child will never reach home.

Adref, adref am y cyntaf', Hwch Ddu Gwta a gipio'r ola.
(Home, home, at once, the tailless black sow shall snatch the last child.)

Madou laughs.

'I didn't take you for the superstitious kind. You're far too intelligent. Calan Gaeaf is an old wives' tale, to persuade children to come home quickly when it gets dark.'

'And I didn't take *you* for a cynic.'

'Are you going to tell my fortune, mirror?'

'Certainly not. I disapprove of fortune tellers, most strongly.'

'Well, there you are.'

'Except for Hallows' Eve. In a darkened room, for one night only, hold a candle to a mirror and you may divine the future. But, I warn you, Joan, the future might come as a terrible shock.'

'Papi, did you hear the news on the wireless? The man in the Paris embassy who was shot? He was the man I saw, who renewed my passport.'

Papi has not heard the news.

'Yesterday, he was shot five times, in the spleen, and the pancreas. Hitler sent his own personal physician to attend him, but it was too late. Is Kater with you? You mustn't let her out in the dark alone. It's the first day of winter for you, though here it's morning, and the sky here looks freshly washed and polished.'

'Mutti, do they know who shot Rath?'

'Yes, a Polish Jew, a young man, let me see. I wrote down his name. Herschel Grynszpan. Hitler deported his parents from Germany to the Polish frontier, so he took his revenge.'

'Mutti, this will be serious. There will be repercussions.'

'I know, but nobody here seems to care. I have to go, Papilein. I have an appointment. But I wanted you to make sure that Kater does not go out alone. You know how she likes to walk. I send kisses to you both. I miss you.'

It is now evening, and the Jew, Billy, arrives at the bungalow in the Beverly Hills Hotel. He, like Papi, fears that Hitler will unleash his revenge for Rath. He lights Joan's cigarette, and they talk long into the night.

'Joan, Grynszpan has been arrested. He has confessed and insisted that his motives were to avenge the Jewish people for the actions of the Germans. He left a letter for his parents. This is very serious. I fear for my people. All those we left behind.'

'I fear that Hitler will unleash his revenge. You know I met him, Billy? Rath. I met him in Paris.'

'The rumour mill from Paris and Berlin says that Rath and Grynszpan were not unacquainted. Rath is known in Paris as Madame Ambassador. He met Grynszpan at Le Boeuf sur le Toit.'

'Ah, so he was a pansy. I thought as much. A crime of passion? How will the Germans cover that up?'

'I don't know, but the revenge will be bloody. Ribbentrop has said that the first shot has been fired, by the Jews, and that they will take up the challenge.'

'Well, we shall wait to see what unfolds. I shall keep the wireless set on. I don't think Hitler will wait long.'

When Billy has left, Madou prepares for bed, removing her make-up with witch hazel, and applying cold cream to her skin. No one anticipates what will happen next. I tremble to think about the consequences, but when they come, the sound of broken glass will reverberate on this day and for evermore.

No Highway in the Sky

The German word sounds so beautiful; glittering stars, shining crystals in a dark sky. I used to love seeing the canopy of bright stars in the early hours of the Californian desert on our way to the studios. *Kristallnacht.* But this was the very opposite of nature's night-time glory. It was man at his very worst.

Mother once told me that breaking a mirror causes seven years of bad luck. When Papi told me about the pogrom, I worried about all of the bad luck that was brought upon the German soldiers who broke the glass with sledgehammers and bricks. Papi said that so much was broken that bonfires of glass lined the streets of Berlin. Small children, turned out of hospitals, in bare feet, tried to avoid stepping on the broken shards. It was a night of broken windows and spirits. The beginning of the End.

I worried about Grandmother and Aunt Birgitte. It had been months since we had heard from them. Papi told me I should save my concern for the Jewish people who were suffering at the hands of the Germans. For the first time, I longed for my mother. Papi told me that the new film contract had not come through, but that Mother could not return until she had completed her papers to become an American citizen. They both knew that the day might soon come when it would be necessary to escape from Europe. Until she returned, I was to go to school in Switzerland. It was time for me to have an education.

But before that happened, I heard the news that Mother's papers were through, and she was headed for Paris. Boni reappeared, in preparation for her arrival, filling her suite with white lilac, and bringing more books for me to read. With all the talk of war and pogroms, I was happy to see my mother, so elegant, so funny, with all her Hollywood gossip.

'Sweetheart, you will never guess. Barbara Hutton has a new boyfriend, you know the shirt salesman from *Blonde Venus*. Now why would she go for a pansy, with all that money she has inherited? I've heard that Cole is furious. I bet he regrets writing *Night and Day* for him.'

She rattled on, full of life and energy. The problems in Germany seemed a million miles away. At least she had news of Aunt Birgitte, who had finally got married, though Mother disapproved of the union.

My mother's suite in The Ritz became a camp for refugees, mainly German people, who had fled their country and knew that Madou would feed and clothe them. I remember her ordering large platters of ham and chicken breast, in her impeccable

French. She would write cheques for clothes and tickets to America for anyone who asked.

As Paris became hotter, we made plans for summer. Mother decided that we should depart for the south of France. Boni and Papi were to come, and Sofi, who was finally ready to be released from the sanatorium. I packed Heidi's things, and buffed up the emerald sisters. Mother and I shopped for summer clothes, and she took me to the House of Schiaparelli, on the Place Vendôme. She had heard that Elsa had designed a one-piece bathing suit with an integrated bra. Mother was ecstatic, conscious as she was of her saggy breasts. 'Thank Heavens I only had one child' was her constant refrain.

Lacy came to visit, and took me out to dinner. I told him all about my worry for Grandmother and Aunt Birgitte, and how much my mother hated me looking fat, and her fear that my bones were growing too fast. I wanted to tell him about my sadness about the broken glass bonfires, but I was too ashamed.

He always listened, and, though he didn't give me advice, just having someone there was enough. Somehow, I was never shy with Lacy. He was playing the part of Iago in a stage production of *Othello*, and he promised to send me a copy of the play. On the way out, he asked me if I still dodged mirrors, and I laughed. He noticed so much. Maybe that's why he was such a good actor.

Top of the Morning

The bellboy sets me down beside the trunk, the suitcases, the hatboxes. Madou removes me from the pile of luggage, opens my leather casing and places me on the bedside table. The studio knew that a vanity – a sturdy travel mirror, the case monogrammed in gold lettering – would be the perfect consolation prize for the failure of negotiations over a new contract.

It is a room of noble proportions. Cream and gold furniture, with a simply marvellous view of the glittering blue sea beyond. The scent of pine drifts in from the balcony, and the linen curtains billow out in the breeze, brushing against me. The light is different here to that of dusty California; softer, limpid, with tones of turquoise and pink.

Madou, with no film career to think of, has allowed herself to tan in the irresponsible Mediterranean sunshine. Her skin is butterscotch, and she wears flowing Schiaparelli beach pajamas in shocking pink. Naturally, she looks divine. The Child asks for a pink dress, too. With her red sunburned face and hideous organdie dress, she looks like a strawberry sundae. Madou abstractedly rubs calamine lotion on the Child's sunburned nose, and wonders privately why her daughter can't tan smoothly brown instead of this lurid pink.

Boni is being most vexing. He moons about, scribbling away at his novel in German on his lined yellow pad. Poor Madou. She deserves constant attentiveness. She admires herself in the mirror. Takes out a pink silk turban to complete the outfit. The Child sits quietly mixing suntan lotion made of olive oil, iodine and a drop of red wine vinegar with her chubby hands. She soaks everything up like a sponge.

Madou's voice has a silky, bored tone.

'Boni, why are you ignoring me?'

'Joan, I have to work. Why don't you swim with Kater? The pool will be most refreshing at this hour of the morning.'

Madou picks up a loose page of his manuscript, and reads it aloud: '*The smell of the soil was strong and grateful.* Now, Boni, that's a good sentence. Papa Hem would approve.'

Boni smiles in a strained way, and takes back the page. She pesters him, like a small child, desperate for attention, while looking at herself in the mirror.

'Boni, I don't want to get old.'

'You won't get old. Life will pass over your face, that will be all, and it will become more beautiful.'

He puts down his work and takes her face between his slender hands, cradling it, just looking down at it.

'Your eyes are bluer here than in Paris and you are tanned. How brown you are, Joan.'

'You love me?'

'Yes, but I'll do everything I can to break away from you.'

'I understand. Boni, I do.'

Her face has changed. Like a mirror, he thinks. Time and again it has reflected whatever is held before it. Now it is composed and beautiful.

'Bird,' he says. 'Still on my branches, but with wings ready for flight.'

Leap into Life

Mother and I, resplendent in our new bathing suits and beach pajamas, made our way below the hotel to her candy-striped cabana, which nestled among the rocks, carrying our books, sun hats and beach robes. The Hotel du Cap was one of the most beautiful I have ever seen. It was a huge, white wedding cake of a hotel, perched atop a cliff. The restaurant overlooked the sea, and the swimming pool was carved into the rocks.

After a lazy morning, swimming and reading, we made our way to the restaurant to meet Boni. The food was delicious. I remember the hotel's ice sculptures in the shape of dolphins, mermaids, and swans, dripping in the heat. The seafood was the best I'd ever tasted; snow crab, midnight blue mussels, and langoustines cooked in garlic, partnered with crispy warm bread.

Boni opened the wine list and ordered the finest wines and champagne. Madou seems irritated by his presence: 'Boni, you are drinking too much. Everyone knows that Fitzgerald is a drunkard, and Papa Hem drinks only because he is a real man, but you are too sensitive.'

'My beautiful puma. You must not worry. It won't change anything.'

Mother was in one of her tetchy moods.

'Why does Willie surround himself with all those boys that he picks up on Moroccan beaches? Of course, Noël does that too, but he does it politely, with discretion. You see, that's why it's a relief when I'm with Papa Hem. He's a *real* man – and a *real* writer.'

Boni winced and continued to drink.

'That stupid man, Chamberlain. He thinks he can persuade Hitler? Does he think that going to the Berchtesgaden will impress the Führer? The British insist on behaving as though they are an empire.'

'Maybe that is the attitude that will save them in the end.'

'Boni, don't be so stupid. I thought you were supposed to be a great expert on war.'

'My darling, I am making an observation on a national characteristic, that is all.'

Mother gave him one of her *looks*, and left the table. Boni rose and followed her to her suite as she gave her final orders: 'Kater, stay with your governess. Try not to get your nose burned.'

Free at last, I asked my governess's permission to paddle in the sea. She nodded her consent and followed me out of the restaurant.

On a slim crescent of white sand, I took a moment to cool my toes in the cool sea. At this time of day, the beach was usually deserted, but that day there were a few people stretched underneath bright striped beach umbrellas. They didn't look at me. I thought they must be English.

Behind me, I heard an outbreak of noise: shouting and shrieks of laughter. The voices sound American.

'– Gee, Kick, how can you run so fast with such thick ankles? –'

'– Bobby, you move on over to the right –'

'– Pat, quit the tears, you're on Jack's team –'

'– has anyone seen Teddy? –'

I turned my head, tilting the brim of my canvas sun hat, so that I could see more clearly. Sun gods. White teeth, blazing blue eyes, tan skin … a halo of light … I knew about light. Mr von Goldberg would have died for this light, this skin.

They were all laughing. Dimpled. Teasing. Mustn't spy on them. That would be wrong. Mother always said it's rude to stare.

I stooped to retrieve my peignoir and beach rug. Then I looked up and he grinned at me. A skinny boy with unruly golden-brown hair and freckled skin.

'You wanna play?' he asked.

I shook my head and made my way to the steps, my governess hurrying behind. Mother would not permit me to mix with American children; especially those she did not know.

The sun was now broiling, but my governess insisted on wrapping me in the peignoir. I walked towards her, and I glimpsed a tall girl, with blonde hair and huge blue, vacant eyes. She was sitting on the rocks, watching the young people.

By the stone steps that led back to the hotel, I looked back at the beach. There was a man, also blond, with the most wonderful smile I'd ever seen in my life. It wasn't a Hollywood smile, because it wasn't for the cameras, it was for real. He ran up and carried the young boy on his broad shoulders, spinning him round and round.

'Quit it, Joe, quit it,' he cried. The young boy is thrown in the sea. Nobody noticed. He ducked under and came back for more.

'Do it again, Joe, do it again.'

My governess was cross.

'Why are you staring, Kater? You know your mother would not approve.'

'I'm sorry, Fräulein.'

We made our way back to the hotel to change for dinner, but my head was full of this family: they had to be a family for they all looked so much alike. I knew one thing: I would return to the beach the next morning.

The most vital thing was that my mother should not know how I was fascinated by these people. Mustn't show any interest while in her presence. This, I told myself, was very important. I was becoming an expert at keeping secrets from her.

Twentieth Century Blues

Madou is in a mood of nostalgic regret. She often turns to me when she is feeling blue, because she knows how I understand and love her so completely, even as I truth tell, and chastise, and scold.

She is growing bored with Boni, who loves her with such intensity. She craves new adventures. She wants to work. All this fuss about sex. I try to amuse her, to take away her sadness.

'To me, passionate love is a tight shoe rubbing blisters on my Achilles' heel.'

She smiles, that wistful smile, which I love so much, and lowers her hooded eyes.

'There's something terribly sad about happiness, don't you think, mirror?'

'Not at all. There is no sense in grief. It's a waste of emotional energy.'

'I believe that being in the depths of sadness is just as important an experience as being exuberantly happy.'

'With your success, Joan, comes many pleasurable trappings. An extravagant number of gowns, and jewels, and a still extravagant amount of publicity. But there's a penalty to pay, and that's loneliness, a deep loneliness.'

She pauses to think about her career so far. Her fights with the studio. Mo's desertion, John's death in her arms.

'Those studio types – they want to tear out your intestines.'

Madou knows that success has spoiled her, that she can't live an ordinary humdrum life.

'People are jealous of your success, Joan, especially a woman who dares to be different from other women. It's the one unforgivable sin in society. People will never forgive you for being successful. It's so pleasant to feel sorry for people.'

'I never took my career seriously. Duties are what make a life worth living. Lacking them, you are not necessary to anyone. Sometimes you speak out of turn. Anyway, I don't need your treacly compassion.'

'There's no need to be so unpleasant.'

'There's no need to be so sensitive. You, who know me so well, as well as my conscience knows me.'

'You're not a mystery to me, darling. You're transparent as glass.'

She laughs and concedes defeat. But she is worried. There are bills to be paid, and she wonders how she will get the Child back to America if the war breaks out. She will speak to that nice

American ambassador, and see if he will help them. She has seen the way his hungry eyes follow her around the dining room, even though he has his pretty dark wife and children in tow.

She will approach him today, but she must dress for the part; something translucent and billowing, and white. She looks so good in white. He won't put up much resistance. She hears he has a taste for Hollywood stars. She sprays perfume onto her neck and wrists. Narcisse Noir, it's such a heavenly smell.

The Big Bluff

There was a buzz of excitement in the lobby of the Hotel du Cap. Mars was about to collide with planet Earth. An end-of-the-world party was planned. Mother told me that the women were all agonising about a suitable dress to wear for the last night of their lives. The men took out their binoculars and spent hours discussing the exact timing of the collision. I was beside myself with excitement.

Mrs McLean took out the famous Hope diamond from the hotel vault. It was supposed to strike down dead anyone who dared touch it, but now that the world was coming to an end, there was nothing to lose. To my surprise, Mother let me fondle it. Of course, she dismissed the whole thing as nebbish, but joined in the discussions of the red glow of Mars, which was coming nearer and nearer every second.

Mother thought it highly amusing that the only man in the hotel most visibly affected by the coming of Armageddon was a famous philosopher called Will Durant. Looking ashen-faced, he packed up his car and drove off at high speed, according to Mother, right in the direction of Willie Maugham's villa.

On the fated night, there was a magnificent beach party. The men dressed in tails and the women in their finest evening gowns of satin and lace. Mother's body was moulded in cream silk jersey, her face bright and lovely.

Enormous crystal bowls of caviar nestled among flame-red lobsters, and pearly-grey oysters. Champagne in tall tulip-shaped Baccarat goblets sparkled in the late sunshine. The men took out cigars, and the women sipped Pink Ladies. They talked and chatted animatedly as the velvety dark descended. It was the most lovely end-of-the-world party.

Eventually, the dawn came up over the silvery sea, indicating that the world was not going to end that day. We were all quite sorrowful to pack up and return home to the hotel. I unhooked Mother's evening dress, cooled her shoes, and soaked the adhesive tapes binding her breasts.

I couldn't stop thinking about the family on the beach; they were as American as apple pie. I dressed for lunch, planning my attack. Once my mother and Boni had left the table, I wolfed down my lunch and begged to go back down to the beach. For once, my governess agreed.

The family were there. One of them, a young girl, of maybe eighteen, ran up to me: 'Are you Miss Joan Madou's daughter?' she said.

'I am.'

'Gee, do you think you might ask her for an autograph picture for my collection?'

'Sure.'

'My father used to work in Hollywood. Now he's the American ambassador to the Court of St James. My name's Kick. We have a villa close by, but we come to the hotel to swim in the pool.'

The girl, so pretty, so friendly, held out her hand.

I took it and made a curtsy, which made her laugh. I laughed too.

Later, I told my mother, who seemed to know all about the American family. I was so relieved that she thought they were a suitable acquaintance. That summer, I got to know them all.

The eldest was Joe, the hunky boy with an Irish smile and the bluest eyes. Then there was Jack, the handsome, skinny boy with a wicked grin, a real ladies' man. Kick, who had asked for the autograph, seemed to be the eldest daughter, though she wasn't. Opinionated Eunice terrified me with her sharpness. Pat was the closest to me in age, but she was slim and athletic, with not a pimple in sight. Then the little ones; Bobby, Jean, and Teddy. I worshipped them all, and would have given anything to be one of them.

My special friend was Rosemary, who was the oldest girl, but was the damaged one, the beautiful one with those large, blue vacant eyes. We were the misfits; the shadow children. We would sit for hours on the beach holding hands and watching the calm sea.

Wait a Bit, Joe

Madou is as good as her word. I get the full story when she is back in her suite.

She has made the acquaintance of the American ambassador, with the hard blue eyes, and the lean, wiry body. She calls him Papa Joe. He is angry about the war. He knows that England cannot defeat the Germans. He has told her over and over again that it's not America's war and they should keep the hell out of it. She knows that he is thinking of his strapping sons, who are like Greek gods, and who have been raised to fight wars. He promises her that if war breaks out, he will get them all home safely. He tells her that one day, his eldest son, Joe, will be President of the United States.

They have become friends.

She has told him about her fights with the studio, and he has advised her to fire her agent. He has given her the name of a man to call. Madou is grateful. She is now getting ready to show her gratitude the only way she knows how.

I warn Madou about the ambassador. I'm not sure that he should be trusted. He looks like a scoundrel to me. And what about Boni? We must not stoop to the silliness of taking sides, but Boni is a prince among men. I fear I have gone too far this time. She stops talking to me, for a time.

Kater, who seems to intuit so much – really, she's 105 in a child's body – fiddles with her doll, and pretends that she doesn't know what's going on with her mother and Boni. Personally, I feel that she's far too old to play with dolls. She should put away childish things. She cares for that doll as if she's a real person. No mother could be more attentive. She cares too for the emeralds, but I see the greedy look in her eyes, and I know that she covets those jewels. She cleans and polishes them and puts them away in their velvet beds, and then locks them in the safe, because she does not trust the maids.

She grows and she grows, there are dimples on her thighs and upper arms. In the heat, I can see that her thighs chafe together and leave unsightly marks. She looks uncomfortable all the time. It is too absurd that Madou continues to dress her like a little girl. You can't cheat the wings of time.

She suddenly glances at me, as if she knows exactly what I am thinking. As if she agrees with me. How impertinent. I've seen the way that she looks at her devoted mother. She is giving me exactly the same look, as if she sees right through us. I'd wring her neck, if she had one.

Man by the Roadside

He appeared on a three-masted schooner. A gorgeous dark-haired boy with bulging tattooed biceps. There was great excitement at the Cap the morning he arrived. He waved to the crowd who had gathered to watch. He dropped the anchor and rowed ashore.

I had never seen such a lovely schooner. She was built of the finest teak, and had a shining black hull and cream sails. She was majestic; gently bobbing in the milky depths of the Mediterranean against the hard, blue sky. Her name was *Orlando*. Mother was mesmerised.

'Boni, do you think that boy is coming to have lunch here?'

'My darling, I neither know nor care.'

Mother glared, and turned back to her book. Our cabana was close to the American family's. They were nowhere to be seen. Their rented villa was high in the hills, but they still took several cabanas to be close to the pool and the restaurant.

Mother often disappeared into the ambassador's cabana after lunch. The ambassador's wife didn't seem to mind. I suppose she was busy with all those children. One day she invited me to lunch. I was terrified. I didn't know what to wear. Those children always looked so American, so relaxed.

We had lunch around a large table, and the children were asked to discuss a topic. It was incredible. Every opinion was considered, respected. They were listened to. And they were so much fun. So noisy. Only my special friend, Rosemary, was quiet, but she listened to the chatter with a beautiful, dreamy smile. My, she was lovely.

Jack was ever courteous. He filled my water glass and smiled across the table. Not one of the children asked me about my mother. They talked mostly about Mr Chamberlain and England. Bobby asked if I wanted to fish for octopus. He had a new underwater gun that he wanted to try out. They always seemed to have the latest gadgets.

Bobby told me that Rosemary needed to take her nap after lunch, but that the rest of us should swim. Bobby made everything seem easy. I asked him if Jack would be coming, too. Bobby assured me that Jack was coming, and told me about his scheme to lure the octopus with his spearing gun. It was simply a matter of ensuring that he hit the octopus between the eyes, as quickly as possible, so it didn't ink us all.

Everything turned out just as Bobby had planned. For the first time in my life, I felt part of a family. I had never felt so happy. In the cold water, I felt light as air, and as slinky as an eel.

* * *

Mrs Maxwell was giving a party. I loved her because she understood what it was like to be unattractive in the midst of the beautiful. I hated being on display, and she always made sure to sit me next to the people who were kind to me and who knew never to mention my mother.

The American family were invited to the party, and I decided to take a deep breath and ask my mother for an evening dress. I was tired of being an eternal child. Mother and Boni were friends again. He had a new car, which he loved. He called it his grey puma. He told Mother that she mustn't be jealous of his grey puma as he equally adored his golden puma. Mother was amused. She loved the thought of having a car as a rival.

'Mutti, may I have a real evening dress for Mrs Maxwell's party? In black silk. And evening shoes like your gold slippers, and a little embroidered purse?'

Mother, still glowing with her renewed love for Boni, was all graciousness, all smiles: 'What does a child want with an evening dress?'

Boni looked at her with a tender glance and then smiled gently at me.

'Well, if that's what she wants, that's what she will have. I will choose the dress pattern and we will have a dress made up for you. But not black. A child does not wear black.'

There was no point in pleading any more. At least I would escape those hideous pink puff-sleeved Alice in Wonderland efforts that seemed only to draw attention to my ample proportions.

On the night of the party Mother looked mesmerising. She was wearing a silver lamé sheath dress with diamond clips and Mo's sapphires. My mother seemed to be the only person on the Côte d'Azur who could achieve an even suntan. The sun would not dare to burn that nose or those noble shoulders.

My dress was hideous. It was made from white net and had a wide cummerbund encrusted with multi-coloured glass beads. I looked like a fake Christmas tree. Mother slapped calamine lotion onto my pink nose and pinned a large net bow to my head.

Mrs Maxwell's party was like an Aladdin's cave. Hundreds of miniature lanterns lit the ballroom, and the air was filled with the scent of tuberoses. Mrs Maxwell assigned me a table as far away from Mother as possible. I hid behind the potted ferns, content to watch the beautiful people dancing. The band struck up 'The Lambeth Walk'.

And there he was. The most handsome man I had ever seen, striding across the ballroom towards me. I looked behind me. He must be looking for someone else. I could hear the sniggers, as he approached. Then he made a low bow, grinned with those gorgeous teeth, and asked me to dance. I saw Mother staring across the room in disbelief. Scarlet to my toenails, I rose and followed him onto the dancefloor. *Honi soit qui mal y pense.* Jack Kennedy dancing with a net tent. Whoever would have believed it!

I remember the night that he danced with me, because when I returned to the hotel room I did something that I hadn't done for a long time. I removed my dress and looked at myself in Mother's full-length gilt mirror. My large, creamy breasts buffed out like proven dough. I ran my hands over my soft belly, and then down to my chunky thighs: 'Hog, heifer, butterball, dumpy, piggly-wiggly, jigglypuff. How could he ever like you? You're disgusting, you're vile, you're a mess. Why don't you kill yourself? Nobody would care.'

I repeated these words over and over again. Then when I was done with myself, I took a large Spanish scarf and draped it over the looking glass.

When My Ship Comes Home

Madou is beside herself. She is dressing for dinner, and needs the Child to bind her into her silver evening dress. All of that French food is taking its toll. Tomorrow she will start another diet. She talks non-stop, as the Child takes out the tape and the scissors.

'Sweetheart, you will never guess. That boy on the schooner is a *girl*. She's an English heiress – oil – and she's obsessed with sailing. Can you imagine? We are having dinner tonight. She's invited me onto her boat. Her real name is Bridget, but she calls herself Peta. Her stepfather is a famous surgeon who transplants monkey tissue into male scrotums: for rejuvenation, you see. Maybe that's what Boni needs, some baboon glands. Of course, Papa Hem wouldn't need any of that nonsense.'

Madou is enchanted. She babbles on: 'Peta has a friend, a doll called Lord Tod Wodley. Lord Tod has his own wardrobe, like Kater's doll: his suits are made in Savile Row and he is given tiny handmade Italian shoes. He has his own gold Cartier cigar case and minuscule calling cards in a Cartier box. And his own monogrammed stationery. She carries him around everywhere. So charming. So English eccentric. Of course, only the English can get away with carrying dolls or teddy bears in public.'

Madou endears herself forever with Peta: when she first sees Lord Tod, she exclaims, 'Who is that?' rather than, 'What is that?'

The affair is intoxicating and giddy. It takes place on the schooner, away from Boni's prying eyes. Madou is sure to take me with her, she only trusts her own vanity to ensure that she is looking her best. I must confess that I rather admire the Pirate. She's really rather charming. Simply marvellous upper arm muscles. She hails from very good stock.

The Pirate strides up to me, fearlessly. She tucks three fingers into her breast pocket and gives a smile of satisfaction: 'You'll do, old chap.'

Madou speaks: 'You certainly will, darling. Now come to Mother for a kiss.'

'Mothers are very underrated.'

Madou lies naked in bed. A ray of light comes streaming through the window, splintering its shafts of light onto my surface. The boat rocks gently. Her mind is full of this sensuous, beguiling boy-girl. Peta tells her fabulous tales of a kingdom she has created on her tropical island.

The island was uninhabited when she bought it. That was its charm. First she built roads, then houses for the natives, a general store, a school, and a church. Finally, she built herself a great house; planting palms, almond trees, and sea grape trees in its spacious grounds. Oleander, hibiscus, and mastic lined the outer walls.

It took 300 men to build the house, a sturdy white Spanish villa with red roof tiles. There were five bedrooms and five bathrooms, a cold room for meats, and a large, spacious kitchen. There was a large living room with a fireplace for the cold nights, and fans on the ceilings for the warm nights. She hung copper ships' lanterns in the rooms, and scattered Turkish rugs on its wooden floors.

She banned alcohol and *obeah* – a form of voodoo. One day, she was mending a road with her workers, when a poisonous snake slithered from a rock. Peta whipped out her knife and sliced off its head. From that moment, she became the White Witch. Her people believed her to have magical powers. She encouraged their belief.

She would drive around her island on a red motorcycle with Lord Tod Wodley on her handlebars to make inspections. She had the utmost respect of her people, and she baptised their children and supervised their schooling.

Madou is entranced by her stories. She loves to hear the details of the parties the Pirate held in the great house for her lady friends. The accounts of derring-do, fishing in the waters, and encounters with blue sharks; surviving the hurricanes that blasted the island;

native uprisings in the middle of the night. The Pirate tells her that she was never bitten by sand flies or mosquitoes as they knew she wasn't afraid of them.

Later, in her room, she taunts Boni with her latest lover.

'You see, Boni, the Pirate is better than any man. She is stronger, and tougher. She is respected by the natives. An African chieftain once gave her a present of a necklace of dried human ears.'

Boni is unimpressed and wildly jealous.

'And she knows how to please a woman. She was once a lover of Dolly Wilde in Paris in the twenties.'

Madou leaves the Pirate's love letters lying around to torture Boni. He no longer rages about Papa Hem. He is far more fearful of his new rival. As she talks, he stares at Madou's reflection. How the light flows over her shoulders. The Moon in her hair.

Just one more night, this one night, once again this
sleeping head on his shoulder, tomorrow one could fight,
once more her breath beside him, once more in all the
falling, the tender illusion, the sweet deception; don't go,
don't go, what else have I?

When she leaves with her weekend luggage, he approaches me and starts to cry. He looks at his face in the glass, almost enjoying it, half ironically, half genuinely, half serious and half something else. Not play-acting, more curiosity, wanting to get himself in tears, waiting for the tears and then there they are: a certain calming down and composure.

He walks slowly to the bar and pours himself a large tumbler of golden calvados.

The Imaginary Baron

The Pirate disliked girl children, though he idolised little boys, so I tried to keep out of the way as much as possible. Mother's infatuation became more intense by the day. He was Mercury to her Nike, Pan and Peter Pan rolled into one gorgeous bundle of bliss. She called him the Pirate, he called her 'Mother' and 'Babe': the only person in the world to get away with calling her that.

Mother said that if she was Leda seduced by Zeus in the shape of a swan, then he was Ganymede raped by Zeus in the shape of an eagle. I hated eagles. I especially hated the vicious-looking eagle on my German passport.

To my dismay, Mother made no attempt to hide her lust from Boni: 'Sweetheart, that flat chest, and those triceps. You know he has an M tattoo just for me. He calls me POW for perfection of womanhood. I'm sailing with him for a few days. You're so busy with your novel, and you must take care of the Child. You know how the Pirate fears little girls. Besides, Lord Tod has taken a dislike to the Child. He's such a strange doll. So vain, too. He's always looking at himself in his tiny hand mirror.'

'Joan, stop this servant-girl chatter.'

'Boni, you can't love. You never give yourself.'

'You always do, and that's the problem with you.'

I left the room when they started to fight. Mother usually invoked Papa Hem to incite Boni's jealousy. But I knew that Boni was jealous of the Pirate in a way that was different. Mother would leave in a rage, and he would start to drink. It always ended the same way.

Later I crept back to check Boni was OK. He was asleep, empty bottles all around him. I saw that a yellow page with his neat handwriting had fluttered to the floor, and I picked it up and read it, knowing that she never would:

She is Madonna of the flighty heart. Nike of Samothrace, broken mirror of a dark god: 'She had no country.'

Here I stand, miserable and with the sharp claws of jealousy in my stomach, longing for you, despising you, admiring you, worshipping you, because you cast the lightning that set me ablaze, the lightning hidden in every womb, the spark of life, the black fire, here I stand no longer like a dead man on furlough with his small cynicism, sarcasm and portion of courage, no longer cold: alive again …

You love the intoxication, the conquest, the Other You that wants to die in you and that will never die, you love the stormy deceit of the blood, but your heart will remain empty – because one cannot keep anything that does not grow from within oneself.

Something had gone wrong, at some point the ray of his imagination had failed to hit the mirror, the mirror that caught it and threw it back intensified into itself, and now the ray had shot beyond into the blind sphere of the unfillable and nothing could bring it back again, not one mirror or a thousand mirrors.

Jack had an idea. 'Kater, you're a good swimmer. Let's swim out to the island. We can carry our clothes above our heads and then we can dress for lunch.'

'Well, I'll have to ask Mother.'

'That's done then. I'll meet you at the beach in one hour. But don't tell the others. It's our secret.'

I was surprised that Mother agreed to my wish, but she was having lunch with the Pirate, so she was probably glad to get rid of me. When I saw her at the water's edge, waving and watching me with anxiety etched over her lovely face, I felt a surge of sorrow and happiness. She only walked away when she saw that we had arrived safely at our destination.

Jack looked so much thinner than when I had first seen him. There were rumours swirling around that he had been very ill, but when I saw his grin of triumph when we reached the island, I forgot about his emaciated body. We ate delicious *croustine*, mopping up the garlicky sauce with thick crusty bread, and Jack drank ice-cold pink wine.

After eating, we wandered to a rock pool, and Jack drew my attention to a pair of jewel-coloured damselflies. They twirled and looped in a slow dance, their spindly, emerald bodies entwined in the warm air, high above our heads. I gasped when I saw them bending together in the final climax to form the shape of a heart. It was the most beautiful thing I had ever seen. I turned my face away, but I knew that he understood how I felt.

Later, he lay in the sun resting, while I sat watching him sleep. I guess that was the last time, as a child, that I felt truly happy.

When We Were Girls Together

Madou is happier than I have seen her in a long time. She has heard word from her mother and her sister that they are well, and that war might be averted, after all. Her sister is moving to Bergen, with her husband and baby. There is no need to send money. They have plenty from her husband who has gone into the film industry. Boni sulks, but she pays him no heed. She knows that he loves nothing better than playing out a doomed romance against the background of an all-engulfing war. The last golden summer with his golden puma. He is in love with the glory of it all.

Papi is in Paris with Sofi. She has returned from the sanatorium. Kater plays happily with the Kennedy children. The ambassador has returned to London for an emergency meeting with Chamberlain. In his absence, Madou decides that she will help herself to the eldest boy. He has a beautiful body, with strong arms and chest, and tiny hips, like a wasp.

The Pirate has left to pick up a dear friend, but promises Madou that she will return bearing gifts; whatever her heart desires. She will bring silk dresses, and jewels and maybe a doll for Madou, so that they can seal their friendship. Madou waves her off from the shore, and slinks away to the Kennedy cabana. When she returns, her face is flushed and dewy. She has not taken a young boy before, and she has enjoyed the taste of fresh meat.

But then Papi calls, telling her that he needs more money. There's always someone who needs her money. Perhaps she can sell her emeralds? What about her new agent in Hollywood? Has he called? He has heard news from Paris that the German situation has changed, again. They will need money to travel.

She is alarmed. But then the Pirate returns, laden with gifts. The Kennedy boy is forgotten, and bouquets of lilac and lavender fill the air. The August sun is hot. Ice cubes are ordered, and Madou traces the cubes around the contours of her naked body, to the Pirate's delight. Later, they dress for dinner. They make a very pretty couple; she in her flimsy gown, she in a fisherman's top and beret. The Pirate tells her of her oldest friend, who waits for them in the dining room. They were once lovers. It was she who presented him with Lord Tod and the doll-child sealed the unnervingly close bond between them.

Madou is delighted. She considers sexual jealousy low-class and bourgeois. She would like to meet this friend, perhaps they can all have fun together on the *Orlando*, where they will not be disturbed. The Pirate confesses that her special friend is no oil painting. She is comely rather than pretty, and is heavy-set, and hairy, though her voice is gentle and sweet.

Madou's laughter is like the tinkle of tiny, silver bells.

Heads Up, Charley

Her name was Viola, which evokes delicate spring flowers, but she looked like a rhinoceros. She had an immense body, large head, short neck, broad chest, and small feet. If she had slipped off her shoes to reveal three toes, I wouldn't have been surprised in the least.

She was the Pirate's dearest friend. I learned later that the Rhino gave her Lord Tod as a way of cementing their love. She was good at presents, just like my mother. I still longed for an evening dress that didn't look like a Christmas tree.

One day a parcel arrived for me. I tore apart the layers of cloud-pink tissue and there it was: the most beautiful dress I had ever seen. It was a midnight blue satin sheath, which miraculously seemed to skim over my bulging hips and flattened my tummy. It had three-quarter length sleeves, and fell to just below the knee.

I had no idea who had sent the dress, but later the Rhino appeared and whispered that she had persuaded Mother that I needed a grown-up dress, that I was no longer a child. Her kindness was touching. Her voice was so soft. She bought heeled shoes to match, and a blue velvet evening bag. Inside was a ruby red lipstick in a silver bullet casing. It was my first lipstick.

She made time for me. Knowing that I loved reading, we would sit with our books in the cool of the evening. She insisted that I should have a chaperone when my mother was partying. 'You never know what could happen,' she would admonish Mother, 'leaving the Child alone in the evenings.' For once in her life, my mother was put in her place. Gloriosky!

Everybody liked Viola. Despite her off-putting plainness and heavy girth, she was pleasant and courteous. She looked like a nurse out of a storybook. She wore a serge navy suit and a white blouse with a pussy-bow, even though it was scorching hot. She always looked so efficient, so capable in her sensible brogue shoes. Her hands were large and workmanlike. Her only concession to vanity was her scarlet-painted long fingernails.

I liked her. She was so attentive. She took a lot of trouble to please Mother, while at the same time being so kind to me. Once she had built Mother's trust, she turned her focus onto me, and I was so flattered, so grateful to have the spotlight on me, no matter for how brief a time.

She seemed to understand me, she saw that I was lonely. I loved the fact that although she clearly admired Mother, she wasn't enraptured, wasn't caught in her spell in the way that everybody else was. There were times that she spoke up for me. She told

Mother, firmly, that I was no longer a child, and that I needed more independence. But Mother wasn't to worry: she would take care of me. Sometimes she would squeeze my arm.

She came to lunch with the ambassador's family. That day, the Pirate was wearing a white T-shirt, which showed off her bulging biceps and tattoos. I was fascinated by the blue coiled serpent that snaked up her arm. It had eyes like jewels. A telegraph was delivered to the table. Mother chuckled and handed over the telegram to the ambassador.

'Papa Joe, look at this. It's insulting. Who do they think I am?'

'Well, Joan, slow down. I'm not so sure.'

The Pirate had given Mother a gold and cabochon sapphire Cartier compact. She took it from her beaded purse, and examined her face for perspiration. It really was so stiflingly hot.

'But that boy, that dreadful cowboy, with the stutter. That string bean. James somebody. Really, Papa Joe? Make a cowboy film with an unknown actor. But I will do what you command.'

'You need the money. What is there to lose? Go back to America.'

'Papa Joe, if there is a war, will you look after the Child? Bring her back home?'

'I'll look after her as if she's my own.'

Mother decided that she would return to America and make the film. It would prove to be yet another of her brilliant decisions.

She put me in Boni's hands: 'The Child is all that matters. You cannot understand maternal love. It's the strongest love of all.'

'Puma, I will protect the cat. You know that.'

'The Pirate will help you, and Viola.'

'I will protect the Child.'

Ace of Clubs

She packs her bags, leaving her vanity until the last, as she always does.

The ritual is familiar by now. Trunk and cases are carted away, then the final act is to fold my leather casing. I am in the dark. But not for long. On the ship, in the hotels, I am opened again and placed beside the bed.

Madou is bidding farewell to Europe, and the France that she loves. This time our journey will be a new adventure: though she is superstitious and fears flying, she plans to go by air. She wonders if she should bring the Child, but she seems so happy here with the Kennedy children, and Boni. There are many people to take care of her daughter, and she will be busy with the film. She worries about what will happen if war breaks out, but she can hardly believe that would be possible when everything in France seems temporarily becalmed.

* * *

As soon as she is settled back in Hollywood, she will send for the Child. Times are different than back in the old days, when Mo made all the living and travel arrangements. Now, we are on our own. And, she reminds herself, the Child is no longer a child. Viola is correct. Independence would be a good lesson. But she feels responsible for not letting her grow up, keeping her perpetually a child, with her doll and her fairy tales.

Perhaps now is the time to sever the ties. Perhaps now is the time for the Child to let her go. Madou had a rude awakening when her father died, and she was forced to grow up. She was being selfish keeping her a child. A little of life's realities would be a good thing. Nobody wants a child to be a soft, prissy creature, as the children of hard-bitten characters usually are. She remembers what her own mother used to say: the weak are more likely to make the strong weak, than the strong are likely to make the weak strong.

Besides, at the suggestion of the Pirate, she has put her daughter under the care of Viola, who trained as a governess. Every well-brought-up girl has a governess. As for me, before we left the Riviera I saw how Viola was looking at the Child. She seemed to see beyond the physical unpleasantness. To see something special, unknown to the rest of us. How charming. There again, Viola is also lacking in the beauty department, so I'm sure she understands how it feels to be a changeling child. She's a darling to spend so much time and money on the Child. Buying exactly the appropriate presents for a young lady on the eve of adulthood: books, make-up, and clothes. Anyone would think she is after something.

Madou usually protests when the focus is on her daughter, but, for once, she seemed to be satisfied that Viola had the Child's best interests at heart. 'Yes, yes,' Madou confides to me, 'Kater is thirteen now, and it is time to let her experience the world.'

Touch of Evil

Mother used to say to me: 'Think twice before burdening a friend with a secret.' When she left for Hollywood, I was happy to be with Boni. He would tell wonderful stories and sometimes he would let me read fragments from his book about my mother. With my mother gone, he could write worry-free, and he worked feverishly in his room, a brandy by his side, along with a supply of American cigarettes.

Hungry, I ordered French fries and steak hâché. I felt full and warm. Replete. Then there was a knock on the door, and I opened it to find the Rhino, clutching something in her arms. She told me that she had someone she wanted me to meet. It was Lord Tod.

I had never set eyes on Lord Tod, though I had heard the tales of his ample wardrobe and fine things; his engraved silver cigar case, and his Cartier watch. The Rhino told me to shake his hand. He had the happiest face I had ever seen. It was smooth and apple-cheeked. He looked like a real boy. He was wearing a striped shirt, Oxford bags, and a beret at a jaunty angle. He terrified me.

I asked her if she had the Pirate's permission to bring him, knowing how inseparable they were, like mother and baby.

She ignored my question, and set him on the side table, legs crossed, cigar in his hand.

'Kater, it's time for bed. I'm your governess now. Your mother's instructions. Undress, please. Brush your teeth. Good girl. Do as I say.'

'But what about Boni? Does he need to eat? Shall we call him?'

'We don't need to concern ourselves about him. He's fine. Everything is OK.'

I felt reassured by her OK. American, calm, just what was required. A word my mother never used because she hated it so.

The last thing I remembered was her putting a blindfold over the doll's knowing black button eyes. An unwilling witness to my evening's event.

'Now, Kater. Little Pussy Cat. You must lie in bed, quiet now.'

Boni woke me early the next morning.

'Kater, we need to leave now. Pack lightly, we are headed for Paris. We are to leave in the Puma.'

'Boni, have you heard from Mutti? Did she telephone from America? Are Jack and the others coming too?'

'No questions for now, darling. We will talk on the way.'

'Of course, Boni.'

'Good girl.'

Boni's face was creased with worry. We left the hotel without even saying goodbye to our friends. Boni was calm and quiet. What was I now? We saw men walking alongside the dusty roads, walking mules and horses, their faces full of despair. After we had driven a few miles, he spoke.

'Kater, war has been declared. Your mother has arranged for our passage from Paris. I want you to remember this journey. Look at the faces of these men. They still remember the last war; they have given up already.'

'Boni, are we going to die?'

'One day, Kater, but not today.'

I was mostly worried about Jack and his family. Would they get back to London safely? I wished I'd had time to say goodbye. I even spared a thought for Lord Tod, but not for the Rhino.

My only hope was that I would never have to set eyes on her again.

Boni talked and talked on that journey, telling tales of war and misery, how there was no glory in war, only the sounds of mothers weeping. When we got to Paris it was dark. I looked for the lights of the Eiffel Tower, but they had been put out.

'Kater, this is Paris. The City of Lights. Now she is suffering her first blackout. Beautiful Paris. We must say goodbye to her properly. Let's go to Fouquet's and bid her farewell.'

And that's what we did. But first he drove his Puma to his garage.

'Guard my Puma from the Boche, my friend. But if you must flee the city, then use her. Pumas are good at escaping.'

That summer's night the Parisians drank the cellar dry at Fouquet's. The sommelier came to Boni with a dusty bottle: 'Monsieur, we don't want the Boche to find this, do we?'

'We don't, my friend.'

Boni poured a small amount into a glass and gave it to me.

'You will never forget this summer's night, Kater, and you will never forget this wine.'

He was right. I never forgot. And now that I am old, I remember every detail vividly. I remember the goodness of this man. Maybe he was the one to whom I could unburden my shameful secret.

'Boni, I don't love her.'

There, it was out. I had said it. I was not the dutiful daughter that everyone supposed. I was what the mirror saw: ugly and vile. But I felt a sure, strong stab of relief at saying the words out loud. Boni would understand. He knew my mother very well.

'Kater, please don't speak about your mother in that way. She loves you very dearly. We must understand. She loves in a different way to the rest of us.'

So it must be my fault. I am to blame. Why had my mother left me with that woman? I must have done something really bad to deserve this. I thought mothers were supposed to protect their children. I had always been such a good girl. But I wasn't a good girl, because I hated my mother. But then again, I didn't have a mother: I belonged to a queen.

Let's Do It

Madou sits at her dressing table, putting the finishing touches to her make-up as 'Frenchie'. A slash of crimson lipstick, clown-like, contrasts vividly with the deathly-pale pallor of her skin.

Boni stands behind her, looking at her through the glass. He is here to support the film, and to offer his advice, though he is only politely listened to. This is a world in which he doesn't belong, despite his best intentions. Madou is in her element playing a bar-room floozie. She knows it's her best work since *The Blue Angel*.

He begins reciting a passage from his work in progress: '*What do you know about graves that open and how one stands in dread of the many colourless empty nights of yesterday – yet they open and no skeletons now lie bleaching there, only earth is there, earth, fertile seeds, and already the first green. What do you know about it? You love the intoxication, the conquest, the Other You that wants to die in you and that will never die, you love the stormy deceit of the blood, but your heart will remain empty – because one cannot keep anything that does not grow from within oneself. And not much can grow in a storm. It is in the empty nights of loneliness that it grows, if one does not despair.'*

'That was your wave.'

'Oh, so you kept it in mind, Joan?'

'Yes, but you aren't a rock. You're a block of concrete.'

In her cruelty, she still moves him. When she stands up with her back to him, he carries on staring at her reflection in me. Then she turns to face him: 'Enough, Boni.'

She turns away, and he marvels at her grace. She walks as though she were walking against a light wind, he thinks to himself.

He leaves the room, wondering if he could have one more night with her golden head resting on his shoulder. His fickle puma.

Madou turns back to me. Really, Boni was so jealous and disagreeable. Yes, the look was exactly right: lurid and effective. So much for 'box-office poison'. And the beanpole actor was charming. He would only ever be a second-string love interest, but diverting, all the same.

She is simply marvellous in this picture. There is a saloon brawl and she insists on not having a stand-in. She whispers to her female co-star that she will kick and punch like crazy, so she better fight back. The scene is electric. Nobody will believe that this hollering, abusive hoyden, rolling around the filthy floor, is the great Madou. The scene ends with the beanpole cowboy throwing a bucket of cold water over the cat-fighting girls. In a fit of unscripted anger, Madou picks up a chair and throws it at his head. He ducks, just in time, a look of horror and amusement on his face.

'CUT.'

Naturally, this is the scene that everyone remembers. She knows that this performance is one of her best. The beanpole cowboy urges her to dress simply, and, for once, to go make-up free. She agrees, and looks perfect as the older western hussy, singing 'The Boys in the Back Room' in her sexy, husky voice. She breathes new life into Lola Lola.

Boni pays homage to her in his novel as the remote and inaccessible Nike of Samothrace, but she is happier returning to her showgirl roots.

The press goes wild for her, and she is on everyone's lips. She is back in business. The picture has furnished her with a new, younger lover, but that soon comes to a rather unsavoury end.

Kater wishes to speak privately to her mother. There is something very pressing that must be communicated. But when she comes to the dressing room, Dot is guarding the door. Who on earth is with Mother now, I see her thinking, with those all-seeing pale, lashless eyes?

'What is it, honey? Your mother is sleeping. She's feeling unwell. Why don't you come back later?'

'I need to speak with her. May I just see her for a moment?'

'OK, honey, but don't tire her out.'

Madou is asleep on her sofa, and the blinds are down. She is murmuring to herself. Her face is white and drawn. Her slender hand holds a soft shawl to her chest.

Kater kneels by her side and Madou caresses her daughter's hair.

'Dearest.'

'Mutti, are you dying?'

Dot intervenes: 'No, honey, she's not dying, but she needs rest. I'll get her to call you later. I promise.'

Madame Doesn't Want Children

She didn't call me. I didn't see her for six days. By then, I guess it was too late. The moral of the story: don't turn to your mother when she has just had an abortion.

I now knew that no man would ever want me. I also knew it was my fault. I was obedient, pliable, always a good girl. I was trained for it. I didn't blame the Rhino, though I despised her. I blamed someone else. If you put an alcoholic in a wine bar and lock the door, you can't blame him for helping himself to the goods available.

That night when I should have been tucked up in bed, I made my way to the drinks cabinet. The pale liquid burned my throat. For once, I felt all warm inside. It was easy to keep this secret. I learned to water down the brandy, so she wouldn't notice. In those days, Mother's drink of choice was champagne.

When I had replaced the bottle, I finally felt that I had the courage that I needed. I took her out of my suitcase, where she had been packed. She was dressed in her travel suit, her long, blonde hair swept back under a natty hat. She looked so different. She was hard and waxy, not soft and fleshy like she'd always been. I pressed down on her belly to hear the familiar 'MAMA' in her cut-glass English accent.

Just like that, in an instant, she was no longer my child, but a doll. Heidi had been the humanised recipient of all my love, secrets, and hopes. But now it was time to put away childish things. It was finally time to grow up.

Papi wanted to speak to me on the phone. I was desperate for news of Sofi. He told me that she was visiting her brother.

Mother was angry.

'Kater, don't bother Papi with your questions. I've just sent Sofi all my old clothes and more besides. She's crazy. But we all know that. Poor Papi. I don't know how he does it. Now come and help me undress.'

'But Mutti …'

'Speak when you're spoken to.'

Mother had come straight from a dinner and had booked a call with Papi, knowing that for him it was morning and the best time to talk. I unhooked Mother's gold dress and began soaking the adhesive tape that made red marks on her body, but she didn't flinch when I pulled it off: 'Sweetheart, I met a man tonight. A real man. He's French. Intelligent. Not like those American actors.

I am going to help him. Fox have brought him over from France. He was in that magnificent picture, *Grand Illusion*. I don't know why Pasternak gives me a dance teacher for a leading man, a gigolo. I mean, with Mo, we know why he gave me leading men that he knew I wouldn't like, but how can Pasternak be jealous? I haven't slept with him, yet. I told him, no, not until Hitler loses the war.'

Mother was delighted with her Frenchman. She used him to torture Boni as she had used the White Knight to torture Mo. It was an effective method. Boni left for New York. I begged him to stay, but he was proud.

'Goodbye, Sadness. Look after your mother.'

'Why do you call me Sadness, Boni?'

'I call you many tender things, Pussy Cat. I call you a gasp of air because your mother breathes up all the oxygen around you. I wish I could turn you to happiness.'

The studio installed the French lover in Boni's bungalow. Mother set about recreating a French village in the middle of Brentwood. She cooked French food (*pot au feu* replaced her legendary goulash), scoured the shops for French wine, and filled the house with the sounds of Edith Piaf in the place of her beloved Tauber. She wore a striped fisherman's jersey and a beret at a jaunty angle over one eye.

I liked Moncorge, and considered him the only man strong enough for my mother. He was a lion, and she, for once, wanted to be his permanent mate. But he had honour, too, and he told her he was determined to leave Hollywood to join the Free French. She told him that if he left her, she would follow him wherever he went.

Mother was angry that nobody in California wanted to talk about the war in Europe. I heard mutterings about a place called Belsen and what had happened to my Aunt Birgitte. But Mother had more important things to worry about, namely me. She decided that enough was enough and enrolled me in a sanatorium to lose weight.

My stay at La Jolla was a waste of time and money. Mother was convinced that I had a gland problem and insisted that I be fed mainly lettuce. Every Friday there was a weighing-in, but the scales remained the same. When I started to *gain* weight, Mother brought me home.

On the nights – every night – when I couldn't sleep, I read. To try to stop myself thinking about Mother and about the Rhino. I was reading another English classic, recommended by Lacy, who continued to show an interest in my education. My favourite book, at the time, was an English one.

'Conceit isn't a disease,' said Alice.

'It is, though,' said the Wasp, 'Wait till you have it, and then you'll know it.'

Bitter Sweet

Madou's career is flourishing in her second act as a cowgirl. Following the unfortunate incident of the douche in the night, the beanpole cowboy is replaced by another leading man, the cowboy of all cowboys. Wayne is *all* man. Madou, with her female instincts, knows that this man needs to be treated with directness. When they finally meet, in her dressing room, she lifts up her skirt to reveal a watch secured to her garter belt. She purrs, 'Honey, we have all the time in the world.' With that he is off his seat in a trice, and pounces on her.

The affair is passionate and short-lived. Her heart is with Moncorge. But she can't deny the chemistry that she has with Wayne. It helps the movie, too, which is another resounding success. Once again, she plays a saloon girl, with a huge heart. Once again, there is a bar-room brawl. The studio is desperate to recreate the success of *Seven Sinners*, but this time, the fight is between men. 'There's no brawling around her,' she drawls, 'except if it's over me.'

Wayne is a darling, but she cares only for Moncorge. She thinks he is the most attractive man she has ever met, and she has met a lot. She kneels before him, removes his shoes, rubs his toes. She finds him film roles, and spends hours helping him with his rusty English. She thinks he resembles Spencer Tracy, but has more sex appeal. Also, crucially, she sees the little boy in him.

Personally, I find him boorish and uncouth. He looks like a pugilist, with that flat nose, and he knocks her around. A slap here, a punch there. She gives as good as she gets. I find their fights so very difficult to witness. She believes that he is the greatest love of her life. Boni thinks differently. He will take his revenge in his novel, where she is killed by her violent boxer lover.

They make an unremarkable film together, but their chemistry cracks and pops. The plot turns on an act of disloyalty. When he discovers her infidelity, he strikes her so hard she falls to the ground. She is not acting. Life mirrors art.

One afternoon, she returns to her boudoir alone, with a blue-purple bruise covering her cheek like a blackberry stain. It's time for an admonishment. She seems to welcome it, as though she is desperate for someone to talk sense into her, and snap her out of the mess she's in.

'It's no use trying to hide it with Pan Stik, Joan, it merely draws more attention to the wound, though perhaps that is your intention?'

'Don't be impertinent. I have an appointment this evening. Boni has returned, and I don't want him to comment. Moncorge was jealous, that's all, and he lost his temper. It's no matter.'

'And frustrated, perhaps? He is a far better actor in French than English, despite your great efforts. There's always something fishy about the French. So tell me, has de Gaulle sent word?'

'You seem to know everything. Yes, it's true. And I'm pregnant again, and he wants me to have his brat, which I won't consider for a single second. That's why he hit me.'

'It's my opinion that some women should be struck regularly, like gongs.'

She smiles.

'One child is enough, as I'm sure you'll agree.'

'Well, yes, I take your point, my dear. What will you do?'

'I'll do what I always do. What I did after the beanpole cowboy. What Sofi does every year, with alarming regularity, and expects me to foot the bill.'

'Well, take care, my dear. Make sure you have a good doctor.'

'I choose my doctors with great care. I have great respect for the medical profession. It will be over in a day, and I can get back to work. Not like Sofi, who never works and takes weeks to recover, leaving poor Papi to fend for himself.'

She finishes her face, and though the bruise is less prominent, the cheek is swollen. She puts on a hat, and draws the brim over her left side. There, she looks perfect. The blow did not hurt, but his words did. Words can bruise hearts and minds. There may be no black and blue marks, no broken bones to put in plaster, but they hurt all the same.

Knight without Armour

Mother was displeased. Her lips narrowed into a thin line, even though she was smiling: 'You've had an invitation, sweetheart. Jack is in Hollywood, before he leaves for the Pacific, and he has asked to take you out to tea.'

'Oh, Mutti, really? Will Kick be there? Or Bobby?'

'No, dear, just Jack, so of course I've arranged a chaperone.'

'Mutti, please, no. I mean, he'll think I'm still a child.'

'Nebbish. He'll think no such thing. You must wear the pale green silk with the white and red daisies and the cummerbund. If it still fits.'

I was desperate to telephone Jack and tell him about the chaperone, so that he could cancel, but when I did he told me not to worry, that it would be fine. That he had a plan.

Mother had been unwell. She had undergone another minor operation, but this time had developed complications. She went to the desert to recuperate, and stayed for a month. When she came back, she was so thin, her skin taut and papery, as though she had lost gallons of blood.

She duly arranged for a chaperone. When the beady little woman arrived, I was pale with shock. She came with her darting, greedy eyes, just like little black currants. She came, carrying her black crocodile handbag with the gold clasp that snapped. I knew the price I would have to pay for my tea with Jack, but it would be worth it. But I wondered why Mother was trying to punish me, again? What was it that I had done wrong this time?

We arrived at the Beverly Hills Hotel. Jack was there in the lobby, grinning. He whispered: 'We'll stuff her so full of eclairs, she won't have the time to be nosy.'

And that's what he did. He seated her at one of the tables and ordered her a plate of French pastries. There it was again. That Kennedy ability to make the impossible simple.

Then he guided me to a table of our own, and we had a wonderful afternoon. We talked about everyone in his family, those people who were my real friends. Not like the pretend friends that Mother brought to the house to be photographed with me for the magazines. And then we talked about the war, and Jack told me how he intended to survive, and that the secret was that you had to believe that you were not going to die. Really believe. He told me that his father was furious with him, but that he was not going to listen. He had signed up with the

Navy. I couldn't believe that anyone could be so brave as to disobey their parents.

Back in my room, I felt different, somehow. Maybe I didn't look so bad, if he wasn't ashamed to take me out. I undressed and walked to the mirror. Maybe if I felt different inside, it would show on the outside. I lifted my head and looked right into his eyes. The mirror laughed: *You absurd little fool. Do you really think you could be beautiful? Do you possibly think he could find you attractive? Are you actually looking at yourself in this mirror? Dimples in the cheeks are one thing, but dimples in the upper arm are quite another. He couldn't avert his eyes from your ample child-bearing hips, ill-disguised by that hideous skirt, as much as he tried. You like your Shakespeare, do you not? Thou art as fat as butter, a bolting-hutch of beastliness, a swollen parcel of dropsies, a huge bombard of sack, a stuffed cloak-bag of guts, a roasted Manningtree ox with the pudding in his belly ... I could go on, but these obese jokes are not funny; let's face it, you have enough on your plate. Well, there it is. Remember, my dear, men often do, but mirrors never lie.*

The Rhino wasn't angry at having been pushed into a corner; she was just biding her time. Later, when I lay on my bed, I felt as though I was separated from my body, that I was floating in the air. It made the pain go away. I filled my head with thoughts of Jack, and the delicious food he'd ordered. Plates of egg finger sandwiches, lobster salad roll, smoked salmon mousse, and tiny, delicate cakes: strawberry shortcake, banana-cream éclair, and chocolate tart.

And then I thought of the hall of mirrors, and the funny shapes and distortions. Nobody could get inside my head. That was the real secret place that nobody could go. Not my mother, not anyone. It was all smoke and mirrors.

Sail Away

I've seen her sneaking into her mother's dressing room more and more often. Picking up a tooth glass from the bathroom and making her way to the liquor cabinet. Kater thinks that nobody knows about her embarrassing little habit. That girl is full of secrets. And secrets lead to lies. And secrets can eat you up, and they can kill you. After everything her mother has done for her: the sacrifices she has made, the opportunities she has put her way.

And now Madou is entertaining the soldiers at the Hollywood Canteen. Night after night, she works, cooking for the boys, entertaining them before they leave California for the Pacific, some never to return.

Now that America has finally entered the war, she is proud of her adopted country. Papa Joe was wrong to say that it wasn't America's war, and his boys are the first to volunteer, as she suspected would be the case. It is her duty to dance with those brave young men, rubbing her body against theirs, leaving them with the memory of a night to remember. When she comes home at night, she is fatigued, and lines of worry are etched on that lovely face.

Today it is her birthday. She is forty. For the past month, she has eaten no solid food. To keep herself slim. She sips beef tea from her thermos. If only her daughter could learn more discipline. Papi telephones to wish her many happy returns. He has a new job in New York.

'Mutti, tell me your news.'

'It's sad, Papi. These boys are so young, and many of them are already far from home. I want to do more for the war effort. I can sell government bonds. But there's something else I can do. The male stars are leaving America to fight. I want to go, too.'

'Mutti, is that wise? What will you do?'

'I will entertain the troops. Many of the big stars do it.'

'Mutti, many of the big stars are not German. Think what they will do to you, if they capture you. It's too dangerous. I forbid it.'

'I know the dangers, Papi, and I fear for Mother and for Birgitte. Did you hear what they did to Boni's sister? She is on trial for treason – at the *Volksgerichtshof*. They say she is guilty of undermining the morale of the people. Boni is out of his mind with worry. These people will stop at nothing.'

'What will you do about Kater?'

'I have decided. She will go to school in Switzerland. The cold air will be good for her. She is no longer a child, and she needs to learn independence. She is changing, Papi. She is … different. Sometimes she looks at me with such a strange expression. As if she is looking straight through me. I must go, I send kisses to you, my life.'

Later, Madou sends for Kater. She is obedient to her mother's wishes, but she is sullen, and there is a faraway look in her lashless, fish eyes.

'Kater, I am sending you to school, in Switzerland, where you will be safe.'

'But who will dress you? Am I going alone? Is it safe to travel? Are you coming with me, Mutti?'

'Kater, you are not a child. And I have been called to the war service by the American government.'

'But, why …'

'Stop asking questions. Divide a loaf by a knife: what's the answer to *that*?'

'I don't know, Mutti.'

'Look up, speak nicely, and don't twiddle your fingers all the time.'

'But why can't I stay with Sofi and Papi? I can go to New York and l will be good and helpful. I won't ask questions, if only you'll let me.'

'You know what I always say, *Queens never make bargains*. Now you must help me to dress for tonight. There are boys going out to the war to certain death, they need a night to remember.'

Madou is becoming just a little self-righteous about her war work. I'm beginning to feel sorry for the Child.

Why Cry at Parting?

She handed me a large cheque, wept, and told me that she was off to win the war; as if she alone could win the war single-handedly with her shiny red nail polish, bayonet to bayonet. Her encounters with her boys, their courage, and her newfound zeal for America gave her renewed enthusiasm for the Overseas Organization, though privately, I knew she was following Moncorge. There was always a man behind her noble motives. Nor did it cross her mind that her presence in the army might put the lives of American soldiers at risk.

She told me many years later that leaving Moncorge was the most painful parting of her life. He left her in Norfolk, Virginia and headed off to Algiers. Her contempt for the actors who did not sign up knew no bounds, and she was angry and vocal about their cowardice.

Before leaving, she sold most of her possessions, apart from her jewels, which she stored in safe deposit boxes 'for the duration'. Moncorge, certain that he would meet his death, gave her his most valuable and loved possessions, three paintings by Renoir, Sisley, and de Vlaminck. Where are they now? They have also disappeared over the years. I know for a fact that she didn't return them to Moncorge.

It was the first time in our lives that we were to live properly apart. To my shame, I did not even think about the fact that my mother might be in danger. I cared more about the fate of Jack. It wasn't until later that I learned what she had achieved during those years. How brave she had been, and how she earned the love and respect of all the people she encountered. How she had been close to death, several times. No, I didn't care. All I cared about was that I was finally going to school.

For once, I did not give a damn that I was living away from America. I had tools to help me with my misery. I helped Mother to pack before leaving for Switzerland. I wrapped her compact in tissue paper and placed it on the top of her bag. She would need her mirror for what lay ahead. Mother left Hollywood without a backward glance after thirteen years, to await orders in New York. And I, first warming my veins with another slug of bourbon, headed to the land of snowy folds and cuckoo clocks.

Why Must the Show Go On?

Madou snaps open her solid gold powder compact, fixes me with her steely gaze and applies a smear of red lipstick. Red makes her feel invincible.

Say what you like about Joan Madou, no woman could be a better soldier. Her uniform is tailor-made. She is given the military rank of captain. No special Hollywood treatment now that she is one of the boys, and she loves it: 'What a pleasant feeling it is to wait for orders,' she whispers to me.

She is permitted to take only fifty-six pounds of luggage. In her suitcase, she stashes a handful of sequinned evening dresses (they don't crush and don't need to be ironed) and her musical saw. She packs a few gold bangles, and silk stockings, and a garter belt. She packs dozens of false nails from Woolworths.

Captain Madou is ready for her flight. She flies to Algiers by way of Greenland, the Azores, and Casablanca. This is her third act. Perhaps her very best. She has rehearsed her show to perfection in America, a superbly slick mix of jokes, songs, and stories, but now it's for real. If the boys are homesick in their own country, then try to imagine how they feel fighting a war in another land.

Her first night is terrifying. There are 20,000 GIs in the audience and they are going wild for the famous star. An announcement is made.

'Miss Madou is delayed, and will not be coming this evening.'

The crowd boos and hisses. But they know it's a gag. There's so much tension and anticipation in the air.

'She is ... unwell, but is being (coughs) attended to, by the general.'

Laughter fills the room.

Then suddenly, at the back of the hall, there is a cry.

'Wait for me, I'm here. I'm coming right up.'

Madou, in her army uniform, dashes up to the stage. The jeers turn to cheers, as they go along with the joke.

In a sudden, practised move, she darts behind a screen, and reappears in a scarlet sequinned dress. There she stands, resplendent, triumphant. She is radiant. She has tears in her eyes for 'her boys' so far from home. She knows how it feels to be far from home herself. She tells them that her father was a war hero, who was awarded the Iron Cross.

She cracks raunchy jokes, and flirts with her band. She tosses autographed garters into the crowd. She almost brings the house down when she performs her famous trick. She tells the room that she has special powers of mind-reading. She flashes a leg, tosses her hair, and licks her lips, suggestively. She asks the audience to concentrate on whatever came into their minds. Then she walks over to a soldier and says, in an earnest tone, 'Oh, think of something else, I can't possibly talk about *that*!'

Then she begins to sing, and there is silence.

Outside the barracks by the corner light
I'll always stand and wait for you at night
We will create a world for two
I'll wait for you the whole night through

As Papa Hem says, if she had only that voice, she would break your heart with it.

She performs her act, night after night, sometimes with only a box for a stage, but she gives it everything she's got. And then she seeks out her lover. She hears a rumour that a Free French army is near; she finds him, handsome in his blue uniform, climbs up into his tank and kisses him passionately on the mouth as all the French soldiers cheer. She worries about death in a tank, as it's the worst of all deaths. You are burned alive.

She flies to Italy. In Bari, she contracts pneumonia. Penicillin saves her life. When she's not entertaining, she visits every ward, working seventeen-hour shifts, existing on coffee, martinis, and cigarettes. The doctors ask her to wear a lot of perfume before heading to the front-line hospital, because the smell of a woman can make the difference between life and death. When she sees the harsh bright lights blinding the eyes of the soldiers, she orders lampshades at her own expense.

The wards are full of rows of beds and poles with jars of blood – the only sound is the bubbling of blood. The only colour is blood. Life is running into the boys from the bottles. She is asked to speak to the German soldiers. They ask: 'Are you the real Madou?' She speaks to them in German. The wounded men ask her to kiss their bandages.

The soldiers scrounge roses and decorate her tent. She takes the flowers when she leaves, so she can decorate her next tent. She sings softly to herself, 'Where have all the flowers gone? … Where have all the soldiers gone?'

She makes radio broadcasts, intended to reach the German soldiers. 'Boys, don't do it. Don't sacrifice yourselves for that lunatic.' She knows what they will do if they capture her. They will shave her hair, stone her, and have horses drag her through the streets. But she will evade them. She is given a small pistol to shoot herself in the event that she is discovered.

She takes lovers; so many lovers. She cannot let them go to their deaths without a last act of love. It's her supreme self-sacrifice.

The Imaginary Baron

My schooling didn't last for long. My little secret was discovered, and I was sent home to my father. I had a new plan, to study drama. Papi approved of my plan to become a stage actor. I was too ugly to be a movie star, but looks didn't matter so much for the stage. I hadn't forgotten Lacy and my love for Shakespeare. I missed Mother when I saw a picture of her in *Vogue*. She looked wonderful in her Eisenhower jacket and army boots.

Mother and Father insisted that I study at the Max Reinhardt School of Theater on Sunset Boulevard. Gloriosky! I was back in my beloved Hollywood, and without my mother.

One day I was rehearsing when a student ran in: 'Kater, there's someone outside for you. You'd better hurry.'

I had no idea why she looked so excited and spoke in such a breathless way. Then I saw him. He was leaning against a red sports car, dressed in navy whites and wearing that huge grin.

'Jack. What are you doing here?'

'I'm taking you out for cheeseburgers.'

'I'll grab my cardigan.'

Back in the drama studio, the girls stopped whispering and looked at me with surprise.

'Who's the mystery man, Kater?'

'Oh, just a friend.'

I fled before they could ask any more questions, but I was conscious of a new respect in their eyes.

As usual, Jack never commented on food or my weight or asked about my mother. He ordered cheeseburgers, fries and Coca-Cola, and we talked for hours about his family. He joked about them all, and was only silent when I asked about my special friend, Rosemary. Kick was in England working for the Red Cross, and Joe was a fighter pilot. He was shy when I asked him about how it felt to be a war hero.

'I didn't have a choice, Kater. It wasn't bravery. Of course, big brother Joe was furious with me for letting the Japs bomb my boat in the first place.' He grinned at the thought.

Over cheesecake, we talked about Antibes, and the End-of-the-World Party, and how we swam out to the island together. I could feel the eyes of the other women in the diner resting on him as he talked and laughed. I never wanted the afternoon to end.

When we had finished tea, he did something that I have never forgotten. It will be with me until my dying breath. He told me that he was going to show me something, and that it would be very important and I should be very brave.

We drove to the Santa Monica pier. When we got out of the car, he took my hand and guided me to a building painted with garish colours. He paid for two tickets, and gently pushed me into the first room. He told me that it was a maze, and that the only way of getting out was winding through each of the rooms. At the end of the first long, narrow corridor was a huge mirror, but it was not like any other mirror I had ever seen. It was huge, like Mother's, but with wavy lines across the middle of the pane.

So he had worked it out. I turned back, shocked, but he just grinned. Go on, Kater, you can do it. It's just a bit of fun. A hall of mirrors. I took a deep breath and stared straight ahead. Why, it was the funniest thing I had ever seen in my life. My head and torso were stretched out long and flat, like a cartoon character who had been stretched like elastic before springing back into shape. My eyes and teeth were distorted and elongated, my hair looked like it was floating away from my head. I laughed out loud and my teeth jutted out like the mouth of a carthorse. I lifted my arms, and then wriggled my fingers, each digit ballooning hilariously as I waved them back and forth.

The next room had four mirrors, each reflecting a different image, bouncing lights back and forth to produce a queasy, strange effect. Four Katers. As if I'd finally met my quadruplet sisters. Pleased to meet you, I said. I've always longed for sisters of my own.

Another of the mirrors was a door, and I pushed through, Jack close behind me. This mirror was curved and bulged, a convex mirror, which made me appear tall and thin. It was me, but it was not me. A thin giantess, with enormous feet.

And then, in a darkened room, I came to the final mirror on the wall, in a beautiful iron frame, spotted and flecked with tiny black marks. A single light shone down from above. I looked into the mirror, and saw the shadow of my mother's face, for just a glimpse, and I looked almost beautiful. A single tear coursed down my face, which I brushed away, and then I felt a surge of anger. My mother was a liar. A cheat. She told me that mirrors never lie, but they do. And here was the proof. All of my childhood I had never known what was real and what was just an image. The make-believe of Hollywood. The distortions, the artifice, the false doors of the outdoor stage set that could make a short actor look tall and a tall actress look short. It was all lies and cheating.

And it was Jack who understood. Who had brought me here to show me all these illusions. And who had done it without saying a single word.

He dropped me back at school. I took one last look as he smiled and waved before climbing into his sports car. I did not know then that I would never see him again. It's just as well. I could bear my own misery, but not his. The first gorgeous young man who had been kind to me.

'Take care, Kater.'

'Take care, Jack.'

We both did a pretty good job of not taking care of ourselves.

Dearest Love

Papa Hem stands peering into me, the bathroom mirror, the razor carefully scraping the soap from his throat. Madou perches on the bathtub, watching him, her beautiful legs crossed.

'Kraut, why are you doing this? It's dangerous. You know what they would do to you if they capture you.'

'It's the decent thing to do.'

'You know what they did to Boni's sister; she was beheaded.'

'I know the risks.'

'But now you suffer. And the damn itching. War's no place for a lady.'

'It's fine, Papa Hem. I can live with crab lice. Those boys went to their deaths knowing they had slept with Madou. It was a price worth paying.'

'You look like a combat soldier. The knitted helmet becomes you. You walk like a combat soldier. You even smell like one. So, what happens next? Don't you think you've done enough?'

'When my leave is over, I'll go back for another tour. If I die, I die.'

'You're brave. Nothing ever happens to the brave.'

'Maybe.'

'You're immortal, my dear Kraut.'

'Have some champagne. The food is lousy, but the champagne is good.'

'And what about Kater?'

'She's safe in Hollywood, which is more than can be said for my mother. I collect war bonds to pay for the bombs that fall on my beloved Berlin.'

'But you can't return to Germany. They will never let you do that. You're putting lives in danger.'

'We'll see. First it's Iceland, and then Labrador.'

'So be it, Kraut. But you'd better pack your thermals.'

'Well, Papa Hem was certainly right about the cold,' Madou mutters as she cracks the ice in her helmet so that she can wash her face and rinse her stockings. She is making do with a compact instead of a vanity. Large or small, I'm always by her side.

Papa Hem might have warned her about the rats. Every night she lays out her sleeping bag on the icy ground. It is cold, rainy, and muddy. She pulls the blanket up to her chin, and the little horrors run over her face with their icy paws, as cold as death.

She is suffering from frostbite, and inflammation of the jaw. She never complains. She makes potato pancakes on a stove. She eats with the men, listens to their stories and their jokes. Sometimes, her stage is nothing more than a makeshift box with a ragged curtain. No lighting, no props. She is freezing, but she eschews a warm overcoat and dons her thin gold sheath dress without demur. They want to see a Hollywood star, not a hag in an overcoat. One of the soldiers shouts out for a prize for a raffle. She smiles and removes her pink and black garter belt, tossing it into the crowd as they cheer. The men can see the goosebumps on her flesh. You'd think she was performing in Beverly Hills, not the freezing Ardennes. The closer she gets to the Front Line, the more amazed the soldiers are. She appears like an apparition in her bright dress among the wild, forlorn places, with shellholes in the trees around them.

She summons the energy deep within her to be Madou. The men sit on their helmets and stare at her bare shoulders. They love her because she is the only entertainer to come within enemy artillery range.

Afterwards, she is invited to dine at the officers' club. She meets a handsome American soldier, who is young but highly decorated. His name is General Gavin. His men call him 'Slim Jim'. He tells her that she must never show her fear in front of the soldiers. They will tell themselves that things can't be that bad if Madou is here. They would never let her come to harm, never expose her to danger; false reasoning, but it's important to reduce the tension.

And then she is captured.

Black Fox

They called it The Battle of the Bulge!

My goodness, that's a battle I know well. Mother's most popu-
lar war anecdote was the story of her capture and release at this
most famous of German offensives, their last attempt to fight
back. She would tell her story, in her husky voice, of the times she
was almost captured by the Germans; once on the Italian Front
Line, and then the second when she was taken prisoner in
Bastogne. It was the handsome, young General Gavin who para-
chuted in and rescued her from German hands.

She had been flown into Huy, Belgium, as a surprise for the
demoralised allied troops. Boy, did they get a lift when the news
spread that Madou was coming to perform. Morale was at its
lowest ebb, dysentery had broken out.

She performed in an old church hall, the men using their
helmets for chairs. She cracked her first joke: 'Fellows, I may have
to break in the middle of a song to excuse myself, and, heck, you
know the reason why!'

The men roared their approval. She was one of them. And, she would tell her mesmerised audience, she never once went to the bathroom. And then, after the show, she went off on an unauthorised tour to see a hospital, and it was there that she was captured by the Nazis, and it was Gavin who rescued her, and she remembered the parachutes, those floating jellyfish, suspended by thirty-two nylon threads. She held the fine, gossamer parachute silk to her cheek, and thought of the flag room in Hollywood where no silk had ever felt so soft.

And do you know something, Mother? I don't believe this tale for one moment. I do not believe for one single second that the American troops allowed you to be captured. But if you believed it to be true, then it must be true. Nobody would dare to contradict you, the great war heroine.

And, in the meantime, I began my own Battle of the Bulge. Just after I saw my thin, elongated frame in the Hall of Mirrors, I saw what might be, and I stopped eating. It was so easy, and I marvelled that I had left it so long. I sipped soup made of Heinz ketchup and hot water, nibbled on wafers, and got thinner and thinner. The rolls of fat slowly disappeared, and my face miraculously revealed cheekbones as sharp as cheese graters.

And then I did something that I knew would make my mother furious. I signed up for the USO. I'd been playing a part all my life. I'd witnessed every great director, every great actor in Hollywood at close range. Maybe I could act, even if I could not dance or sing. And what would the men think when they knew that their favourite star, ageless and fragrant, had a grown-up daughter? Maybe then the famous Madou wouldn't seem so young. That thought kept me warm and full.

Don't Put your Daughter on the Stage

On temporary leave, Madou reunites with Kater in the Zebra Room in New York. Glass wall panelling sparkles, reflecting the two women who sit at a table. Madou, beautiful in her captain's uniform, her daughter dowdy in her USO garb. Kater tells her mother that she is part of a theatre company, where (who would believe it?) she plays the part of a whore called Molly Malloy. She hopes the GIs will appreciate the play. What does her mother think about her daughter playing the part of a whore? Does her mother have any advice for her about performing to the troops?

Madou pulls out her gold compact and fixes her lipstick, before speaking. Then she tells her war stories.

For once in her life, there were real men worthy of her. Soldiers, not Hollywood actors playing a part. She bonds with the 82nd Airborne Division, the bravest of all. General Gavin is a softly-spoken man, highly regarded by his paratroopers, despite his extreme youth. He insists on always carrying a rifle, not a gun. He is unable to resist Madou. He knows that she is courageous, like him, the only star to perform in Battle Conditions.

Most of the other stars fly in for an hour and fly back, but not Madou. She insists on staying with the boys, talks to as many as she can, posing for photographs, performing to each of the individual soldiers as if he were the only man in the world.

There are still those that say she can't dance, she can't act, she can't sing, but try saying that to the GIs and they'd take you down in a flash. The boys are cold and miserable. But this woman looks them straight in the eye and says, 'You're special. You matter.' Which is the equivalent of a St Bernard dog appearing in the snow with a brandy bottle around his neck, to rescue you and save your life. She somehow builds their confidence, has an instant connection. She is one of them. She is no phoney. She is in the mud with them. She has their respect. All those thousands and thousands of American boys, and one German woman.

The 82nd presents her with a white silk jump scarf, and she promises that she will always wear it when in battle. It's one of her most precious possessions. The general gives her another present, a solid gold Flato cigarette lighter in the shape of a jerrycan. She loves it. Three items are always with her: the scarf, the lighter, and her gold compact.

She records a live show, *Madou sings to the Homeland*. She hopes and prays that her mother will hear it and know that she is alive. She knows that the Germans hate her for standing with the

Americans. She hears that Hitler says that he has the means of making her very unhappy. She is everything he despises about liberated women; the battlefield for women is the delivery room, and her workplace is the kitchen. This woman is unsexed. A German woman in an Eisenhower jacket! In those final hours, they do what they can to discover the whereabouts of Madou's mother. She can pay for her famous daughter's treachery.

When she finishes making it all about her, she says, 'You must never show your tears, Kater. You will see suffering and you will want to cry. But you must not.'

'I have learned not to cry, Mutti. I am perhaps stronger than you think. Tears don't come so easy to me.'

'Well, at least you will be nowhere near the Front. Not like your mother. I will never let my boys down. I daresay you will be safe and far from harm.'

'And what exactly would you know about the harm I have been exposed to already in my life?'

'What do you mean? The kidnapper? I paid for you to have a bodyguard. You never came to any harm, like that poor baby. I made sure of that. What have I always told you? Nothing bad can ever happen to you as long as you are with your mother.'

Kater stares ahead moodily. I catch her eye. Funny, how she no longer fears me. She's becoming rather impertinent as she ages. Her tone is sullen and emotionless. She begins to say something and then thinks better of it.

'Go safe, Mutti. There's still time for the Nazis to do their worst. I don't suppose you have heard any news from Grandmother or Aunt Birgitte?'

Berlin is broken. There is dust everywhere, statues with decapitated heads on the ground. Bullet holes pockmark the buildings of the Third Reich. She arrived with the 82nd and performed at the only theatre standing, the Titania-Palast. Backstage after the show, in a makeshift dressing room with a half-cracked mirror she gives an interview. 'What were her impressions on returning to Berlin after all these years?'

She summons up the scene, her voice tired and wooden. The Kaiser Wilhelm Memorial Church reduced to rubble, and the Bahnhof Zoo. Her old apartment, number fifty-four, still standing, peppered with bullet marks, but with pots of red geraniums on the balcony.

She tells of how they got there. Driving through villages, sometimes split down the middle – in Holland, and in Belgium. The German children on one side of the street shouting her name. They knew who she was, and she thought about the parents who must have talked about her to them. How else would they have known her name?

Another French village was war-torn and silent. She couldn't understand why there were bonfires of rubble when all the houses were still standing, curtains fluttering in the breeze. Then she looked through the window and saw that there was nothing behind. Just like the stage sets at the studio. Not a single person had survived.

Aachen was the first German city to fall. Though she was apprehensive about her reception from the German people, she was greeted warmly. The people had had enough. She was devastated by the first sight of her ruined homeland, even though she believed that Germany deserved what she got. Corpses lined the roads. Her unit took over the cinema, which was freezing cold with no fuel. But they carried on with their performances.

The German caretaker of the picture house had taken out his thermos and handed her his precious coffee. The other men worried the coffee might be poisoned. When she asked him why he was giving her coffee, he replied, 'Ah, the Blue Angel.' Apart from her duties performing, she was asked if she would speak into a megaphone and tell the German people to go home, and shut their shutters so they didn't obstruct the tanks.

The reporter asks again how she *feels* about being back in Berlin. Her response is terse.

'The tears I have cried over Germany have dried. I have washed my face.'

Art of Love

My mother once told me, 'Think twice before burdening a friend with a secret.' I thought of this often, but then, again, I didn't really have any friends. As for boyfriends, I was determined not to be like my mother, so I never thought about boys in that way. Besides, I was not sure that anyone would touch me if they knew about my past. And then at theatre school I met Martin. The first thing I liked about him was that he didn't know about my famous mother. Gloriosky!

He was kind and sensitive and good-looking. In certain lights, he looked a tiny bit like Jack. That was enough for me. He was in the same theatrical troupe that performed for the USO. He liked drinking too, so we had one thing in common. Sometimes, after the performance, we would drink together and talk. Unlike every other person I had ever met, apart from Jack, he didn't once ask me about Mother or all the famous people I had met. He seemed interested in me. Now that the war was coming to an end, there was plenty of alcohol and cigarettes. It was easy to shed my inhibitions with a few drinks inside me, but I kept my secret.

There were times when Martin, with his kind, brown eyes, would ask me if I were OK. Was there anything I wanted to talk about? It was so easy to lie. In fact, I had perfected a brilliant matter-of-fact tone, when he asked questions about my childhood. Easy-peasy. Don't let them in. Keep it all to yourself and nobody will know the truth.

My natural shyness helped to convey the mask of innocence. When he asked me if I'd ever kissed a man, I could shake my head with impunity.

He said that after the war, we would be married and have children. We took our show to Italy, and I had my own moment of glory. My mother truly believed that she was a soldier. At the end of the day, she was only an entertainer like everyone else. I was there, too, and I played my own part.

I was the one who was given the task of announcing the news that the war in Japan was over. That moment will be with me for ever. First the ominous silence as the news sank in, and then the explosion of applause and cheering. The realisation that the war was over and we were all finally coming home. But where was my home?

Nevermore

Madou paces up and down, up and down. She still hasn't had news of her mother, but there are murmurs about Birgitte and Belsen. She looks into me and straightens her hat. The telephone rings out harsh and shrill.

'Yes, yes it is she. Who told her I was dead? Goebbels? How dare he say that London is in flames. You have her there, with you? Let me speak.'

'Maria.'

'Mami.'

'Maria.'

'Mami, my sweet, we have to speak in English.'

'*Ja*, my lovely Maria, I am so glad to hear your voice.'

'Mami, Birgitte is safe. I am coming to you as soon as I can.'

'*Ja*, and I am so happy and thankful for what you have done.'

'Mami, you suffered for my sake. Forgive me.'

'Yes, my love.'

'Mami, take care of yourself.'

'Yes, goodbye.'

'Goodbye.'

She telephones General Gavin and arranges for a flight to Tempelhof Airport.

As the plane swoops down over the ruined city, she takes out her compact and applies crimson lipstick as her armour. When the propellers slow to a halt, the door opens, and out she runs, in her uniform and forage cap. Her mother, so tiny, so frail, like a bird, is waiting on the cement ramp. 'Mami. My Mami.'

She only has a few days before her visa expires, so she moves quickly. She makes sure her mother is fed and clothed. Then she sets off to find her husband's parents. She discovers that they have been sent to a camp in Austria. Demanding to see Marshal Zhukov, she sets off to Potsdam. She knows he has a reputation for being tough and brutal, but she is determined. She spends two hours with him, and then she leaves – clutching a pass signed by the man himself – with a jeep and a driver. She sets out across the highly dangerous Russian zone to find them and bring them back to Berlin, and that's exactly what she does.

Once her family is safe, she returns to Paris. She knows that she will never see her mother again, whose final words are etched on her memory: 'I've lived this long, I've outlived Hitler, and now I can die.' But when the news reaches her, she has one last favour to ask of General Gavin. She phones him and says, 'I wish you could help me.'

He replies, 'We'll take care of it.'

No Highway in the Sky

I was not invited to my grandmother's funeral. Mother went with William Walton, the *Times* bureau chief, who, because he was a member of the press, was allowed to mix with Germans.

I sit now, an old woman, fingering my mother's war medals. They were her most treasured possessions. She often said that most children inherit medals from their father, you will inherit them from your mother. I deliberated about bequeathing them to the Museum of Berlin. Perhaps it is time to let them go back to her homeland.

I lay them out on a piece of velvet. *La Croix Pour le Mérite, Ordre National de la Légion d'honneur, Commandeur, Operation Entertainment Medal, Ordre des Arts et des Lettres, Medallion of Honour of the State of Israel, Medal of Freedom, Chevalier de L'Ordre de Léopold.*

There was one medal she was not so happy to have received; a blue and silver medallion with a swastika in the centre – the Order of Glorious Aryan Motherhood. She wrote down her reaction on a slip of paper and left it in its case: 'The unbelievable chutzpah of those bastards!'

My mother could still make me laugh, even from the grave.

Handsome General Gavin had ensured that my grandmother was buried properly, as he had promised. It was many years after the war had ended that I had discovered the story. The general was determined to help my mother, whom he loved, but the anti-fraternisation rule was on, and he was not allowed any association with the Germans. But he made it happen. He ordered four paratroopers, each armed with a shovel, to dig a grave at Schöneberg cemetery. They waited until the early hours of the morning when it was dark.

Many of the graves had been blown open by the Allies' bombs, and coffins were standing on their ends, with corpses hanging out of them. It looked like a film set for a Dracula movie, they told me, but I could think only of Mo's film set in the studio. Then they drove their jeep to my grandmother's apartment, and carried her tiny, light casket into the jeep, and from there to the cemetery. The smell of rotting flesh was all around them, gravestones ripped apart. A scene of utter desolation.

The next morning, Mother flew in with William Walton, and she sat there just looking at the coffin. Then she dropped a clump of earth on the lid, she then turned away and never looked back.

*   *   *

As soon as she was discharged, she was sent back to America. All her boys were desperate to go home, but Madou had no home. She received her orders to fly to LaGuardia Airport. There was no welcoming party to await her. It was raining in New York.

She looked sensational, wearing a grey suit with a mink stole wrapped around her shoulders. If she thought I looked different, she didn't show it. She smiled and linked my arm.

'Sweetheart, it's wonderful to see you again. How was the chocolate in Switzerland? Haven't I always told you Swiss chocolate is the best? And what about this acting school of yours? But why do you have to be in New York? I have to go back to Hollywood, darling. I have no money for you and Papi. I love France, but it's twenty years behind America – holidays all the time, no tempo – just eat, eat, eat. In Paris, I had to sell my furs, just to pay the hotel bill. I watched the planes going off to the sea, and I felt like the girl in the fairy tale looking after the birds flying away for the winter.'

As usual, Mother talked non-stop about herself. Rarely asking questions about my life. She was now in her forties, adrift from the studio, lonely and homeless. She had no money and many dependants. Worst of all, she had nobody giving her orders, telling her what to do.

Her lovers had been pushed away. Papi only ever asked Mother for money. Her affair with the Frenchman had come to an end, so, for once in her life, she was off France. They had reunited briefly in Paris, but she was bored by his jealousy and his insistence that they marry and have a child. On VJ Day she watched the parade alone from the Champs-Élysées: 'Angel child, my heart was heavy with memories and loneliness in the rain.'

Her beloved Europe was in ruins. The Europe that was in her blood had dwindled to a memory, but she still longed for it, forgetting that it was gone for ever. She told me that she even had to sell her jewels.

'Remember when we had rooms just to store the luggage, and now *he* expects me to share a bathroom. I told him that maybe I need liverwurst sandwiches, the solace of the afflicted. I came back to be with you, sweetheart. Like old times.'

When she took off her gloves, I looked at her hands. They were bright red, which frightened me. She said that she had trouble sleeping.

'Mutti, be careful with those pills.'

She lit a cigarette with her GI lighter.

'*Quatsch*. They never touch me. I'm too strong for them.'

She turned and looked at me as if she were seeing me for the first time. As if she had seen a ghost.

'Are you eating, sweetheart? What are they feeding you?'

'I'm on a diet, Mutti. All the girls do it. And I walk so much in New York. It's so different to Hollywood. I cycle in the park, too.'

'Well, I want you to come with me. I've rented a house in Brentwood. With a blue swimming pool.'

'Mutti, I'm not a child any more, and if I'm to do anything in the theatre I need to be here in New York,' I said gently.

She asks me to send a telegram to her general to call off the affair. She wants me to know that she is desired by a much younger man, but he is part of her war adventure, not Hollywood. She has her sentence ready.

'Love is a conjuring trick done with the most beautiful mirrors in the world.'

How Do You Do, Middle Age

That pathetic excuse for a daughter has refused to accompany her mother, so she returns to Pasadena, alone. She opens her compact and fixes her lipstick. At the station, she is gratified to find she is welcomed by the press. It's a reminder of what once had been: 'Madou, did you ever sleep with Eisenhower?'

'How could I, darling? He was never that close to the Front Line.'

'We hear that you've been awarded the Medal of Freedom. Congratulations.'

'It's the thing I'm most proud of. Acting is a demeaning occupation. We are merely circus performers.'

'What did you think when you heard of Hitler's death?'

'Oh, that horrible dwarf. I once tried to kill him. Never trust a man with short legs. His brains are too near his bottom.'

There is no lover to meet her. Mo is long over her, and her husband has stopped answering her letters. All she has left is Boni. She writes to him, telling him that she wants to live in the desert, because in the desert you can't put down roots, and that suits her. Boni writes back. She sits at her vanity and opens his letter, every now and then glancing up at me, to see her own face.

'It takes a strong heart to love without roots. I imagine you dressing for the evening, combing your hair. Your swift walk. Your shoulders. The voice, as supple as your body. You ask to stay friends. Never. Try to grow a small rose garden on the ashes of broken feelings? No, this will never work for me and you. Love should not be spoiled by friendship. The end is the end.'

She crumples his letter and tosses it into the basket. Really. Boni is so dramatic. She looks at me, and panic flits across her lovely face. A wrinkle has appeared on her cheek. She pushes it apart with her fingers. She will have to do something about this blemish.

It's this constant worry about money that's giving her wrinkles. The poor darling needs a picture. But in Hollywood, stars have to carry on behaving as stars, because God forbid that anyone suspects the truth that you're over, gone, yesterday's news. Hollywood is different now. It's another world. Travis, and Dot, long gone. Black, black nostalgia.

It's my place to offer some homespun wisdom.

'Swish your skirts aside from life's realities. Thousands of people have talent. I might as well congratulate you for having eyes in your head. Your motivation is your pay packet on Friday. Now get on with it.'

Yes, she needs to make another picture. She needs to reinvent herself. The studio has offered her a role about a gypsy, and she likes the sound of it. She mustn't let people think she's all washed out – a whiff quickly turns into a stench.

She no longer commands the highest salaries, and she has her pride to think of …

'Pride. Pride tastes awfully good, especially when the crust is flaky and you put a meringue upon it.'

She bursts into laughter. I always know how to lift her spirits. As the light fades, she pours herself a drink. The pleasant, familiar warmth steals through her veins, her troubles slowly beginning to fade. More than anything, she wants money and success, but she knows there's a penalty attached: loneliness.

She takes out a sheet of notepaper and writes a final letter to Boni: 'My feet are cold every night without you, and presently I suppose I will be cold throughout.'

Nights of Love

We married in secret. It was a squalid affair in a register office. I wore a cheap black dress and carried a bunch of supermarket American Beauty red roses. Mother was furious, but she put on a good show for the photographers. The day after the wedding, she marched me off to her gynaecologist to have a diaphragm fitted. No babies were allowed. Madou was not ready to be a grandmother.

Martin and I were too drunk to do anything the evening of the wedding, but the next night, the evening after the wedding, I was scared. Scared of intimacy. Scared of myself. There was no booze in our rented apartment. Not a single drop. It was time to face the music.

Over and over again, my new husband told me that I was so sweet, and so innocent. He knew that he was my first boyfriend. He told me that he would never hurt me. That he loved me. Words I had longed to hear for so many years, would have taken them from anyone, and, now that they had arrived, were terrifying.

I wanted to tell him who I really was, but I had kept the secret for so long that it had become part of me. I cradled my sin, like I once had cradled my doll. I fed it, I protected it, I loved it. Now I tried to hide it by wearing a long, white cotton nightgown, which I pulled over my knees.

He was kind and tender, kissing me gently. But he didn't understand when I pulled away and began reciting a poem.

A sudden blow: the great wings beating still
Above the staggering girl, her thighs caressed
By the dark webs, her nape caught in his bill,
He holds her helpless breast upon his breast.

How can those terrified vague fingers push
The feathered glory from her loosening thighs?

Martin was sweet. But he wasn't a poet.

The marriage lasted barely a year. I took cash jobs to buy booze. It was easy to stop eating, when I needed the money for bourbon. My diet still consisted of soup made of ketchup mixed with hot water. I lost the pounds and gained the men. I would take anyone who would have me. Anyone who promised to love me, even a little. My lost years are a little hard to recall. They merge together in a blue haze. I know that I put myself in danger, and the more dangerous the better. My sin with strangers. One-night stands.

These were my favourite. Better than food. I felt nothing. That was the point. Nobody could penetrate my small, secretive heart.

I finally got a proper job as a dresser to a drag queen called Sophie Tucker. His real name was Walter. He was over six feet tall and bald as a pigeon. His wardrobes were made of cedar to house his extensive collection of sequinned dresses. His accessories and wigs were carefully catalogued in archive boxes. It was like the old days of Hollywood, the smell of coffee and wig glue. I was expert at binding him, stuffing newspaper into his shoes, sewing on loose sequins.

He fed me, tucked me into bed at night, worried about me, and loved me. I never forgot him. He was a better mother to me than anyone could ever have been. Then I ran out of money. I called Mother and she immediately wired money to bring me home to Hollywood. I came slinking back to Brentwood, and climbed into her bed. Mother was thrilled that the 'love of her life' was back. If she smelt the brandy on my breath, she never mentioned a word.

The next morning, she made a telephone call to Papi to discuss the divorce: 'The Child is back. She has come to her senses. It was just one of her girlish infatuations, like Jack. Papi, we have to try with detectives to prove that Martin is a homosexual, and then we can get a divorce for the Child. She will live with me. She wants to resume her acting at the Academy. But she can help me here at the studio. Have you sent the pills?'

I resumed my studies at the Max Reinhardt Academy on the corner of Fairfax and Wilshire Boulevard. I worked hard by day, drinking hard at night, trying to cope with my early-morning hangovers. It was sad to be a divorced drunk at the age of twenty. My first major role was the lead in a play called *Mourning becomes Electra*. Mother was excited and invited several of her Brentwood friends. Halfway through the first act, an old air-raid siren suddenly reactivated. The audience knew that it couldn't be an actual air raid, so they sat listening to the play, and trying to ignore the wailing.

Mother just couldn't bear it a second longer. She stood up, and, with a majestic wave of the hand, stopped the show. The audience was horrified and fascinated. She proclaimed that she would stop the noise, and off she flounced, people trailing behind her to watch the drama outside. She somehow found a ladder, climbed up the post with her skirt hiked to her hips, showing her stunning legs, and much more, and then, with a theatrical flourish, stuffed her mink stole into the offending horn.

Back on solid ground, she pulled down her skirt, herded everyone back into the theatre, told the cast to carry on, and gave a final instruction to 'Dim the lights.'

I made myself a promise that I would never ever allow her to come to another show.

* * *

We moved to a small cottage in Beverly Hills. Mother paid for my legal fees and in return I became her handmaiden, just like old times.

'My angel, a cosy net for mother and child. There's only one bedroom, so we will share a bed.'

I wondered how long it would take for her find a new lover and for me to be assigned to the couch in the living room. Mother was to star in a new picture, playing a gypsy. She was ecstatic. She phoned Nellie, now back as head of Hairdressing, to discuss her wig.

'It must be coal black, Nellie, dripping with grease. You know that those gypsy women smear goat's grease on their hair to make it shiny – that's why they stink so badly. Make the bangs long to add mystery.'

It *was* just like old times. We drove through the Paramount gate at dawn, the sky rosy and the air crisp. Mother had been given her old dressing room, and when we arrived, Nellie was there, holding the greasy wig under her arm. Mother was delighted. She loved playing that role. She smeared dirt on her face and body, covered her arms in gold bangles, and made necklaces of fake gold coins.

She took a dislike to her co-star, who, newly married, was immune to her charms. She couldn't forgive him, so she found ways of making him pay. She rubbed rotting fish on her skin so she stank to high heaven. On the day of the campfire scene, she grabbed a fish-head from the cauldron and sucked the head, eyes and all. Her co-star ran for the bathroom. The next day on-set she pulled up her dirty petticoats, scratched her crotch ('All gypsies have lice, you know, sweetheart'), moved her hand seductively down her legs, and then tore off a hunk of bread and popped it in his mouth. She insisted on smearing his face with goose grease – so that *it* looked real. He hated her for it.

Mother began playing another game with me. She was furious that I wasn't sleeping around at the studio. I didn't want to compete with her. And I knew that she wanted me to behave worse than she did so that she could play the fine lady.

'Mutti, why do you sleep with everyone who asks?'

'They ask so nicely. Then they are so happy afterwards … don't you find that?'

So, to please her, I stayed out all night and returned to her dressing room in the morning. She was applying her lashing of kohl onto her eyelids. She stared at me intently in the mirror.

'Well, did *he* get you?'

'Oh, he wasn't special, Mutti. Very average.'

She smiled serenely in the mirror.

I was such a good liar.

Pageant

'I do wish you'd give up this sort of thing.'

'What exactly do you mean by "this sort of thing"?'

'You know perfectly well what I mean.'

'Are you attempting to criticise me?'

'I should have thought you'd be above encouraging silly, callow young men who are infatuated by your name. It's so terribly cheap.'

'Nonsense. Anyone would think I'm eighty the way you go on.'

'Don't use sex like a shrimping net, Joan. It's awfully undignified.'

'One more word out of you, and I'm leaving this room.'

I know what she's up to. The film is a flop, and she is comforting herself with a succession of dreary, besotted young men. She's done with older men, with their thinning hair and paunches. She longs for smooth, silky bodies, and strong muscles. Boys like the soldiers she gave herself to during the war. Boys who are grateful, appreciative, and to whom she can teach a few tricks.

She's making a damn fool of herself. She can't fool me. I know her too well. Ah, well. *Devouring time, blunt thou the lion's paw.* That's one fight she is never going to win, but she will give it her best shot.

When the phone call comes in, she's insulted. A one-night show in Las Vegas? But when they mentioned the money, she relents. She calls her daughter, who tells her to do it. That she just needs to recreate the one-woman show that she did in the war. Just a few songs, some gags, the musical saw. How about creating the most spectacular gowns ever made? Now she gets it. She returns to her vanity and stares into the glass. Can she still do it? She needs the money. She has no investments. She needs to buy jewels and luggage. Boni once said, 'A refugee should always have a packed suitcase ready to go at any time. Buying houses is a waste of money.' And that's what she is, a refugee. A thousand dollars for one night is not to be sniffed at.

'Maybe it's not such a bad idea. Vegas worked for Tallulah.'

'But she's so vulgar, darling.'

'I rather like the idea of Café Society?'

'More like Nescafé Society,' he sniffs.

'There's no need to be unpleasant. But I need the right act and the right clothes. Jean Louis from Columbia must make the gowns. But he won't come cheap. I must speak to the head of the studio.'

I can see that she is excited. To have the adoration of all those people; it will be like the war again, and just for one night. A few days later she calls her daughter to tell her the good news.

'Sweetheart. You will not beee-lieve this, the head of Columbia says he will do it on *one* condition; right there, in his office. *In the daylight.* In return for Jean Louis and his seamstresses. Naturally I agreed. I'm thinking swansdown, bugle-bead gowns that mould to the skin. Irene is creating a new foundation. It's a soufflé of silk, weightless, but with the strength of canvas. The dress will look nude, with strategically placed rhinestones. Anyway, I have to go. *He* is coming.'

With deep concentration, they take minute strands of wispy hair from along the hairline, braiding them into tight little ropes, then long hairpins are twisted into the scalp and the face is pulled up even further. That instant facelift.

Nellie places the golden wig over the hair. She is ready. During the day, it will loosen, and the whole procedure will happen again. It makes her scalp bleed and her teeth ache. No matter, she is a soldier. She doesn't feel pain.

She has another trick up her sleeve. Travis, long gone, has been replaced with Irene. Irene, a doughy-looking woman, creates the secret to her magnificent body: the 'foundation'. They guard the secret closely. They create the base from thick, flesh-coloured silk.

Getting into the foundation takes effort. She steps into it, fastens the slim inner belt around her waist and then secures the elasticated triangle between her legs and the sides of her vulva.

She bends over and scoops her breasts into the bra-like structure. Each nipple must be in exactly the right place or the whole process has to begin again. Then she stands upright and is zipped up the back. The diaphanous gossamer overdress is draped over the body. The zip of the outer garment overlays the inner garment zip. There must be no giveaway of what lies beneath.

The only other problem is the neck, where the foundation stops. She camouflages it with a sparkling diamond necklace, so that the line is obscured. Now she can barely move. She becomes a statue. *Galatea*. Breathing is a conscious effort. She likes the test of physical discipline. Movement is constricted. Bathroom breaks not permitted. This is the body she craves. The body she had at the age of twenty-two. It is perfection. No one can see the price she is paying, how much it hurts. All that matters is the diaphanous fabric that moulds and sculpts her body.

If, heaven forbid, the zipper breaks, the foundation is replaced with one of several others hanging in their garment bags. From this moment on, Madou will never be without her foundation. Only three people are entrusted with the secret: Irene, Kater, and me.

Madou's *One Night Only* in the Congo room of the Sahara Hotel is a sensation. She appears at the top of a staircase, shimmering in a gown that seems barely there. The crowd gasps and goes wild. The statue has come to life, and is slowly descending the staircase, her head and gaze straight ahead – a trick she has picked up from the Vegas showgirls.

Having found her key light, she sings a handful of songs, which bring the audience to tears. The applause goes on and on, and flowers are thrown onto the stage. She has what she has always wanted – to be the only star of show, not sharing the stage with anyone else. Just Madou and her beloved audience. For one night only.

Golden Earrings

Mother's *One Night Only* was a sensation. It was the hottest ticket in town. Celebrities flocked to Vegas to get a ringside seat at her one-woman show. Her plan was to take her act around the world, but she needed someone to direct. It had to be perfect.

Finding Burt Freeman was another example of her extraordinary ability to nose out the right person, to find the Pygmalion to her Galatea. He was a classically-trained conductor, who also wrote the perfect pop songs. Together they created a new show, and they would take it around the world for seventeen years.

He wrote songs for her that complemented her strengths and concealed her weaknesses. Like her, he was a perfectionist and they spent hours and hours rehearsing. He taught her how to make a song her own, to slow down, to relax, when to breathe.

He found her a lighting genius. He listened to her advice, arranged her hotel rooms, ensured her dressing room was stocked with champagne, sent her flowers, lilacs and lilies, never roses. He was young and handsome and virile, and she fell desperately in love with him. He refused to sleep with her, saying he never mixed business with pleasure. I think this may be why their incredible partnership lasted so long. And whatever she did to tempt him, he went home at night.

Burt was not a god, but he was almost a saint. She adored him, believed him to be a genius, but she never forgave him for resisting her charms. I needed the work, so I agreed to be her dresser. However bad our relationship had become, we always worked well together. I had huge respect for Burt. He knew exactly how to handle my mother. Together they created magic.

Mother lived for that very first moment when she appeared at the top of a curved staircase in her nude dress, and the audience gasped at her impossible beauty. Each new dress had to be more sensational than the last. It took ten seamstresses three months to make each one. The diaphanous chiffon was dyed to the exact colour of Mother's skin. Then every bead, every sequin, was hand-sewn into place. One creation was covered in tiny mirrors that glimmered and shimmered in the light. I managed to avoid that gown.

Drawing on her experience during the war, she executed a one-minute costume change into tails and top hat. The audience went into a frenzy. For the final act, she transformed herself into a circus ringmaster in tiny black velvet shorts, black tights, and a scarlet coat. She loved flicking her whip at an imaginary tiger.

One day after rehearsals, she let herself into Burt's villa. She cooked goulash, scrubbed his floors, filled his fridge with his favourite food, and waited for him. He had been playing tennis. He was surprised to see her, but escaped into the shower. She washed his tennis clothes and laid out his meal. He sat, he ate, and then he went to bed. But first he called his driver to take her home. Her revenge was to tell everyone that he had gonorrhoea.

He was the first man who had ever said no and meant it. Back home, she heard the news that Moncorge, who was back in Hollywood, was getting married. She was livid. Another one was slipping away from her grasp. She began following him; into shops and restaurants, just to catch a glimpse of him and his lover. She called him obsessively on the telephone. One day, she follows them into an antique shop and makes a scene. He is furious and orders her out of the shop. Back at home, she is shaking and crying.

'He's getting married, Kater. He's a damn fool. He's making a terrible mistake. I always knew he was a stupid peasant. No matter. He will come back to me. She looks just like me, but she's nineteen. She's had abortions, and now she's trapped him. What do I do if I see them? Am I expected to shake her hand? I'm not a good enough actress for that. Now, help me into this dress.'

We were invited to a Bel Air party. Mother resplendent in an ice blue chiffon gown, golden earrings a-dazzle. I remember this party so well because it was the first time I had seen Mother blind drunk. What I didn't know was that it was the first of many times that I would take her out, carry her back to the car, undress her while she screamed obscenities at me, and then put her to bed. I also remember this day because it was the day that I finally stopped drinking. I knew then that I was not going to end up like my mother. That my life would be different. And that I was unable to save her from herself.

London at Night

I am back in the limelight. Just the two of us. Madou and her eight-foot mirror commanding the stage. The good old days have returned.

London had made an offer she couldn't refuse. She is performing her one-woman show at the Café de Paris, introduced each night by a famous leading actor. She has had a new dress designed. She calls it 'the eel' – slinky and glittering, and she moves like one in cold water. She hates the cold of London, so she adds a floor-length white fur coat, with an eight-foot circular train. 2,000 swans sacrificed the down from their breasts. Willingly, of course, for their queen.

Thousands flock to see her show.

'Ladies and gentlemen, Miss Joan Madou,' says the famous actor.

She slithers down the famous curved staircase like a glacier glinting in the sunlight. Her dress is a masterpiece of illusion, transparent enough to make you think you are seeing everything and opaque enough to make you realise you are seeing nothing. Houdini must have designed this gown. She seems happy in a sacred way. Is her smile for you, or simply for herself?

Then she is in the spotlight.

'I get no kick from champagne,' she sings softly, barely above a speaking voice. 'Mere alcohol doesn't thrill me at all.' This is not exactly true.

With the final line of this first number, she points to the audience and sings, 'I get a kick out of *you*.'

Then she says: 'I'm going to sing for you a few songs from my records and a few songs from my films, but first I want to sing the song that brought me into films. I was a student in a theatre school in Europe and a very famous American film director, Mr Mo von Goldberg, came over there to make a film about a cabaret singer called Lola Lola. He had looked at all the actresses and couldn't find the one he wanted for the part, and finally he looked at this student, and one day I received a call to come and make a test for the part and I was told to bring along a very naughty song. Well, I was so sure that I was never going to get the part that I went there without the naughty song. The director had great patience with me and he said, "You know that you were supposed to bring a song," and I said, "Yes, but which song?" And he said, "Well, as you didn't bring a song, sing any song you like, so long as it isn't a naughty song." And I said, "I would like to sing an American song because I like American songs." And he said, "All right, sing an American song." So here's the song that brought me into film.'

And she sings: 'You're …' long pause '… the cream in my coffee …'

And at the end of this second song, she says, 'As you all know, I did get that part, but surely not because I sang that song so well. And when the film was finished, I was asked to come to Hollywood to make more films. One thought intrigued me very much: to go to America. I did not know America, but I knew American songs.'

And on she goes, all through her repertoire.

She sings 'Falling in Love Again' in that voice, like opium smoke. The applause is rapturous.

Each costume change is more thrilling than the last. An inky black gown created from ostrich feathers, designed with a slit to the hip to showcase her fabulous legs, elicits a gasp of shocked delight from her adoring audience. They are thrilled to be in such close proximity to this goddess. They could reach out and touch her, if they dare.

The press, invited back to her dressing room for a glass of champagne, say that it is the most daring dress that has ever graced a stage. I have been wheeled back and plugged in once more, the cables coiling Medusa-like at my feet. The only light comes from my polished surface surrounded by the glaring bulbs.

'Darlings,' she purrs, 'there's nothing underneath except a garter belt to hold up the stockings.'

Of course we all keep the secret of her foundation. That daughter of hers has managed to inveigle her way back into her mother's graces. She takes her money and then bitches about her to anyone who will listen. I have to say, though, Kater is looking quite lovely these days. She has finally shed those pounds. She still manages to avoid my gaze, as if she still fears me and suspects me of harm.

Also backstage are the veterans who flock to her show, several of them in wheelchairs. She is especially kind to them. She stays with them all night, exchanging cigarettes and war stories.

'Darlings, my suite at the Dorchester is so vulgar. Like a stage set. Who is this Oliver Messel? One of Noël's friends, no doubt. Yellow silk wallpaper in the bedroom, and only two mirrors. The bathroom is an abortion. The toilet seat in scalloped gold, like a seashell. You should see it. Deborah Kerr was in tonight and Niven. Every table is sold out. Now, I need you to be ready when I return to Vegas. First I fly to Paris for fitting. I met an intelligent man, a critic. I dine with him most nights. He emerged from my sofa like a little white worm, you know, like the ones you find in flour. But he's so brilliant. You should have heard what he told me about Olivier. You wouldn't know him. Oh, yes, Tynan. That's him.'

Concerned about her feeble vocal range, she has begun taking cortisone. She has heard that it improves the vocal cords. Slippery slope, my dear.

In the Shadow of Happiness

I never believed in 'Love at First Sight'. That was for picture stories and Hollywood. Mother perfected the art of falling in love again (and again and again). Love, I realised, was not for me. Then I met him. I smiled when I saw him scowling at me on a Sunday when the theatre was dark and I was rehearsing. He was fixing cables and moving lights. He hated movie stars, and he hated daughters of movie stars who thought they knew something about the theatre. He would take a little convincing, I thought to myself.

I had a little on my side. I had lost weight, and, now that I was sleeping better, my skin recovered its bloom. I was beginning to look more like my mother. Sometimes I caught a glimpse in the mirror, the blonde hair, the full Cupid-bow mouth, and felt a sliver of shock and fear. The plain fat child had long gone, but she was still there, deep within. She was a part of me and I pitied her. My ugly duckling. My poor sin.

I asked Bill to marry me, after a week of working night and day on a show, and he was too tired to say no. It was the best decision of my life. I kept him well away from Mother.

For our wedding, I wore a simple cream silk jersey dress. Bill had tears in his eyes when he saw me. Someone must have told Mother because when we returned to our apartment, someone had broken in and strewn red rose petals over the bed. A bottle of champagne sat meekly in an ice bucket. Mother pretended to be delighted, but she was furious. To anyone who would listen, she complained incessantly about her daughter's betrayal.

This time, I wanted the world to know. I called my mother's old lovers, Mo, Lacy, and Boni, and told them my news. They were delighted. They all said how much they still loved my mother. How much she was missed. How much she loved me. Lacy sent me a volume of poems by Shelley, with an inscription saying 'He knows everything there is to know about love.' I told Sofi, and she wept and wept.

Mother was still banished from my apartment. I gave in and invited her to meet Bill. She was all graciousness. She smirked at the linoleum on the floor ('Just like Berlin, sweetheart'), and tasted the tuna casserole without a word. She left shortly afterwards. Bill thought she was charming.

A few hours later, a limousine arrived. Boxes were carried into our home. Smoked salmon from the cold rivers of Scotland, Russian caviar, French cheeses, bundles of white asparagus, tiny honey cakes scattered with dried lavender, and cases of Dom Perignon. Bill was astounded by her generosity. But I knew what it meant. It meant that with him, you only get tuna, with me you get caviar. I told him we should hold a party and get rid of it all. He didn't understand my tears, but he held me close, and agreed to the party.

She hoped and prayed that I would leave Bill and return to her, but I knew, and she knew, deep down, that she was defeated. Later that night she called: 'Angel, I know someone, he's like your Bill, so Italian, but he's a little less good-looking, more low-class, more down towards Naples. He hits a ball and then runs "home" in that childish American game ... he's dumb, but sweet. Joe somebody.'

'Mutti, I need to go.'

'This air conditioning: cook or freeze, typical America exaggeration – we never had it back in the day. Do you remember? I suppose that now you have a husband you don't have time to remember. But you must not forget to douche. You don't want to have a baby. They're nothing but trouble. And now I need to buy you a house. You can't live in an apartment with a baby.'

When she began to slur her words, I knew that soon she would fall asleep.

'Mutti, don't forget to put the phone on its hook. Please don't forget. Put down the phone.'

* * *

'Why don't you get an abortion? It won't be so easy to leave your husband if you have a child to consider.'

I was thankful that Bill wasn't around to hear this. I glared at her and told her of my plan to make my own bassinet. 'You know, Mutti, like the ones in the movies. With lace and blue ribbons. I know this baby will be a boy.'

'Well, you know you will lose the beautiful blue eyes with that Italian husband of yours.'

We discussed the bassinet with Bill.

'If that's what you want, darling, that's what you will get. We will all make it together, as a family.'

Mother threw him a sour look.

'Look at her. All her life she has hated being fat, now she's as big as the massive house I bought for her, and now she doesn't mind.'

My husband had the grace and sense to ignore her, and he was already sketching designs for my cradle.

It was the most beautiful bassinet, and as I sewed on the thick blue silk ribbons, Mother made sandwiches and coffee. The baby came; a boy, as I had wanted. He had fair hair and blue eyes. The day he was born was the happiest day of my life, but, when I first held him in my arms, I cried and cried.

Bill was worried and shocked. How could he understand when he had never been introduced to my sin? So I told him. I told him everything. And he listened, and he held me and he told me it wasn't my fault. I was a child, and it wasn't my fault. In the end, my beautiful baby banished my sin, and I slowly began to stitch myself back together.

On the day of his christening, Mother laced me into my dress. I begged her not to pull the laces too tightly. I could hardly breathe. The baby slept soundly in his cradle. His face was a rosebud, but I didn't wish him beauty. I wished him love and joy. Mother, dressed in black, as though in mourning, sighed and muttered something under her breath.

The newspapers described her as the most beautiful grandmother in the world. She hated being old enough to be a grandmother and decided on a different role. That of Fairy Godmother.

On With the Dance

Those press guttersnipes constantly comment on Madou's age, describe her as a 'glamorous granny'. Of course, she lies about how old she is. Who wouldn't, when she looks half her age? She seems to be even lovelier than ever. She is back at her best with her show. Fame is hers once again. She has more money than she needs and, true to her heritage, commissions a new piece.

It will be a bracelet to outdo all others; a ruby and diamond jarretière cuff. Along with her diamond rose brooch and her gold seed pearl and diamond Van Cleef compact (both presents from Mo), it will be among her most precious possessions. Now, she buys her own jewellery.

She buys her daughter a house, and a ranch for Papi and Sofi. The money keeps flooding in. But she works for it. She performs two shows a night, never complaining. She sits for hours for dress fittings, and then walks and sits, ensuring that it looks good in all conditions. The camaraderie reminds her of the war, get the show on the road, is the dress OK, where are the musicians;

it reminds her of the happiest days of her life, when she was one of the boys.

She has no time for lovers. As soon as she returns to California, the first thing she does is to clean Papi's house from top to bottom. She leaves casseroles in the oven, and stocks his fridge.

I am the only one to see her as she really is. Yes, she is thinner than ever, her waist twenty-one inches. But when the wig is off and the make-up removed, there is no disguising that she is fifty-five.

Onstage, she is more radiant and poised than ever before, breaking hearts with that voice: a voice that sounds like midnight; like cigarette smoke and perfume and brandy, and amber lighting.

And still they come, in droves, wanting an intimate glimpse of a goddess; waiting for the moment when she would cease to be a statue and become flesh and motion. And when she finishes, she raises her arms above her golden head and bows, and the flowers rain upon her like manna from heaven.

Dishonored

Mother bought me a brick house that could never be blown down by the big bad wolf, but I paid a large price. She summoned me to the rented house in Brentwood to help her pack for Vegas. I was expected to be there, always at the end of the telephone, forever at her beck and call. Before leaving, she pressed her body against my husband in a suggestive way and kissed the baby, carrying away a soiled bib as a reminder.

Mother loved being rich again. She bestowed lavish presents on my little boy, whom she loved because he had inherited her thin, elegant bones. When she saw him reading a book of fairy tales, she arranged a surprise. On her next visit, she arrived dressed in a gown of layered pink chiffon. A rose rested in her bosom. She even tried to find real glass slippers, but had to make do with plastic. He was enchanted by the 'pwetty lady'.

She purchased yards and yards of silver-tipped Russian sable to make a fur stole – a ten-foot runner of skins that wrapped around her body like a second skin. She called it 'The Animal' and later

304

grew to hate it. It cost her a fortune to insure, so she decided to lose it. She left it under her seat at the theatre, but it was returned. She left it in taxis, but it was returned. When she was shopping in Bloomingdale's, she let it slide off – somehow it found its way back to her and she was forced to smile graciously and offer a reward.

Finally, on a boat to Europe she had had enough, so during a storm she went to the upper deck and threw it over into the sea. Finally, rid of The Animal, she called Papi to call the insurance company. Two hours later, the captain returned it to her, beaming with pride. It had flown off the edge and landed on the head of a third-class passenger. She said that the day she cancelled the insurance someone would steal it.

When she discovered that I was to have another baby, she smiled her thin smile.

'Doesn't he let you douche? And he still expects you to work?'

That evening we dined with Mother and her friend, the little French sparrow with the spectacular voice. The sparrow turned to my husband and asked him how it felt to live off his mother-in-law. He asked her to repeat the question. She did. We rose, without a word, and left the table.

'You see,' Mother said accusingly, 'I brought her up to have perfect manners, and now look at her. Why does she need a second child when she already has a perfect son? I told you, women's brains are too small, they can't think straight.'

The next day, she telephoned as though nothing had happened. There were many times over the years that I banished her from the house. The first time was just after my first baby. When I looked at him, so perfect, so innocent, I felt a rush of protection, so fierce it was frightening. And then I felt a rush of hatred for my mother. I didn't want her near my child. And then always something would happen to change my mind.

One day, a veteran came to see me. He pressed a coin in my hand and told me a story. He was just a boy in the war and he was afraid of dying. Mother gave him a coin and put it in his hand. She had told him that as long as he had her coin he'd be fine.

He told me that he was fine, and that he had made it home, and that he wanted to return his charm. He told me that he wanted to say to *her* as long as you have this coin, you will be fine. And then I felt a sudden rush of love for her as strong and swift as I had felt the rush of anger.

Tonight is Ours

When she least expects it, she falls in love. He is her last great love; twenty years younger, and virile. She has many names for him. Gypsy King is her favourite. When she is feeling ill-disposed towards him, he becomes 'Curly' – a joke about his premature baldness. To the world, he is the king of a successful Broadway show. To me, he is a mediocre musical star who treats her shoddily. When her first Vegas tour is over, she follows him to New York and rents an apartment on Park Avenue to be close to him. Her rooms are furnished in Siam red and gold; it looks like a brothel. She makes sure that the lamps are always dimmed, installs fluorescent lights underneath the huge king-size bed, and fills the rooms with mirrors. In her apartment, she will always look beautiful in the low light.

She stocks the fridge with his favourite food and drink, champagne and Russian caviar, and showers him with presents. He arrives late at night, after the show, often drunk, and they tumble into bed like teenagers. She is thrilled to see how her crisp white linen is streaked with his stage body make-up. In the morning, he remembers little of his professions of love.

Sometimes she stays with him at her daughter's house. She tells Curly that they can 'put the babies to bed as if they were ours'. She doesn't see that he doesn't want to play house with her, he can do that with his wife. He leaves again without making plans to see her again, and she is desperate, depressed. She sits waiting for his phone calls.

When friends call, she asks them to get off the line, so she doesn't miss his call. Sometimes, he only has thirty minutes to spare. She can see that he is checking the time in the gold Philippe Patek watch she has given to him. *Tick tock, tick tock, hickory dickory dock.* She makes a telephone call to her daughter.

'Sweetheart, I think I might be pregnant. I haven't bled for ages. Wouldn't it be wonderful to have *his* baby?'

'Mutti, did you speak to the doctor, like I asked you to?' asks the daughter. I note that she doesn't dare say that it might be the menopause.

'No, I don't need to see a doctor. Why would I need to see a doctor? I told you, I'm pregnant, I'm not sick. He needs an excuse to get rid of his mad wife. Did I tell you about Orson? An intelligent man like that! Falls for a Mexican hoofer. Why? Does he like orange hair underarms?'

She never liked Rita Hayworth.

She is having trouble sleeping. She has begun taking suppositories to send her off. They enter the bloodstream quicker than
pills. She calls her suppositories her 'Fernando Lamas' – 'You
know, sweetheart, the most boring man in Hollywood. He could
always send me to sleep.'

'Mutti, don't mix the pills with champagne. It's dangerous.
Please don't do that,' says the nagging daughter.

'Nebbish. I don't drink. Besides, these pills don't touch me.
Anyway, the King is adorable. He told me that he had loved me
ever since he was a boy. I know he has other women, but he loves
me better than anyone else. And you know what I told you: once
a woman has forgiven a man, don't reheat his sins for breakfast.'

But when she is alone, she suddenly looks tired. She takes her
pills and washes them down with a mug of champagne. The maid
will think that she's drinking coffee. She drifts into sleep, waiting
for a phone call that never comes. I watch over her. Mirrors never
sleep, just as mirrors never lie.

I Lift up My Lamp

While Mother was wowing the crowds around the globe, I was becoming famous too, on a much smaller scale and a smaller screen: television. I loved watching television and appearing on it. Mother was scathing about it and predicted that it was a fad and would never last. For her, it was just too small a screen. For me, there was a special relationship between a television actor and the audience who invited her into their homes. The actor must seem grateful for the invitation, and, if you succeed, you become a friend. You mustn't make a fool of someone in their own home. There's a special kind of intimacy – the kind that terrified my mother. She would scream at me: 'Do you think anyone on their deathbed wished they'd watched more television?'

She changed her mind when her King disagreed with her about the small screen. He had been a TV director, before Broadway, and it was he who convinced her of television's huge potential. He told her that I was part of the development of the medium, and that she should encourage her daughter. Oh, my! How I wished he hadn't taken my side.

She marched into the TV studio.

'Don't let me disturb your important work. I'm only here to support my wonderful daughter. I don't want to be in the way.'

Then, in the darkness of the studio a voice would boom: 'The light needs to be higher on her face, her nose looks too long. That hat is throwing a shadow on her face.'

And so it went on, until I forbade her entrance, after having apologised profusely to the staff, who, were, of course, charmed and enchanted by her interest.

I became something of a household name, and *Life* magazine requested a lead feature. Of course, they also wanted my mother on the cover. The image was Narcissus looking into the pond. I was photographed on the top of the page, looking down at the reverse image of my mother below. Her blonde hair was streaming behind her in a mass of curls, her arm outstretched, as she looked upwards towards my reflection. Mother told everyone, 'It was my idea that I should be at the bottom and my beautiful daughter at the top. *She* is the star. Not me. Besides, my hair looks better spread down. No, no, no. I must be at the bottom.'

There was another person who saw the potential of television: Jack Kennedy. On the 'Tonight Show', he impressed viewers with his good looks and charm. He talked not only politics, but about his love of football and his wife. She was beautiful, and stylish, just like Jack's mother, who was so kind to me. I remember in Antibes, Papa Joe saying 'image is reality'. They were always ahead of the curve.

Then I saw on television that Jack was president. It should have been his brother Joe, but his plane exploded over the cold English Channel, and there were no bits to bury, no grave to visit. So now it was skinny Jack, who had danced with me in Antibes, and taken me to tea and for hamburgers, and who always made me feel pretty. It was Jack who rescued me from the Rhino, who saw exactly who she was because he recognised the fear in my eyes.

I wished Jack could see that I had turned out to be OK. I had shed the rolls of fat, developed cheekbones you could slice cheese with, and had legs as long and slender as my mother's. Now when I looked into the mirror, I liked my reflection. I marvelled at the smoothness of my skin, my silky blonde hair that flicked across one hooded eye, the curve of the Cupid's bow. My old enemy winked back at me: 'More than passable, my dear girl. Really quite charming.'

Mother, at the age of sixty, looked like my sister. Every year, she seemed to look younger. She convinced herself it was the apple vinegar that she sipped religiously that kept her skin so fresh, her tummy so taut, that maintained her superhuman energy levels. Her bathroom cabinets revealed a different story: cortisone, Butazolidin, phenobarbital, codeine, belladonna, Nembutal,

Seconal, Librium, Darvon. Who were the 'Dr Feelgoods' prescribing this stuff?

I refused her offers of 'help' for my own depleted energy levels.

'You always needed your sleep, dear. Just like your father. Why don't you try a little of this,' and she passed me one of her tiny bottles, which I declined.

I helped her to pack for her world tour, and told her that I would meet her in New York where I would resume my duties. I made her promise to give my love to Aunt Birgitte when she saw her in Berlin. Mother glared when I mentioned her sister's name, but said nothing. When we said our goodbyes, she made a parting shot: 'You know I'm dragging myself around the world like this for you and the children, and for Papi. How else can you afford to live in luxury as you do? And who else pays the bills for Papi's ranch? And Sofi's crazy doctors?'

I didn't dare remind her that Papi's 'ranch' was a tiny shack in the middle of nowhere, out in the dusty San Fernando valley where he bred chickens to try to earn a living, trying to claw back some shreds of dignity. Or that my poor Sofi had been driven crazy by the many abortions my mother had forced upon her so that the secret of my parents' dead marriage was never revealed.

I breathed a sigh of relief when her car came and she slipped into the back seat, elegant in her tailored suit and fur stole. As I watched her car drive away, I wondered how it was possible that she could still frighten me so much. I was a wife and mother and a successful TV star, but she still had the capacity to turn my knees to jelly, without ever raising her voice.

The Party's Over Now

'You're embarrassing yourself again, Joan. What was it you once said about knowing the moment when love has flown out of the window?'

'When you arrive two hours late, and he hasn't called the police.'

'He only comes to you when he's drunk.'

'Don't be pert.'

'And the new baby.'

'As ugly as a hairless monkey. She does it on purpose to humiliate me. More headlines about the most glamorous granny in the world. Do you want to know what she said to me? She said she wants to live a normal life. I told her that I think that very few people are normal, deep down in their private lives. What a thing to aspire to. Normality!'

'Now where do we go? London?'

'Ah wonderful London; the higher the buildings, the lower the morals. Yes, and then Berlin.'

'Are you really ready for Berlin, Joan, dear. Is it wise?'

'I've told you, I never hated Germany. I hated the Nazis. I have Burt to protect me. It's his idea.'

Burt tells her she will perform at the Titania-Palast theatre in Berlin. She will return triumphant and it will be a test of character for Germany after fifteen years of shame. I wonder just how they will react to their erstwhile Fairy Queen. It was Hitler she despised, never the German people. Let them spit in her face, if they dare.

Madou wants a new gown for her show. It must be a sensation. She is addicted to the gasp of wonder when she is first seen by her adoring audience. She is reading the poetry of Gunnar Ekelof. Her thoughts drift to Boni and the goddess that stands at the head of the sweeping Daru staircase of the Louvre. Boni always saw beauty in her motion and her stillness because he knew the concentration it required.

She studies pictures of 'The Winged Victory of Samothrace'. The gown so artfully draped around the voluptuous torso, clinging to the right leg that strides forward in motion. Nike, descended from the skies and guarding the ship's prow, fighting the wind, proclaiming victory. Madou is struck by the paradox of violent motion and stillness. The gown is rippling in the strong sea breeze. She studies the striking feather pattern on her wings. How can she recreate this look?

She needs a wind machine. She needs silk chiffon to ripple in the breeze. Strips of silk strategically draped across her breasts and hips. Instead of wings, she will have her swan's-down coat.

Before she faces the press in Berlin, she looks at me and tweaks her wide-brimmed hat. She wears a black, well-cut dress, a mink coat, high-heeled shoes, and white gloves. Her only adornment is the small French Légion d'honneur ribbon. There is something monkish about her, so severe, and yet she has a cool, polished eroticism.

The press conference is full, and they shout her name as she enters the room. She speaks in a soft voice, answering questions from *Der Tagesspiegel*.

No, she has not been to the *Tiergarten* section of town. She recognises the zoo where she had played marbles as a child. No, she does not have mixed feelings about being back in Berlin. You don't go to a city to be sad just because you were once a child there. She is here to make money.

The only indication that she is less than confident is her chain-smoking, though she smokes slowly, and with precision. She refrains from speaking in Berlin dialect. Her world tour will start in Berlin and will end in Washington DC.

How does she stay so slim? She eats veal steak and green salad, and drinks tea with honey. She thanks the press and retires to her suite at the Hilton. When they ask questions about her sister, she is shocked and says, 'I have no sister.' She leaves in a sea of flashing light bulbs.

When she performs at the Titania-Palast theatre, she is dignified and poised. She never sheds a tear or betrays a shred of sentimentality. The crowd is respectful after the last song (she never gives an encore). Thunderous applause erupts. She takes a deep, low bow in her swan's-down coat, looking for all the world like a swan in human form. When she has sung her final song, 'My Blondest Baby', the audience delight her by throwing flowers onto the stage.

She encounters a less positive reception in Bad Kissingen, where she is booed by a throng of teenagers, who hold up a banner saying 'Traitor' in black spidery writing. In Dusseldorf, a young girl spits in her face. Madou wipes her face, calmly, and carries on. When someone in the audience hurls an egg onto the stage, the crowd erupts and gives her a standing ovation for refusing to be driven out by a Nazi.

She flies to Israel, where she's told she can't sing one song in German. She says, 'No I won't sing one, I will sing nine.' She does and the audience cheers. When she sings Richard Tauber's *'Frag' Nicht Warum Ich Gehe'*, the audience weeps. Have they lost their minds, one wonders? She donates all the proceeds of her first concert in Tel Aviv to a rehabilitation centre for the Israeli army. Later, she insists on performing for the army, whose applause brings her to tears. She asks Burt to make a sound recording of the applause.

Back in her suite, she is exhausted, and pale. These days, she always seems to find herself alone. She is painfully thin, and seems to have lost her appetite. She tells no one of the pains in her abdomen. The excruciating pain in her right leg. She will carry on. No complaints. Always the soldier.

Rancho Notorious

I can't remember the exact year when it happened. Those years of having babies merge and blur. But I remember that it was after her return to Berlin. She was resting before another tour. We were in New York when she suddenly gripped my arm, and, speaking in German, said, 'It's my leg, my leg. Get me into Tiffanys so I can lean against the counter and rest.'

I knew it was serious, because Mother loathed Tiffanys. The saleswoman could barely contain her excitement when Madou walked through the door. Mother leaned against the glass counter, while an array of jewels were proffered.

'Hmm, the stone is OK, but the setting is ugly. What kind of man would buy *that* for his mistress?'

As soon as the pain subsided, she indicated to me that she wanted to leave. The shop assistant looked disappointed.

'What happened. Mutti? Are you in pain?'

'It's my leg, it just collapsed. Now we must get to Knize for the fitting. I don't want you to fuss.'

For the next two hours, she stood still as she was fitted for her trouser suit. But I was alarmed, and insisted that she saw a doctor as soon as she returned home. She constantly complained about American doctors, but was delighted when this one prescribed strong painkillers. He became the first of her more obliging physicians.

Mother searched for reasons: was the pain worse in the humidity or in the cold? She discovered that it subsided after a few glasses of champagne, so she began drinking in the morning, and carrying a plastic bottle, filled with champagne, in her handbag. She refused to tell anyone about her problem; stars must never have flaws, never become mere mortals.

Her new favourite drugs were Dexedrine and Chlorodyne, the latter stored in very thin, cobalt-blue bottles with a cork stopper. Those bottles went with her everywhere, and she thought nothing of washing down that viscous black treacle with copious amounts of champagne.

I kissed her goodbye, said that I would see her the next time she was in California, and told her to keep her leg raised when she flew back.

There's a Younger Generation

The two of them are arguing again.

She thinks she has the Child back under her thumb. Every night now, the table in front of me in the dressing room is loaded with liquor and pills. In the early days of her touring, her habits never appeared to affect her performance. She was perfectly in control, as she slithered down the staircase in her long fur coat and tight dress. Once she complained that her leg hurt, so someone suggested that she use the banister rail to steady herself. She was furious, screaming that only old ladies needed banister rails. She would never stoop so low.

But over the past few months she has been losing control. The crew were at a loss. Burt was smart enough to see that he would not be able to stop her from doing whatever she wanted. So he called Kater and begged her to become her mother's dresser. The television jobs were drying up and the husband was no breadwinner. There would be good money, Burt coaxed. And surely she could see that she was the only one who could keep her mother's show on the road.

So here she is. Old times again.

'Sweetheart, look at my panties, I'm staining again. I thought I was pregnant. This time, I am keeping the baby. Now, where are my firecrackers?'

'Mutti, the tampons are in the bathroom cabinet. The one over the basin. Let me find them for you.'

It would be pointless for either of us to try to explain the menopause to her. If she decides that she is to have a baby at the age of sixty, then that is what she is going to do. Mother Nature is no match for Madou.

'I have a pain in my leg. I need some of those vitamin shots, the ones they give you in the backside.'

'Mutti, it's all this travel, and living out of a suitcase. You need to buy a home.'

'I bought you a home, and Papi a ranch. Why you need a big house, I will never know. You know what Boni says: Suitcases are more important than houses.'

'OK, Mutti. But just maybe you should think about it. Now what about your finale? I was thinking a line of chorus girls, dressed in tails and top hats.'

'Borrrrring. I was thinking of my ringmaster's costume, but you know, have a real lion. Maybe I could put my head in its mouth, you know like that ridiculous Mae West film. It is Vegas, after all.'

Her daughter burst into laughter. 'Mutti, I don't think that's a good idea. Who else did you see?'

'That terrible woman Taylor was there tonight, with Wilding. He likes her to dangle her enormous breasts in his face, and yet he couldn't take his eyes off *me*. Sinatra, too. Frankie is sweet, tender. He is so grateful when you do *it*. But you know, he drinks too much with those pals of his. And he's so jealous. Just like Boni and Mo.'

'Did you see the King? Did he come to the show?'

'No, and he didn't call. He knows I am here. I know it's all because of that Swedish horse. I think he'll finally get a divorce from that whore. Rossellini told me *everything*. What she put that poor man through. No wonder he sought comfort in my arms. How could I say no? Anyway, Kirk came. We had a cosy dinner at his beach house.'

'Did you see Noël?'

'Yes, I did. I told him he doesn't understand how it is that one man can be a woman's whole life. That's because he does it to boys in the ass.'

'Mutti, tell me about your legs. Did you see the doctor?'

'You and your doctor fetish. Doctors are only any good when they're specialists, and I don't know what's wrong with me, so it's no good going. Like surgeons. They just want to cut you up. Why? Anyway, the cortisone stops the numbness. You should try it. But then you keep having all those children and playing house, so you probably won't. But you know me, I never complain. I was too well brought-up. I always put others before myself. What would *you* know about sacrifice?'

Kater pales and begins to speak, and then thinks better of it. I must confess, she really has become a rather charming woman. Marriage and motherhood become her. She is slender as a wand; her complexion is flawless. She abstains from alcohol and never touches junk food. That girl I remember, who always avoided my gaze, has blossomed into a very beautiful swan.

Show Business at War

My sons adored their grandmother. When she was 'resting', she would come to 'her' house, and take over. Dressed in her white nurse's uniform, she would walk them in the park, and take them out for tea. What she lacked as a mother, she more than compensated for as a grandmother. But she was never to be called Grandmother, she was always Massy.

After seventeen years together, touring the world, Burt has decided to quit. Mother was sanguine when he told her that he was leaving.

'I'm lucky to have had him for as long as I did. Now he's writing stupid songs about raindrops on heads.'

'Mutti, your show is perfection. You don't need Burt. You just need a new conductor. Your show runs like clockwork.'

Mother began to undress.

'You know who was there at dinner tonight? The Duke of Windsor and that elegant skeleton. Do you remember when she made him wear that awful kilt and dance a Scottish reel? I always regret that he turned me away that time. She spent the whole night staring at my jewels.'

'How are your legs feeling? Do you want me to arrange for you to see a proper doctor?'

'There's nothing wrong with my legs. You know my mother had a problem with bad circulation in her legs, but that's because she was *old*.'

'OK, Mutti, but let me know if you change your mind.'

'I never change my mind. Neither about books or men.'

Mother was furious because I was pregnant again.

'That report from that dreadful man, Kinsey. "Put it in, pull it out." Why do American people have to be told this sort of thing? You should ask that husband of yours what he thinks about it. You have so many children, you must do *it* a lot. All those times I've looked after your children when you go away for your dirty weekends. I've boiled your nappies, made the formula, scrubbed the floors, and what do I find in your fridge? Jell-O. You should never give a child that stuff.'

'Relax, Mutti.' I can see she is in one of her moods.

'Last night Michael took me out to dinner. I had to sleep with him because that woman's in Rome doing her Cleopatra picture. I felt sorry for him. He asked so nicely. He did that thing to me that sounds like an Irish airline. We broke the double bed in my room. Afterwards it was all cosy. Well, you wouldn't know about that. You, so faithful, thinking you're above everyone else with your *happy* marriage.'

Long practice had taught me to ignore Mother's barbed comments. I always felt that I had disappointed her by my insistence on a normal family life. My husband was bewildered by my delight in the quotidian; children's pencil cases, for example. What were they? Many things that civilians (as my mother called non-celebrities) took for granted, were a delight to me. Standing in a line, for example. Going to a café for a cup of coffee. This, she could never understand.

And I still had my secrets. But she had hers, too. What had really happened to Aunt Birgitte? Why had she told the press that she was an only child? And why had she cut Birgitte out of every family photograph, leaving only the beautiful daughter, with the long blonde hair, sitting beside her parents? So we both had our secrets. And we would probably take them to the grave.

We Were Dancing

'The apple doesn't fall far from the tree.'

'What on earth do you mean? She is not the least bit like me; all those children and that boring husband. How closely women clutch the very chains that bind them.'

'She's happy and contented.'

'Nuts. She was happy with the life she had with me. She's having all these children to spite me. And she's having all these boys. A daughter is for life. She's doing it on purpose.'

'Darling, that is quite untrue, and you know it. She's had her problems.'

'Oh you mean her weight. She just needed a little discipline.'

'Yes, indeed. Look at her now. Quite the beauty.'

'When you are beautiful, you have the world on a string. And who would not want that? Particularly if you can get hold of that string without any effort. The ugly girls do not fare so well. The glass slipper does not fit. Prince Charming is oblivious to their frantic efforts. The Beauty does not have to try hard. Everything that is good, everything she desires, falls right into her beautiful lap. General rules do not apply. She has an extra-special set of rules all of her own. Even as a child, she gets the extra candy, the special dress that she doesn't really need. And then when her bracelet is full of charms, and the boys swarm around, and her mother says, "I don't know how she does it, my little Beauty", she knows that she can rely on her looks to get her heart's desire, once she sees how it works. And the more it works, the more value she puts on this asset. She has no real joy, but she does notice that.'

'And what of the Ugly Duckling? You cannot know how this feels. You, who have been gifted with beauty from birth.'

'Lucky is the Ugly Duckling. Don't envy the pretty duckling. You will have time to be alone, to read, and to make friends. In the realm of love and happiness, beauty lies like a feather on the scale of values.'

'You are still beautiful, Joan. Perhaps even more so. But he won't leave his wife. They rarely do. Men are creatures of habit.'

'Perhaps you're right.'

'You're not a mystery to me, Joan. Do you mind? You're transparent as glass.'

She lights another cigarette. She's smoking far too much since the war, and it's bad for her legs. She worries about touring without Burt by her side. Her daughter can be there some of the time, but she has her family to think about. If only her daughter preferred women. Let's face it, homosexuals worship their mothers.

Later, the King calls. Then he turns up, with a whisky bottle under his coat, smiles that boyish smile, and she forgives him, promises that she won't ask any more questions, won't demand anything, will just take the little she can get. She is scared of being alone. She is so thin that she seems to be held together by her clothing and her jewels.

He leaves after half an hour. Absence is to love what the wind is to fire. It blows out the small one and lights the big one.

The Happy Mother

One of my children was ill, so I couldn't go on the next tour.

Mother told me that the first night at the Palladium without Burt was terrifying, but she refused to let it show. The courage it took to stand alone in the spotlight on a darkened stage filled with hundreds of people. She followed the same routine, though she stumbled a little through the first song. Her audience was spellbound. She has made it. Alone.

In Wiesbaden, she fell off the stage for the first but not the last time. She had failed to see the edge of the stage in the darkness. She carried on, even though the pain was severe. Mo von Goldberg was in the audience with his son. Later they had dinner and talked about old times. It was only in the safety of her hotel room that she called me.

'Kater, I fell. But I had to carry on. Mo was there. My shoulder hurts.'

'Mutti, listen to me. You need to see a doctor, immediately. There's an American hospital in Wiesbaden. I'm going to call them now and arrange for you to see a doctor.'

'You know everything. Only you would know that there's a hospital in Wiesbaden. It's not too bad. I tied my shoulder with a Dior scarf and it felt better. You see, I couldn't see the edge of the stage in the dark.'

I wondered whether Mother had had too many glasses of champagne.

It proved to be a broken collarbone. But soldier that she was, she carried on with the tour.

It was pitiful to think of Mo seeing her tumble. Her humiliation. His embarrassment. His fallen angel.

The next fall was more serious. The story became famous. She was in Washington, enjoying the applause as she sang her final song. In honour of her orchestra, she pointed to the pit, and then, without warning, toppled over into the darkness below. The audience gasped in horror. She lay there, immobile and hissed, 'Don't touch me, clear the theatre, clear the theatre.'

Blood was seeping from her legs. She remembered the doctor's command, to stay still. When everyone had left the theatre, she asked to be carried to her dressing room. Then she phoned me. I remember every word of our conversation.

'Mutti, what is it? Is everything OK?'

'Sweetheart, I fell.' Her voice was soft and fragile.

'Did you hurt your legs?'

'Yes. There's blood everywhere.'

'Which one?'

'The left.'

I knew that this was bad: the left leg was the one with hardly a pulse.

'Mutti, listen to me very carefully and do everything I say. I'll book a flight first thing in the morning and be with you as soon as I can. Do not remove your support stockings, they will pull away your skin and will need to be cut away carefully. Wrap a clean towel around your leg.'

'But I've already done it, they were covered in blood.'

I was terrified about the dirty floor and the threat of infection, but the voice on the other end of the phone remained calm. She would need a tetanus shot. Who could help her?

'Don't raise your leg high, keep it flat.'

I could sense that her leg was raised already.

'Mutti, ring Teddy Kennedy. He will know the best doctor in Washington. Now keep warm and get to your hotel and stay warm.'

Fear trickled through me at the thought of what could happen with an open wound that could not heal without a proper blood supply.

* * *

When I arrived at the hotel, it was worse than I had imagined, the wound as large as a fist. But she was bandaging her leg, ready to go onstage in the evening. The show must go on.

'Mutti, what did Teddy say?'

'About time you got here. That dreadful conductor man. He did this to me. I reached towards him and he pulled me down, like a rag doll. And where was Burt when I needed him? Singing his song about raindrops falling on heads.'

'Did you reach Teddy?'

'I told him I won't go to hospital, so he arranged for a doctor to see me here.'

For once, that night she had to cancel. She was distraught at letting down her fans.

We turned her hotel suite into a first-aid station. Disinfected the tiny kitchen in her pantry, and stocked it with medical supplies. Because she refused to go to hospital, the doctor advised us to keep the wound as sterile as possible until she came to her senses. She refused to cancel her tour, would listen to no one, except her favourite quack who administered a shot of 'vitamins' into her groin. Fortunately, there was a week's break before the journey to the next venue.

On my way to fetch supplies, I was accosted by the conductor, a lovely, gentle man, who was white with shock.

'I promise I didn't pull your mother off the stage. She says I did it to her, but I would never hurt her, she stumbled and fell.'

I assured him that it wasn't his fault. She had her version of the truth and she would stick to it. In the meantime, I watered down her Scotch, and removed her glass whenever I could, throwing it into the nearest plant pot. The plants had never looked so good.

Remarkably, she recovered, and her enforced sobriety did wonders. She continued her tour in Montreal. I stayed with her. Her first-night performance was the best I had ever seen. Her skin was luminous, her gait steady. She was sixty-three and had never looked better. She had designed a new foundation of pink soufflé that moulded her body, and a sheath of glimmering pearly bugle beads gave off an iridescent light. No one in the audience would ever have noted her agony or guessed that beneath the glitter her leg was oozing and bleeding.

She stood there for an hour, singing her heart out, steady as a rock. Then she strode from the stage where we waited to change her bandages in time for her second show that evening. When I changed her dressing, I saw that the edges of the open wound were turning black. That evening I phoned a prominent surgeon and begged him to see my mother. She consented to see him, only after I told her in no uncertain terms that if she didn't see a surgeon, then she would have to face amputation of the most famous legs in Hollywood history.

She packed a bag, and we left for the airport. From now on, I would be at her side, whether she liked it or not.

The Dream is Over

The King is viciously cruel. Says she has the red hands of a house-wife. Calls her 'old' and tells her that he will never leave his wife. Still, she comes back for more. She is depressed when he doesn't call. She is jealous of his wife, calls her a bad mother, claims she's insane. Madou wants to kill herself but she doesn't know where to do it: in Billy Wilder's summerhouse? No, that would be unfair. He's been such a good friend.

She comes to her vanity and looks deep into me, still so lovely. She lights a cigarette, slowly blows smoke rings into the air, turning it a soft, misty blue. I take a deep breath and tell her the truth: 'Darling, you must pack up this nonsensical situation once and for all. It is really beneath your dignity, not your dignity as a famous artist and a glamorous star, but your dignity as a human – only too human – being. The King is attractive, beguiling, tender and fascinating, but he is not the only man in the world who merits those delightful adjectives … Do please try to work out for yourself a little personal philosophy and DO NOT, repeat

DO NOT, be so bloody vulnerable. To hell with goddamned "amour". It always causes far more trouble than it is worth. Don't run after it. Don't court it. Keep it waiting offstage until you're good and ready for it, and even then treat it with the suspicious disdain that it deserves … I am sick to death of you waiting about in empty houses and apartments with your ears strained for the telephone to ring. Snap out of it, girl! Life is for the living. Well, that is all it is for, and living DOES NOT consist of staring in at other people's windows and waiting for crumbs to be thrown to you. You've carried on this hole-in-corner, overcharged, romantic, unrealistic nonsense long enough. Stop it Stop it Stop it. Other people need you. Stop wasting your time on someone who only really says tender things to you when he's drunk. It's your career that matters. Don't end up like those other faded stars; all alone in the back of limousines, with only bouquets for company.'

'Enough! I've had enough of listening to you. What do you know about love? You, so perfect. Well, perfect things belong in museums. I can still *get* a lover who is twenty years younger than myself. And he is the most inventive lover.'

She tears off her blonde wig, and releases the tiny braids that give her a natural facelift. She brushes out her thinning hair. It is a relief to see her, hand trembling, pick up one of her sleeping pills. She downs it with a glass of champagne. She walks to the vanity table to turn off the lamp. She looks into me.

338

Whose face is this, she is asking? She experiences a stab of shock when she sees her profile in the fading light. She puts out the light and I can no longer see. But I am still here. I am always here.

Kismet

'The witch is on her broomstick,' said one of the grips.

'OK, don't worry, I'm here now.'

'Kater, look at this dressing room. Can you believe it? Garden furniture made of sticks. Dangerous for the dresses. And orange cushions. I expected better of *Broadway*. What is this! An Adirondacks porch or the dressing room of a star?'

'Mutti, go and do your rehearsal and I will do the room.'

I phoned Bloomingdale's and begged the salesman to let me hire his selection of French furniture from the shop floor. When she returned from rehearsal, the room was bedecked in blue and gold French château. She loved it. Then I sorted out the flower room. Her idea was to employ 'flower boys' to throw nosegays, just as she launched into 'Honeysuckle Rose'. The boys complained endlessly about the arrangements, that the pink ribbon was synthetic and not real satin, that the pink was too deep. She loved them and they remained devoted friends.

In New York, Mother was reunited with her Italian lover – 'just like your Bill but better-looking' – who had flown in from Palm Springs to see her concert. Frankie was a generous man, showering her with flowers and presents. She had my father flown in from LA to witness her latest triumph. Papi was frail, and the cuffs on his shirt were frayed and grey, his suit hanging from his thin frame. He was barely recognisable from the dapper, fastidious man I remembered as a child. He carried a stick and an air of pride, but he was a broken man, longing to get back to his ragged dogs and chicken farm.

I asked him about Sofi, who had been locked away for her own safety. So many unborn babies had been ripped untimely from the little room in her body; the woman who had longed to be a mother, and was denied the only role that she had ever wanted. Over the years, Mother doled out pills to Sofi like candy, and now her fragile mind had collapsed.

Papi told me how Sofi, pale as waxed paper, would sit for hours picking away the skin on her fingers, mourning the babies she had lost, weeping silent tears for hours on end. I had failed Sofi. I had let them destroy her and stood by while they ensured that they did the job properly. My poor white queen.

I flew to London to prepare for Mother's arrival. As soon as I got to the Savoy I asked to see the manager and took him up to her luxury suite.

'Please listen to me and listen carefully, and everything will be fine. On no account must you ever repeat this, but my mother must never fall or injure her legs in any way. She suffers from a circulation problem and if she receives even the slightest wound, her lack of circulation would make it impossible for it to heal. Please remove all of the rugs from the sitting room and the bedroom. One of the bathrooms will be her dressing room. I will need a plank of wood to lay across the tub. Please send for twelve large white towels and lay them on the plank. I will need another dozen small towels for hair. Get rid of this mirror, and install a long, floor-length mirror and ask your electrician to install three lights above it; Miss Madou always does her make-up in the hotel and not in her dressing room. We will need a shelf for three wig stands right over here. Please remove this bath mat. You will need blackout blinds in the bedroom as Miss Madou has problems sleeping. Please tape the edge of the carpets. My mother prefers lilies and carnations. She despises long-stemmed red roses. If they arrive from fans, please give them to the chambermaids. We will need a record player and shelf for her books and newspapers. I will need a six-foot long table to lay out her swan's-down coat. When she rings for room service, night or day, answer immediately and make sure that the chef does not keep her waiting. When you hear the phone, then grab your menus and run. Please fill the fridge with champagne, and make sure it is always ice cold. Do not fill her water glass with ice; Miss Madou is European, not an American. Do not expect her to sign a room-service check, just bow and leave immediately. Please remember that she is always right. Never question her, never contradict her. If you do what I say, it will be easier on everybody concerned and we might all make it without a nervous breakdown.'

I gave the speechless manager a very large tip, and told him that more would follow. By the time she arrived, the suite was prepared.

'Sweetheart, I just had tea with Vivien and Larry and you would not *believe* her hair; so lustrous and thick. I asked her what pill she was taking and she laughed and pulled off her bandeau and she was completely bald underneath. Bald as an egg. Her wig-maker is called Stanley Hall and he is fabulous. He uses real hair and you can *not* tell the difference. The English are the only people who know how to make wigs.'

She ordered dozens of wigs, perfectly dyed to match her own hair, and from that moment on she wore them constantly. Her hairdresser braided her own fine hair, pulling up the skin on her face, and then she placed the wig with its velvet bandeau over the top so you could not see the line between the real and the fake. The effect was fantastic. She wore Stanley's wigs for the rest of her life.

I was still worried about her legs, and forced her to see a doctor. He told her that she needed immediate treatment for advanced arteriosclerosis. He warned her that if she refused treatment she risked gangrene and amputation of both limbs. Not even the threat of losing those beautiful legs that had made her name was enough to deter her, or make her listen.

'He says that my legs are being deprived of blood supply and that causes the swelling. Nebbish. I'm going to see a real doctor, who says he can improve the circulation by injecting me with vitamins.'

She got around the problem of her swelling legs by wearing trousers by day, and invented tall boots to wear with her Chanel suits. By night, she wrapped her legs with bandages and wore floor-length gowns. Nothing could be permitted to mar the perception of perfection. No one knew what she suffered. The doctors told me that if she ever had a fall it would be extremely dangerous, perhaps fatal.

And then there was a year of deaths; the little sparrow died and Papa Hem put a gun to his head. 'Sweetheart, if *I* had been there with him, he would never have done it.' At that moment, I knew that they had been more than just friends.

She dressed herself in flowing black robes, took out his letters from their strongbox and retired to her room for days. She lit votive candles around the silver-framed photograph that sat beside her bed. She always loved playing the grieving widow. She searched for clues as to why he had done it, and why he had deserted her; in her heart, she never forgave him.

Suite in Three Keys

Whisky opens the veins, and she can't sleep since his death, so she pours herself a liberal glass. Her photograph of Papa Hem stands on her dressing table. Bottles of pills keep him company, and her trusty blue phials nestle among lipsticks, ointments, and jars. The lights over me are exceedingly bright and it takes a few moments for her eyes to adjust to the blinding glare. Stacks of telegrams and letters on one side; cigarettes, ashtray and a lighter on the other. She lights a cigarette, sucking in those glorious cheeks, smoking, as always, slowly and methodically. In the background behind me is her swan's-down coat, so heavy it needs its own table to rest upon before it is fluffed out for the show.

Shake out the pills and wash them down with Scotch, darling. It seems to stop the trembling in the hands. Hands needs to be steady to apply make-up. Brushes and tweezers and scissors are laid out like surgical instruments. Create the face, fill in the lips, enlarge the eyes. A chilled glass of champagne is always at hand.

She still has the stamina of a young girl. She is a little fuller in figure, and needs help to squeeze into her foundation. Has she put on weight again? That would never do. Perhaps you do need to lay off the Scotch, darling. Are the leg bandages in place? Check there's a threaded needle and pearls handy so you can sew one in at the last minute if need be. Now the swollen feet need to be pushed into her Ferragamo shoes. She wants to scream with pain, but she must walk steadily to the stage. Don't trip over the cables on the floor. Steady, steady on.

Find the key light. Adjust the microphone stand. There are pictures on the screen behind her, documenting her life: Berlin, Hollywood, Paris, a World War II soldier, Las Vegas, Israel. The crowd applauds loudly. She stands erect, the soldier. Takes a bow with perfect posture.

She returns to her dressing room. She removes her make-up and transforms herself from a goddess to a woman of her age. She feels so weary, so tired, but she can't sleep. She takes notepaper and writes to the only man who has never deserted her, and who loves her and who truly understands: 'The days go by, Papi, and there are a hundred things to do, although I get up early; once again, I am unable to sleep since the Hem thing. I am unkempt and far from home. I send you a kiss.'

Princess Ololah

My mother agreed to an operation to save her legs. But some things had to happen first. While she was in surgery, I unzipped her large leather bag and emptied the contents onto her bed. A mixture of anger and pity washed over me as I scanned the stash of drugs and booze. Mother had all the duplicity and cunning of the true addict. She had poured Scotch into bottles claiming to be cleaning fluid and lotions. Bottles purporting to be mouthwash were filled with vodka. Her pills were stuffed into sewing kits, Tampax boxes and make-up cases.

As soon as the anaesthetic had worn off, she asked for her bag. She was enraged when she realised what I had done with her contraband. Deprived of her loot, and in extreme withdrawal, she screamed obscenities, drove the nursing staff mad, until she was prescribed Thorazine to keep her calm. Suddenly she became charming and funny, minded her manners, and we chatted and watched TV together. That was until she discovered that the drug was used to soothe inmates in a lunatic hospital and that spelled the end of Thorazine and her good temper.

He saved her legs. They turned from icy blue to a rosy pink as the blood circulated freely around them. She had been lucky this time. She blamed everyone for the circumstances that had brought her here; Burt, the conductor, me; everyone except the drink that had caused the fall.

Eight weeks after the operation, we were back on tour. She was still furious with me. She told me that she was plotting her revenge. We had a row.

'Kater, give me one of those filthy cigarettes.'

'Mutti, the doctor said no. It's bad for your legs.'

'The legs are perfect. Am I to have no pleasures? And just one drink.' Her tone is sweet and wheedling.

'It's dangerous. You are taking too many pills.'

'You hate me. You've always hated me. I gave you everything, but it wasn't enough. You were such a sweet girl. So docile. So obedient.'

'What happened to Aunt Birgitte, Mutti? Where is she? Is she alive?'

'I've told you. I don't have a sister.'

'You said you saw her in Belsen. Did she die?'

'I don't know what you're talking about. Now leave me alone. You have your own secrets, leave me with mine.'

Her sleeping pills were beginning to take effect. I switched off the lights and tucked her into bed, and, just like in the old days, she curled up her body at the very edge of the bed, and fell asleep.

Waiting in the Wings

Now you are recovered, darling, you can drink as much as you like. Empty the miniature bottles of booze into a mouthwash bottle, no one will know. Order more bottles of champagne as befitting a star. You only drink one or two glasses to steady your nerves. The Scotch is needed to wash down the pills, because everyone knows that booze opens your veins.

The King is here in her dressing room. She can't contain her joy. Now that her legs are healed, she seems younger than ever. They go to dinner. She is dressed in a simple, black sheath and still, at the age of sixty, outshines every woman in the room. One comes up to her, peers at her face and asks, 'Who did it?' She responds: 'God.'

Back in her room he is staggered by her beauty.

'I can hardly believe you have a married daughter with children.'

'I married very young,' she snaps, irritated by his compliment.

He pours her a drink.

'Do you love me?'

'Joan, love's an awfully big word.'

'No it's not, it's tiny. Am I too old for you? Is that it. Do I repulse you?'

'No, it's not that. But I have a wife and child.'

They fight and he leaves. He returns and then leaves again. He promises he will call, but doesn't. He says he will leave his wife and child, but he doesn't.

She tours Australia and writes in her journal: 'I am lonely, lonely, lonely, down under.'

She has to make more money.

Her husband writes to her, but always ends with the same request: 'I need some money urgently, if you can. Forgive me.'

She writes the cheques and sends packages of food and wine.

She's spent her life playing the unhappy abandoned women who give up everything for love, so she begins to play the role in real life. Drunk and alone, she writes to her daughter: 'The King, he keeps showing up from time to time and I don't have the nerve to end it. The children get all the love that remains, so all is not lost. I am lost, and that is a shame. Waste, waste, waste. Kiss your heart and all that is in it.'

Witness for the Prosecution

Mother ended her tour in Washington. She told me she was having lunch with Bobby. I was sad not to see him, but I needed to be at home with the children for Thanksgiving. I often thought of Jack, the first boy I had loved. He told me once that he had never wanted to be president. That he wanted to be a writer. But after Young Joe's death, he felt his father breathing down his neck, and he was powerless to resist.

Powerful parents can do cruel things to their children, and they are never challenged, never judged. When your mother is a goddess, a war hero, a legend, she can get away with anything. If I told anyone that she had left me in the care of a predator, who would have believed me? How can you see clearly when you are looking into the sun? I looked at my own children, and I wondered how she could do it. I had no sympathy for myself, but I had it for my own children.

I bore no ill feeling for the Rhino. She was kind to me. She was attentive. She had every opportunity. You wouldn't leave someone locked in a wine cellar if you knew they were an alcoholic – of course they would help themselves.

We had never celebrated Thanksgiving when I was a child, but I made sure that my boys were American through and through. I would spend hours in the kitchen making cranberry sauce and pumpkin pie. I could never be a better cook than my mother, but the children didn't complain, and they tolerated my delight in unknown traditions, just as they tolerated my joy every time one of them began school. I, who had never known school, was amazed and delighted by a lunch box and a satchel.

I held my children close to me and promised I wouldn't leave them again for a long, long time. It was Friday, and I walked them to school. On days like these, I sometimes wanted to cry with happiness. How had I arrived here, with a husband I adored and four children – thankfully all boys? I don't know what I would have done with a daughter. I would be worried that she might turn out to be beautiful like my mother, and I never wanted that curse upon my imaginary little girl. That fairy in the tale of Sleeping Beauty who gave the baby the gift of beauty – what a curse that turned out to be! Sometimes I wanted my beautiful mother to sleep for a hundred years. All I had ever wanted was contentment – the Cinderella of emotions.

I was busy at home and awaited her return from this, the final leg of her tour. She was thrilled when Jack rang her. He had seen her concert and asked her to the White House for drinks. She seemed edgy when she called me on the phone. She disapproved of my childish delight in Thanksgiving. She found it unseemly, too American.

Bobby had wanted to hear my news, and they had laughed about my girlish crush on Jack. So she had noticed? I truly believed she was too busy sleeping with his father and his older brother to have noticed our special friendship. I thought of us swimming to the island, and seeing the damselflies. The time he crossed the dance floor to ask me to be his partner. Mother's jealousy at anyone who superseded her place in my affections. How I had tried so hard to conceal my love.

She returned to New York the next day. She came to our house (the one she had bought with her hard-earned money), and let herself in with her key. She was always exhausted at the end of a tour, but today she was triumphant and flushed. She was looking elegant in a cream tweed suit, and carried a large black leather purse.

'Mutti, you're back. How was the White House? What can I get you?'

I remember her face was hard and lovely.

She looked at me for what seemed a long time, drinking in every detail. Her silence was unnerving.

'How was he, Mutti? The president, Jack. Did you see him?'

She held out her purse and unlocked the clasp. Then she slowly reached into the lining and took out something silky and sheer, pale pink edged with golden-brown lace. She thrust it under my nose.

'Kater, smell him. It's the president. He was magnificent.'

Kater Through the Looking Glass

Let me tell you a story about a little girl who once upon a time fell down a rabbit hole. She is sitting in a drawing room with her cat. Outside, the snow is falling so gently that it seems to be kissing the windowpanes. Kissing all over. The snow will cover the trees and the fields in a white cosy quilt – go to sleep, darlings, until the summer comes again.

Above the flickering fireplace is a large looking glass. The cat has been naughty and needs to be punished, so the little girl lifts the cat up to the looking glass and threatens to put her through it. 'If you're sulky and not good directly, I'll put you through into Looking-Glass House. How would you like that? Oh, Kitty Cat, wouldn't it be nice to be through the looking glass?'

To the little girl's astonishment, the glass begins to melt away like a bright, silvery mist. The first thing she sees on the other side is a clock with the face of an old man, grinning at her …

Later on, in a garden of talking flowers, she bumps into the Red Queen. The Red Queen gives her a biscuit, but it is so dry that the girl thinks that she is being choked. The Red Queen gives advice: 'Speak in French when you can't think of the English for a thing – turn out your toes – and remember who you are.'

'Remove the pudding. Remove the pudding.'

Often the commands are confusing: 'The rule is jam tomorrow, jam yesterday, but never jam today.'

The little girl tries to change the subject: 'May I put your shawl straight for you?'

Suddenly, she sees the White Queen approaching. The Red Queen takes the White Queen tenderly by the hand and, gently stroking it, speaks: 'She means well, but as a general rule she can't help saying foolish things. She never was really well brought up, but it's amazing how good tempered she is! Pat her on the head and see how pleased she'll be.'

The White Queen puts her head on the girl's shoulder and says, 'I'm so sleepy.'

'She's tired, poor thing,' says the Red Queen. 'Smooth her hair – lend her your nightcap and sing her a soothing lullaby.'

'I don't know any lullabies. And why do I have to take care of two queens?'

The White Queen begins to sing softly:

First, the fish must be caught
That is easy: a baby, I think, could have caught it

Then she suddenly screams and seizes the girl's hair with both her hands: 'Take care of yourself! Something's going to happen!'

The Red Queen is alarmed by this unsavoury outburst from her rival. She looks at the girl and says coldly: 'All the ways about here belong to me.'

The little girl speaks softly: 'It's a great huge game of chess that's being played – all over the world.'

The Red Queen moves quickly and effortlessly in this game of chess: she is a queen, so she can move anywhere on the board. The young girl is a pawn, but a pawn can morph into a queen if she can navigate her way across the board to the other side, evading the Red Queen.

But the young girl has had enough of the Red Queen's games, and cries, 'I can't stand this any longer … you, you are the cause of all this mischief.'

She begins to shake the Red Queen by the shoulders, but the Red Queen has dwindled down to the size of a little doll.

Why Does Love Get in the Way?

'This refusal to see me is absurd. She ordered me out of my own house. Told me to get out and never come back.'

'Darling, you have the heart of a lion and an utter lack of imagination. Of course she threw you out. Rather a betrayal, don't you think?'

'But she's a happily married woman. Why would she begrudge her own mother a bit of harmless fun? Do you know he looked at his watch the whole time, just like Papa Joe. And then when it was over he asked me. "Did you sleep with the old man? Was he better than me?" Of course, I lied.'

'What will you do now?'

'Go back on tour, like in the war. These people need me. I bring so much light, so much happiness. I have bills to pay.'

She looks tired.

'Billy has called. He wants me to be in his film. How can he expect me to play the wife of a Nazi. Is he nuts? Only Billy would have the nerve to ask me to do this film.'

'Maybe you should. Mr Wilder is a marvellous director.'

'You know Boni got married. To that actress, who wants all his paintings.'

'So another one falls. No matter, you still have me.'

'And Papi. He's the one that matters. I would never divorce him, and that's why the others left me. They wanted children and a home. I never wanted another child. I had one perfect daughter. And now she's gone.'

The Tragedy of Love

Don't look back. Don't look back. You can't see the present, you fear the future, and so you look back. It drags at your heart that you can't do anything but look back.

I thought it would be easy to cut my mother out of my life. But just try it when she's as famous as mine. Some ghosts can never be laid to rest. For the sake of my own sanity, I stopped seeing her, and refused to take her calls. The weeks turned into months. But she is everywhere. Her voice softly singing in the elevator of the department store or airport; her image in card shops, television screens, picture frames. People forever ask, 'How is your wonderful mother?'

This preoccupation with the famous is hard for those who carry it due to birth. We pay a price. We know that this adulation is not for heroic endeavour or courage or valour, and we know what misery is unleashed on the ones that have only a ringside seat. That *thing* that is revered, worshipped almost to the point of canonisation, is so nebulous, so fragile.

Make your ego porous. Will is of little importance, complaining is nothing; fame is nothing.

I never knew what it felt like to have a mother that nobody knew, or cared much about. It's different today; stars are not stars today. They don't shine so brightly.

A week before another Thanksgiving. I shopped and returned home alone, switched on the TV set and then suddenly from nowhere – a candy-pink suit … a dark-haired woman scrambling over the back of a car with splodges of red spoiling her lovely clothes. My knees buckled and I sat.

It couldn't be true. Not him. Not the man I had loved so dearly. I saw him, tanned and handsome, diving off a cliff, bowing in a white tuxedo asking for a dance, driving me to tea in his red sports car. His smile and those blue, bluest of eyes. Kind to his sister and to me. The most alive young man I had ever met. So sexy, so sure of himself. I would mourn him for all of my life, for the youth he wore so well.

I Travel Alone

At the age of seventy, Madou has found a new lover. Her lover never lets her down. Never turns up late to her door with a whisky bottle inside his coat. Her lover is always grateful, worships without complaint, is undemanding, is completely hers to control. Her new lover will never leave her for another, younger lover. Her lover is always punctual. Curtain. 9.30.

She has her demands. She requires a very large fridge.

'The largest that you can find. It must be completely empty and then I need a second, smaller fridge and you must fill it with champagne and liverwurst. And then, you must pay my daughter to be my assistant. I can't do this without her. She knows what I need. And I need, what do you call it now? A record player. Don't forget the record player. Last of all I need a mirror, and it needs to be an eight-foot mirror on castors and with lights.'

Down slams the phone. Hands tremble as she reaches for a drink. She needs to give up the booze. It's making her fat. She's finding it hard to fit into her clothes, and every calorie shows in that tight-fitting dress. But she's hungry all the time. Her swan's-down coat is looking shabby and her dresses have seen better days. But it's all right. No one will see under the lights. Her face is nice and tight. No need for the hair braiding in this day and age. She has a marvellous surgeon. Simply marvellous. Of course, they're always nervous with *that* face, even though they pretend not to be.

Her lovers have gone now. All the better, as she doesn't have to pretend. She can remove her wig, release her body from the foundation, take off her make-up, pour herself a drink, and play her records. She waits for her daughter. But she doesn't come.

Like Lola Lola, her first creation, Madou inhabits two sets: her dressing room and her stage. It has become her world. She couldn't be happier. Her fridge is full, though she barely eats, just sips champagne from morning until night. It helps the aches in her body. Now she enters the stage to rapturous applause.

I have been wheeled on so she can check her lighting. I can see that she has had a few drinks just to calm her nerves, but she has smeared her lipstick. Her wig is askew. She forgets the words to some of the songs, but no matter. The crowd don't seem to mind. She looks old and frail.

Then something happens. It's as if a light bulb has suddenly come on inside her and she is transformed. She flirts with her audience, stands erect. The old soldier is back. Then I see what she sees: the King. He is in the audience.

I Wish You Love

This time when she called, I told Bill I would speak to her because, despite everything, she was still my mother, and I guess children have a deep capacity for loving their parents, no matter what they have done. But I have made a decision. She will never again be allowed to hurt me. I will do my duty, as she has taught me, but I build an invisible wall around me, and her words will spring off the wall, and rebound, and I will be safe.

'Hello, Mutti. It's been a long time.'

She was breathless with excitement. It was as if she had seen me yesterday.

'Angel. It was *him*. The King. Can you believe it? After all this time. He asked to see me, but I refused. He wanted to come to my room, but, you know, the wig and all that nebbish, so I said no. Besides, I hate him. I gave him everything, everything. He deserves that crazy wife. And that sick kid.'

'Mutti, I heard from Papi. He's been sick. But he's OK now.'

'It's all that ghastly food he eats. Sofi doesn't feed him properly. I always said, if you can't cook, don't cook. Cooking is an art form. Papi, who dined with me in the best restaurants all over the world, and they eat in that greasy diner.'

'Mutti, Sofi died.'

Silence.

'Well, at least he has that other woman to look after him. You know, the one he sees when Sofi is in the loony bin.'

She doesn't ask me how she died. That beautiful, gentle soul who suffered so much at the hands of my parents. I thought of how they had tortured her. Made her wear my mother's cast-off clothes and shoes. Made her walk behind them every time they went out. Made her kill her babies, over and over again. She was the nearest thing to a real mother I ever had. Flesh and blood, not an icon. And now she is dead. She was stabbed to death by another inmate. And she was all alone.

Where Have All the Flowers Gone?

A tall, eight-foot mirror on wheels stands alone on the bare stage, with the sweeping staircase. The vast concert hall is empty, except for one person. A little old lady. She bends to her knees and gathers the flowers that have been strewn over the stage. She takes them back to her dressing room and places them carefully into the huge, empty fridge. She will need them for tomorrow. After all, she has paid for them.

She puts on a record of one of her concerts, not for her singing, let's face it, the talent is feeble, but for the applause. Over and over again, she listens to her adoring audience clapping and cheering, and then she smiles. On no, is she going to play the B-side, I wonder?

So many falls. At a concert in Sydney she stumbles and falls over a cable. In her bedroom in Paris, she falls and breaks her hip. In London, she is drunk and falls forward on her face. She is dragged backstage by her heels. She has broken a leg. Enough is enough.

Her daughter finally comes and puts her to bed. They talk about the old days. Madou begins: 'I'm a daughter of the military. You know what that means ... I was taught discipline. When I was a child we used to go for long rides into the country in summertime. But I was never allowed to run to the lemonade stand with the other children, I was told, "Control your thirst. Control hunger. Control emotion." It has served me well.'

'Mutti, remember when we went to Hollywood and we had the blue tree that melted in the sun?'

'We laughed so much. Didn't we always laugh?'

'We did, Mutti.'

'The emeralds, and the grey coffins and the *Normandie*. It was another world.'

'And the blue swimming pool. And Boni.'

'No one can become stranger than the person you once loved.'

'I guess so, Mutti.'

'Do you remember the balloons that popped in my face. That was my favourite picture. Mo never made me look more beautiful. I should have stopped then. Now, I look like a toad.'

'You were always beautiful. Perfect.'

'You know what Boni said? "Those who are perfect should be placed in a museum."'

'Like Nike of Samothrace? In the Louvre.'

'You were perfect to me. That's why I never wanted another child. Look at you now! So beautiful. Now who would have thought that you would have turned out to be a swan?'

Madou walks to her dressing table, snaps open a gold cigarette case, and lights an American. She sits on the stool and blows smoke directly into me; she knows that the smoke softens the lines on her face. She speaks to her daughter while she stares at her image through the cloud of blue fumes: 'You know that story you loved so much as a child? The one about the midgets and Snow White, and the talking mirror?'

'They refused to bury her in the cold ground, so they made her a coffin of glass.'

'But in the true German story, it wasn't the stepmother, it was the mother who was jealous of the daughter and wanted her dead. Do you remember?'

'I have to go now, Mutti. Back to New York and the children.'

'Of course you do. You know what I always say; children come first.'

Just a Gigolo

Papi didn't want their Berlin furniture, and the next time I went back it looked wonderful in Mother's Paris residence in the Avenue Montaigne, which was small but beautifully formed. She loved her upscale fifth-floor apartment in the leafy, tree-lined avenue, close to the Eiffel Tower, and the Rue du Faubourg Saint-Honoré.

She had a tiny kitchen and a parlour filled with a gallery of photographs of her family, her lovers, and herself. She called it her wall of death. Her cream sofa was scattered with silk cushions. Mirrors make a room look twice the size, which is why the walls were lined with them, mostly smoky-glass, so kind to the face, she told me. On the side cabinet was her photograph of Papa Hem, and piles of books and newspapers. She lay in her bed, wearing beautiful bed jackets in pink and baby blue.

She had a new lover.

'He's perfect because I never see him. He sent me a fan letter, saying he had adored me ever since he saw me as Lola Lola as a child. I noticed that his letter-heading said 'Doctor', so I wrote back to him and we began a correspondence. He is a cultured man of science, even though he lives in the San Fernando Valley. I gave him my number.'

She told me that he was such a charming man, Dr Simon Bliss. A lover of poetry and history. During their third telephone conversation, she realised that he was pleasuring himself. She played along. On the seventh call, he asked for a favour. Could she send him a present through the post? What colour, darling? she had said, in that husky voice. She heard him groan in response. He promised he would send her a cheque. She told him that she would be sure to send them in a fitting state. She took out a clean pair and rubbed them between her legs. That would do nicely. She popped a signed photograph into the package.

'He always rings first thing in the morning, or last thing at night. It feels good to enslave a man again.'

I got it: he sees Lola Lola in those frilly panties, not the decrepit old bag, the ugly old witch holding out the apple. He doesn't see the crêpey thighs, the thinning hair, the saggy breasts.

Sometimes she sings to him. Her mind is pin sharp. She recites Rilke. It's the voice that he loves. The voice that never ages.

Of course I knew what she was after. She waited for the moment when she had his close attention, and then she asked for a prescription, something to help her to sleep at night. She's so lonely. No problem, he says. It will be my pleasure, ma'am.

She tells me all this, watching my face for any expression that might give away the revulsion I feel for her. I keep my face impassive.

'You know, darling, I am so nice and tight down there. It's been such a long time. I will need to send for some lingerie. "*You never know*, said the widow."'

'Be careful, Mutti. The phone calls are expensive.'

'He always calls *me*, sweetheart. He's a good man. He's a doctor. I thought you liked doctors?'

I hand her a tumbler of watered-down whisky, and her pills.

'You need to sleep.'

Later, when she is asleep, I tidy the apartment and clear away the empty bottles. Mother's diary is on her bedside table. A flick of irritation washes over me. Inside, it is written 'Kater never comes. I see nobody.'

I pick up a pen and write in bold letters: 'Kater is here.'

You Were There

After she has polished me, the English maid hovers nervously.

Madou's apartment is spotlessly clean. She makes a note every time the curtains and the bedlinen are laundered. Her clothes hang in the oversized wardrobe; her suits in varying colours of cream, pink, and blue.

'Where is my Chanel, with the gold trim?'

'Don't you remember, Miss Madou. You sent it for auction.'

'Nebbish. Why are you lying to me? Have you stolen it?'

'No, ma'am. You sent many items for the auction. The beautiful gold cigarette cases and the wristwatches.'

'Now I know that you are lying. I never sell my clocks or wristwatches. Now pack your bags and leave. Before you go, make me some black tea, with lemon.'

She can't afford to lose another maid, but what is she to do? Later, the phone rings and it is her daughter. Another of her lovers has died. As Papi says, it's 'the thinning of the ranks'. She hopes he has left her money or a painting that she can sell. She has booked an appointment for live cell treatment at Dr Niehans' famous La Prairie clinic by Lake Geneva. The wonderful doctors inject fresh cells taken from foetal sheep and they make her look years younger. It's a miracle treatment. She will fight and she will win this last battle if it's the last thing she does.

Her daughter rings from New York. She has bad news about Papi, who has had a stroke. She will make sure to send him that pear vodka that he likes so much, and that lotion for thickening his hair. Poor Papi, with no one to look after him, though he has never asked Joan to live with him. Unselfish, you see. Always thinking of others. But she is not prepared when his condition deteriorates. And then the news comes, and she is suddenly stricken with fear. He has always taken care of everything. Poor Papi. She won't go to the funeral. The photographers will be there, you see. She'll send Kater.

She orders a wheelchair. It makes it easy to get around and clean the apartment. In the evening, she wheels the chair to the window and looks out at the trees. The rain falls softly. She wheels herself to her desk and takes out some writing paper. She has always loved poetry, and, lately, she has tried to write some of her own. Just for amusement. She writes in her beautiful copperplate:

Isn't it strange
The legs
That made
My rise to glory
Easy, no?
Became my downfall
Into Misery!

The wheelchair helps, but she continues to fall. One morning, she awakes to find herself on the bathroom floor with a pink plastic sheet covering her body. She tells her daughter that her maid pushed her over and then covered her with the shower curtain because she felt sorry, but I saw her, drunk as a lord, stepping out of the tub and clutching the shower rail as she fell.

One evening, when she is sitting in her wheelchair, she hears a noise, a knocking. A man has got into her apartment with a camera. She must not let him have a picture. It will be splashed all over the news: the grieving widow in Paris. *Think, think.* She grabs a towel and wraps it over her head. Then she screams at him to get out, get out, get out. She grabs her phone and calls the conçierge. It was her maid – she has been betrayed.

'Please call my daughter. She will know what to do.'

*   *   *

Hungover and hungry, she is snarling like a leopard. Kater has hidden her bottles and she needs a drink.

'How dare you treat me like a child. I invented hot pants and phone sex. What the hell have you done in life except breed children?'

'Mutti, let me cook you some scrambled eggs?'

'So it's your turn to overfeed me, and make me fat. I know what you're doing. Being a fat child was a sign that you were cared for. That you were well-fed. But you always blamed me for that.'

Then her expression changes and her tone becomes wheedling. Speaking in German, she asks for just a small drink, to open the veins, claiming that it is what her doctor friend has advised.

'OK, Mutti, just one drink. But then you have to eat. I'll feed you myself if I have to.'

'I send out for food, from the Maison d'Allemagne. They bring me lentil stew, veal sausages, and potato salad. It's delicious. But how am I supposed to pay for it? I can sell my New York apartment, but that's for you and the children.'

'We don't need anything, Mutti. We are doing just fine. What happened to your maid?'

'She stole from me. She couldn't clean the apartment. And I explained how to polish my medals and she could never clean them. Remember when I cleaned the pans so well you could see your face in them? Well, not you, because you had that phobia about mirrors.'

So she *had* noticed. Wonders would never cease. Kater seems unperturbed.

'I've had an offer from Universal. I told them I can't leave Paris. But I need the money. I always need the money.'

The Countess of Paris

One of Mother's favourite games was planning her funeral. She loved talking about it in rigorous detail, forgetting that most of the mourners were already dead. She wanted to be buried in her black plastic Balenciaga raincoat, which had stiffened over the years: 'Darling, the worms will never get through that coat.'

She wanted to be buried in Paris: 'De Gaulle will proclaim a national holiday. Imagine the fans! Their devastation. They will line the streets of Paris to watch the procession. The pansies will come dressed as me in hot pants and pillbox hats with veils. They never let me down. Papi will organise everything. He will wear his dark blue Knize suit. Nellie and Dot will arrive to do hair and make-up – for once, they'll have to do it themselves, as I will be dead. They will be sobbing. Travis will dress me. I want an army wagon, with six horses, like Jack Kennedy.'

I glared at her, and she had the grace to look away. On she went: 'Then at the church, there will be two boxes of roses, white and red. Everyone whom I have slept with will wear red, and all the others who wanted to, will wear white. The white roses will glare at the red roses, and they will all be furious and jealous, just like when I was alive. The King will be sobbing with remorse, Boni will be drunk, and Moncorge will be smoking by the side of the church. Now the only thing you have to do is get my body out of here without anyone noticing. I don't want anyone to see me. Pop me into one of those black bin bags – you might have to break my arms and legs to get me in – and then secrete me in one of my trunks and take me to the basement garage. No one must see me.'

I had to laugh. She was so funny and so serious. Only when I agreed to all her requests would she stop.

She wasn't afraid of death. She would often say, 'When you're dead, you're dead, that's it,' but her favourite maxim was, 'I'm worth more dead than alive. Don't cry for me after I've gone. Cry for me now.'

Other times, she would say something to me that was so innocuous, a memory of something that had not taken place, a comment about my appearance, or the unruly behaviour of my boys, and I would feel that *thing* in my throat, trickling down into my chest, the sudden surge of white-hot anger, and I would snap back. Then she looks like a frightened child, and I feel guilty and remorseful. Now she is the child, and I am the mother, and I don't want this power, this responsibility. What has happened to the Red Queen? She is as limp as a rag doll.

There were so many things I wanted to say to her. Unanswered questions, but every time I plucked up the courage, she would sense it coming and change the subject before I started. I was too afraid to persist. I was afraid of hearing the answers. Maybe ignorance was bliss.

She became obsessed with her last film. She was planning the outfit, the hat, like in the old days. She didn't know it then, but it was the last time she ever went out of her apartment, ever felt the breeze on her face, the earth beneath her feet.

Just Let Me Look at You

They send a snip of a girl to meet with her and talk through her conditions. They would never have got away with this in the old days. The girl walks straight up to me.

'What a lovely antique mirror.'

'There will come a time,' she says, 'when old, smoky mirrors are the best. They are much more romantic. To put it plainly, a woman looks younger in them. I don't know why anyone would want to see every pore.'

She agrees to make the picture, but she wants her own costume and dresser. She does her own make-up, as she always has. She tapes up her face and then puts on her wig, brushes the hair with a sordid little comb, and, like magic, suddenly, she is there again. But even the tape can't hide the wrinkles. No matter, she finds a hat with a veil.

When she is wheeled onto the set, mirror in hand, she feels the shock waves in the room. This is her? The Legend? The most beautiful woman in the world since Helen of Troy? She can hear them whispering behind their fans. Then she stands. She asks for the full-length mirror she has requested. She looks closely at her face, and then the key light. She finds the butterfly. Then all at once, she comes alive and begins to direct the film crew. She is *Her* again. The face glows, and she moves gracefully. The years melt away like soft butter.

Then she starts to sing her song, softly:

There will come a day
Youth will pass away
What will they say about me?

When the end comes, I know,
I was just a gigolo
Life goes on, without me.

There is a sudden sharp realisation in that room that this is it. This is her final performance. Ever. And she is extraordinary. Tears in the eyes, darlings? You could swim in this river of tears and not get to the other side.

She accepts the applause, this wonderful trooper, then she shrugs, and becomes an old woman again. But just for once, for once, she has become magnificent again. She has shown these idiots what it is like to be a star.

Paris When it Sizzles

The next time I flew to Paris, I told Mother that a man called Schell had called. He wanted to make a film about her life.

'I have to earn money, like always, so I'll do it, but no pictures. I won't appear in it. Just my voice. The voice that launched a thousand ships.'

She told Herr Direktor that she would be 'contracted for forty hours of blah blah blah. That is *it*. No pictures.'

He came to see us. She was in bed, as always now. She looked ravishing in a pink Dior bed jacket, with a drawstring neck. He wanted to make a doc–u–men–tary.

'Well, if he wants to know about her life, he can read her book.'

But, no, he wants to ask her about her life, with no prepared questions. He switches on a machine, and they begin to talk. He asks her about Berlin, her childhood, meeting von Goldberg. 'It's all in my book,' she says. He begins to laugh. He'll come back tomorrow and they can start again.

'Has your life always been rootless? I can see that it is an inevitable part of your life as a movie star.'

'I have none of those kitschy feelings.'

'Do you feel old?'

'We all regret our youth once we have lost it.'

'There are some contradictions about your life that I would like to explore with you.'

'There have been fifty-five books written about me.'

'Have you read them?'

'Why would I waste my time on such trivial pursuits?'

'Do you mind criticism?'

'Not at all, as long as it's unqualified praise.'

'How is your relationship with your daughter?'

'Perfect. I've said everything in my book.'

'But sometimes truth and fiction seem to elide.'

'The truth is not the same as my truth.'

'Do you think this film will be exciting?'

'I wasn't contracted to be exciting.'

'What did you think of Orson Welles?'

'He taught me a mind-reading gag. People should cross themselves when they speak of him.'

'Are you afraid of dying?'

'People should be afraid of life, not death.'

'Looking back now, what do you think of your career?'

'I was an actress. I made films. Period.'

He sighs. She tells him that he's unprofessional because he has not prepared questions. He responds that it's a deliberate choice not to send her questions.

When he does send her questions she simply says 'Yes' or 'No'. Stalemate.

He leaves and asks his production assistant to send her flowers. She sends one long red rose, in cellophane. Mother is furious when she sees it and sweeps it from the table. How dare they send just one rose, when she used to have an extra room just for flowers.

They start over again. She must not let the mask slip. She knows what he's doing, and she won't let him see her vulnerabilities. They watch her movies together. She knows every still, every shot, every image.

'I was a snot-nosed kid before I met Mr von Goldberg,' she says. 'He made that kid beautiful. With his camera.'

Together they recite Freiligrath's poetry:

Oh, love as long as you can love!
Oh, love as long as you may!
The hour will come, the hour will come:
By graves lamenting you will stay.

Her voice falters and she begins to weep. He stops recording.

Let's Say Goodbye

I am the only one who sees her now.

''Ello, who is zis speaking? I am Miss Madou's maid, 'ow may I 'elp you?'

'Joan, stop this nonsense. It's Billy. I know it's you. I'm in the lobby. Come on and open the door.'

'Miss Madou is in Switzerland. She cannot be reached.'

'Joan, stop this nonsense …'

She slams down the phone. Another one rings. She picks up.

''Ello, who is zis speaking?'

'Mutti, what happened?'

'I fell over and broke my hip.'

'OK, I'll book a flight.'

'No need. I'm fine.'

For once, she sounds lucid and sober.

'They fixed my hip. I've got everything I need.'

'OK, Mutti, but I'm still going to come over, just to make sure.'

'Please yourself.'

She has cut off all contact with her lusty doctor. He offers to fly to Paris to save her, so she cuts off contact. He must not see her; nobody must see her. Impossible. Unacceptable. Not on! A sly grin spreads to the corners of her mouth, as she reaches for the whisky bottle. No need for her daughter to come along. Don't want her watering down her medicine. She's not a heavy drinker. She can sometimes go for hours without touching a drop. She locks it away, in the box beside her bed. She is the only one with the key; it's called a *dietrich*, it can open any lock.

She glances at her reflection on the wall. It's her intimate friend. It knows all her secrets. It will take them to the grave. She thinks about mirrors from Lohr, so elaborately worked that they were accorded the reputation of always speaking the truth. But who wants a mirror to speak the truth?

Tell me, glass, tell me true!
Who is the fairest? Tell me who.

They've all gone. Moncorge, and Boni, and now Papi. She thought Papi would live for ever. Her Shakespearean twin. Her golden boy. But she still has her friend, the mirror.

Mirror, mirror, in my hand,
Who is the fairest in the land?

The HMS Disgusting

After my mother broke her hip, she put herself to bed. For ever.
It was late when I arrived at the Avenue Montaigne. Mother was
asleep, a book upended on her chest. Her clocks ticked away,
and the record player needle hissed. I lifted the arm and turned
it off. The rest could wait until the morning. There was a small
sofa in the living room. I curled up like a cat. Sleep came
quickly.

In the morning, I assessed the situation. It was much worse
than I could have possibly imagined. My mother, so obsessed with
germs, had come to this? She looked at me with a crafty smile:
'I've just decided to take to my bed. It makes life easier. I have a
hot plate here, and my phone. I got this claw thing, so I can reach
for my books.'

I saw what she was up to. She could drink as much as she liked
without fear of falling over. Much safer to stay in bed perma-
nently. She never thought it might be better to give up the drink.
She was happy in her mattress crypt. Mother always loved to set

up camp, like the good German soldier that she was. But, my God, the mess.

I removed all the empty bottles and attempted to clean the place.

There were boxes upon boxes of Kleenex. Piles of newspapers and books. On one side was her office. Piles of stationery, notepaper, envelopes of all sizes, stamps, pens, rubber bands, string, magnifying lenses, files, and dictionaries. On the other, her pharmacy: pills, jars, tubes. On a shelf, her drink, decanted into mineral water bottles.

At the side of her bed, on a low stool, a row of Limoges pitchers. I grimaced, as I took them to the bathroom to empty and bleach. She must have been paying someone a lot of money to do that particular job.

She told me about her new friend, David Brett. He lived in a council flat in Yorkshire. They had begun a phone friendship. Again, the sly smile hovered above her lips. I inspected her white telephone. It was filthy with stains and splodges and numbers stuck on with tape.

Mother was obsessed by the fact that she now looked like a toad. I found some recent photographs across which she had scrawled a message: 'How Ugly can you get?'

'A photographer tried to get another picture. He hired a crane to get to me, so now I keep the curtains drawn.'

'Are you sleeping, Mutti?'

'I wake at 2 a.m., every night. No sleeping pills make me sleep, which doesn't help the toad look.'

'You look fine, Mutti.'

Then she looked at me, through her walled mirror, as if she were seeing me for the first time.

'Kater, you look just like me.'

We played our little games. She made excuses not to wash, and then complained to her friends that I refused to bathe her. I watered down her Scotch, but she somehow found a devoted shop girl to smuggle in more. She sipped black tea, laced with booze, and, now that no one could see her, ate whatever she liked.

Her fans were legion and they telephoned day and night. They sent her frankfurters and marinated herrings. She told them, 'I see nobody. I never see my daughter' – even though I was there, cooking meals for her that she would never eat.

She would spend hours responding to fan mail by letter and telephone.

'Who was the most difficult actor to work with? Shall I say Ray Milland? I make it all up, anyway.'

'Good idea, Mutti.'

'Is he dead?'

'Yes.'

'Good, then I can say him.'

Her favourite was still her council flat Yorkshireman. She spent hours and hours on the phone with him, racking up huge bills. He was devoted, and would help her with bills, accountants, doctors, lawyers. Despite my protestations, she gave him my number and told him to ring me any time, day or night.

He would ring me up in his flat Yorkshire drawl and reprimand me for neglecting my wonderful, beautiful mother, who lived only for me. Said that she tells him her innermost secrets. Tells him that she spends every Christmas alone.

When her Hollywood friends called and asked what she was doing, she would say, 'I'm the same. In bed with a book and a bottle.'

At the age of eighty, she conducted telephone flirtations with Ronald Reagan and Mikhail Baryshnikov. When the president left the White House, the last telephone call he made was to my mother.

At 10 p.m., she was at her liveliest and wanted to chat. She would flick through a copy of *Vogue*, complaining about the latest fashions.

'Look at this abortion. They don't know what to do any more. UGLY. That *mennuble*, what's her name? Madonna. She copies me all of the time. Do you remember the review dress?'

'Yes, it was blue velvet and then you changed it to green.'

'Good man, Travis. He *listened*, and that's what made him so great. Do you remember the black ostrich feathers? I invented those shoes, do you remember, and then Chanel copied me. She was such a fake. She was a decorator, not a designer.'

She flicked through the pages.

'Braids, big deal. I wore them in *Dishonored*. And remember when I wore braids when I played the statue, the one that comes alive?'

'I remember, Mutti, but did you know that Lacy died?'

'He was in love with me, but he used to write such boring letters. Anyway, *you* liked him. Do you remember when I wanted dark eyes and I put those drops in to make my eyes black? The things we did then, and now they write books and say it is art. We just made a film – then made another one. Such stupidity. It's business, not art. They ask me why I wore tails, it's because I didn't want to show the legs for once, and I looked wonderful in them. No other reason. Why do they always want to see big meanings in films? Idiots. Did you see that last picture of Garbo?'

'I hear she has kidney disease.'

'That suits her. Smelly pee. She'll die of it. She looked terrible in that photograph – ugly and so old. You know she used to count every piece of sugar to make sure that the maid didn't steal it. And those feet! They could never do a long shot because of those gigantic feet.'

She picked up one of the photograph albums.

'Look, here *she* is in the mink hat. Remember that terrible banquet and all those corpses, like concentration camp victims, long before we knew that they would exist for real.'

When she suddenly began talking about her mother, I saw she was getting tired. Was this the time I should ask about Aunt Birgitte?

'In many respects she was a hard woman.'

Her hands stroked the bedspread nervously as she said this. Her sleeping suppositories were beginning to take effect. She murmured, 'That strange feeling we had in the war. I've never found anything to equal its strength, it was a splendid carelessness that held us all together.'

I removed the heavy album from the bed and turned out the lights. I went into the parlour where her wall of death greeted me. Chevalier smiles, Coward mocks, Piaf broods, Papa Hem looks right through me.

I stood and looked straight into the huge mirror above the fireplace. At last I was not afraid, because I knew the one thing he did not know or understand.

It was time for me to speak to him: 'Beauty is not skin deep.'

You are the fairest of them all.

The Blue Angel

Every morning she wakes sober and resumes her hellish daily journey, sipping Scotch until the angry monster emerges and rules her day. She is awaiting death and despising life for its fragility – for not coming into line as she demands. In the old days, everyone in the studio had jumped to her every command. How dare life disregard her demand for immortality?

It's her ninetieth birthday, and she is all alone. Deserted by that family she loves so much.

Devouring Time, blunt thou the lion's paws.

Her beautiful legs, the symbol of her fame and beauty, are now withered and emaciated. She has chopped her hair with cuticle scissors, and it sits in sparse, grey clumps, where it was once golden and lustrous. Her skin, so luminous, is now like parchment.

Her teeth have blackened and cracked. She awaits death, and faces her private hell alone; just the way she wants it.

She wears the Légion d'honneur, France's highest commendation. She is too poor to pay her rent, but she can't be turfed out of her beloved France, so the city of Paris kindly meets the bill. She would kill herself, if she could, but if she does, her life insurance will be invalid, and she must leave something for the Child. After her stroke, she speaks only three words; 'Yes', 'No', and 'Kater'. She is a shell, but to me she was the most beautiful woman I have ever seen.

She turns her face to look at me.

It's the blind side of mirrors that make them work.

There are no great beauties any more. Actors may be good, but beautiful they are not. Cock and bull, my dear. I'm old-fashioned, I love the moonlight. You don't hold any mystery for me, darling, do you mind? Consider the public. Never fear it nor despise it. Coax it, charm it, interest it, stimulate it, shock it now and then if you must, make it laugh, make it cry, but above all never, never, never bore the living hell out of it.

Remember what I told you: wit ought to be a glamorous treat like caviar; never spread it about like marmalade. How foolish to think that one can ever slam the door on the face of age. Much wiser to be polite and gracious and ask him to lunch in advance.

'That's quite enough from you, dear.'

She remembers the sound of the soldiers marching in step, and the clip clopping of the horses from her home in Schöneberg. Mother playing a Chopin waltz, her fingernails touching on the keys with a delicate little click. She used to call me Paul when she was happy with me. Skating with Birgitte on the Neuer See. The sparkling jewels on Unter den Linden. I came from a family of clockmakers, on my mother's side. Father died of syphilis and it made him mad. My uncles, Otto and Williband, who were killed in the war. Spring driving along the Kurfürstendamm in an open-top car. Marguerite Bregaund was my first love, but I've never loved anyone. Not really loved. The rats' paws were so cold.

Where have all the young girls gone? Long time passing. Grief does not diminish; it just becomes a habit. She would have liked a Spiegelkabinett of her very own, so she could admire her pretty face. Now it's too late for all that. Mirrors distort, and they do NOT tell the truth.

Birgitte betrayed me.

*   *   *

She'd told everyone that her sister died in Belsen, but that was a lie. Birgitte and her husband ran a cinema for the Nazis. Her own sister. A cinema. Entertaining those Nazi beasts.

But when she cut out her sister's face, it was to protect her, not to disown her. If they found out, they would punish her, so she told them she was dead.

Homosexuals worship their mothers, worship them. As for you, Kater: you were never pretty enough to be raped.

Mirror, Mirror on the wall, who is the fairest of them all?

She reaches for the champagne that she has secreted under the bed. Drinkers often conceal the truth even to themselves. I know all her secrets. I'll take them to her grave. I won't betray her. She pours herself a glass and picks up the gold Cartier clock from her bedside table. *Tick tock. Tick tock.*

She smiles and hurls it, right at me, and screams: '*There's an end of all thy beauty.*'

Epilogue

The past is never where you left it.

My mother was lying on her bed like a limp rag doll. I was shocked by how much she still frightened me, even in death. When I was a child, she used to make me repeat, 'When I'm with my mother nothing bad can happen to me.' But it did happen, Mutti. And you did nothing to protect me. And now I don't know if I can ever forgive you.

Her mirror is smashed into fragments. All that bad luck. I pick up a piece, and look at myself.

'Did you feel robbed of your childhood when it happened?'

'No, Mother did that all by herself.'

Her maid handed me a final letter, a poem:

If a Surgeon
Would Open my Heart
He would see
A gigantic sea

Of Love
For my only child
He would be stunned
At the force of it
The violence
The fury of it
All Entangled in
One human heart

She got her Paris funeral, and thousands came and lined the streets to pay their respects. Then we took her to Berlin, and that day it was flower market day, and when the German people saw her casket, they threw flowers, just like they did at the end of her shows. Hundreds of flowers. My mother would have loved it.

I buried her in Schöneberg, next to her mother. The greatest performer in the world is laid to rest in a sun-dappled garden, and on her grave I lay lilies of the valley.

Author's Note

This novel is a through-the-looking-glass telling of the life of Marlene Dietrich. It is a work of historical fiction, not a biography, but I have learned from many biographies of Dietrich and of other female stars from the golden age of Hollywood. I owe a particular debt to Maria Riva's superbly written and extremely candid memoir of her mother, *Marlene Dietrich by her Daughter* (Knopf, 1993), and to Donald Spoto, *Blue Angel: The Life of Marlene Dietrich* (Cooper Square, 2000). The book by 'Boni', from which a few brief passages are quoted, is Erich Maria Remarque's *Arch of Triumph* (translated by Walter Sorell and Denver Lindley, Appleton-Century, 1945), a semi-autobiographical novel about his affair with Dietrich, whom he christened Joan Madou. To capture the unique voice of Dietrich, some of her own words are quoted from *Marlene Dietrich's ABC* (Doubleday, 1962). The voice of the Mirror reflects the style and often the words of Dietrich's friend Noël Coward.

The titles of the chapters narrated by the Daughter are Dietrich films (and a couple of her songs). Chapters narrated by the Mirror have the titles of Noël Coward songs (with the exception of 'Through the Looking Glass' and 'Where Have All the Flowers Gone?').

Although all characters are fictionalised, readers familiar with the Dietrich story will recognise her husband Rudolf Sieber in Papi, the great Austrian directors Josef von Sternberg and Billy Wilder in Mo Goldberg and Billy, the irrepressible Travis Banton in the Head of Wardrobe, the actor Brian Aherne in Lacy, Ernest Hemingway in Papa Hem, Burt Bacharach in Burt Freeman, and so on.

I learned much from Randall Thropp, costume and prop archivist at Paramount Pictures.

Thanks to Arabella Pike and Susan Watt. Susan has been a scrupulous editor, whose ideas and insights have been of immeasurable value. I especially enjoyed our evening together at Wilton's Music Hall witnessing Dietrich come back to life in the dazzling one-wo(man) show, *Natural Duty*. Thanks to Charlotte Webb for her careful copy edit and to Heike Schuessler for the glorious jacket design.

My children, Tom and Ellie Bate, read an early draft and made helpful suggestions. Thanks to young Harry for asking 'How's Marlene going?' Sally Bayley helped me to find the device of the mirror voice, and Stephen Pickles has spent many a long hour discussing all things Dietrich, and passing on several marvellous anecdotes.

Heartfelt thanks to my husband, Jonathan Bate. He is my first reader and my last. My father's favourite song is 'Falling in Love Again': I hope he enjoys this novel. My sisters and I grew up watching black and white Hollywood movies; they were the backdrop to our lives. This book is dedicated to my sister, Christine, the Joan Crawford to my Bette Davies.